ACCIDENTALLY
EVER AFTER

USA TODAY BESTSELLING AUTHOR

DAKOTA
CASSIDY

Published 2017 by Dakota Cassidy.

ISBN: 978-1542560801

Manufactured in the USA.

Email dakota@dakotacassidy.com with questions or inquiries.

Darling readers,

I've gone and mucked it up again, sticking my nose where it surely doesn't belong by using snippets of famous fairy tales and ideas from various television shows to suit my twisted needs. Enormous thanks to: *Outlander*, *Game of Thrones*, *Galavant*, *Shrek*, *Once Upon A Time*, and, in one facet or another, every Disney/Pixar movie with a princess or memorable villain in it ever made. Basically what I'm saying is, I've maybe toyed with some classics (eep!), but it's all done with utter and total respect.

I don't care what anyone thinks about the non-feminist properties attached to my wish to be a princess; I'm honest enough to tell you that when I was five, I wanted to be Cinderella. I didn't much care about the prince then, but I sure wanted talking mice, a coach, hair that floated around my waist, and that darn ball gown. Nowadays, at almost fifty, I just wanna wear a floaty dress while small forest creatures clean my house. But my love of a good fairytale remains.

Also grateful thanks to Mindy Dawn Fletcher for the brilliant title, my ever-awesome BFF Renee George for the brainstorming, and my amazing DH for some of the whacky parodies on names you're about to encounter!

Dakota XXOO

Author Note: For anyone new to The Accidentals, I've included a link to *Interview With An Accidental*, a quick (and mostly painless) interview-style introduction to the women who are the heart and soul of this eleven-book series, originally published traditionally. If you're a repeat offender (YAY to repeat offending, you rebels!), skip right to chapter one!

Acknowledgements
Illustration: Katie Wood
Cover: Valerie Tibbs, Tibbs Design
Editor: Kelli Collins

Accidentally Ever After

Chapter 1

Once upon a time, in a land far, far away (or as some call it, Jersey), there were three lovely maidens and a zombie off for a day full of mirth-filled Christmas shopping and friendship.

Okay, that's not totally true. Yes, there's a zombie, but there are only two maidens full of mirth and friendship. The third maiden is so unlike the other two maidens, she wouldn't know mirth if it slapped her on the ass and called her Snuggle Bunny.

But she totally gets friendship. Swear it.

Back to the story. Allow me to introduce the players in our tale: The first of the trio is our fair Marty Flaherty. With hair fashioned of spun gold—or in some circles, a box of Clairol #222—light of heart and blessed with a gift for perpetual optimism (see Pollyanna), one can surely see the charming Marty comes by her title with ease.

A cosmetic/fashion guru/werewolf, our Marty is an admitted shopaholic, and happily married to her life mate, with whom she shares the blending of two cosmetic empires and a young daughter named Hollis.

The second maiden, equally as fair, is our ever-elegant and oh-so-tasteful Wanda Schwartz. Warm, nurturing, a paragon of decorum, lovingly titled "halfsie" by her BFFs. Which translates to half vampire, half werewolf. Wanda is also happily married, and has an amazing manservant named Archibald who loves to cook gourmet meals.

And then there's Nina Blackman-Statleon…

Fair maiden number three. Though, I warn you, this storyteller is only using the word "fair" to keep things on an equal playing field so when all is said and done, there's no bandying the word "unjust" about. #storytellereyeroll

Ahem…

Anyway, Nina is the trio's resident vampire, adorned with almond-shaped eyes the color of coal and luxurious raven hair totally untouched by any sort of finery. In other words, according to the two previously mentioned maidens, a total babe without even trying.

Dark, broody—dare I say crusty?—and easily provoked, she's a lover of whatever doesn't irritate her. Which is next to nothing except for five things: All animals, the elderly, children, someone in paranormal distress, and Barry Manilow. Mother to little vampini Charlie, surrogate mother to zombie Carl, and happily married wife of Gregori.

On this bright, crisp pre-winter day in December, the women and their zombie Carl find themselves fresh off their recent OOPS (Out In The Open Paranormal Support; a crisis hotline, as such) case. A harrowing encounter, wherein they came to blows with the goddess of disorder and chaos, Eris, in a mythological battle to the bitter end to save their friend and client Quinn Morris from certain death.

It was all manner of crazy, people. Fire-breathing horses, serpents, even a Cyclops (hand to heart—swear it's true) were among their foes—all of which they valiantly conquered like the true warriors they are. That skirmish included Carl, our sweet, sweet zombie, who defeated said Cyclops by using a mighty blow to his big, scary eyeball with, of all things, a copy of Jane Eyre.

Obviously, fine readers, the three fair maidens and one zombie were in dire need of some R and R. So on this unusually chilly, early December day, the gregarious and light-of-heart maiden Marty suggested a shopping trip to the outlet mall in Jersey (I think like exit 92 off the turnpike, for those of you who speak Jersey), one of her and Wanda's favorite places to unwind, regroup, and most importantly, spend quality time girl-bonding.

Little did they know this particular day would not only change their lives forever, but take them on a treacherous journey filled with pitfalls, magic, a new pair of shoes (so cute!)—and bad, bad dudes.

Lots of bad dudes…

"Oh my God, Wanda! Would you look at this? Only twenty bucks!"

If Antonia Vitali had heard the name correctly, a woman named Marty held up a short, flirty skirt she'd pulled from the rack and was now waving it at a woman named Wanda, who was plowing her way through a pile of seventy-five-percent-off silk scarves.

Wanda's elegantly coiffed head popped up, one long chestnut strand of hair out of place from her rabid hunt for the perfect scarf. She'd walked into Discount Designers as though she were royalty and had proceeded to methodically work her way through every sale rack in mere minutes. Tall, stately, wearing clothes Toni could only guess cost more than her entire wardrobe.

"Shut the front door, Marty!" Wanda squealed, her eyes glazed as she blew the errant hair from her face. "I don't know what to look at first. There's sooo much!"

"Look at the door first, halfsie. See the one that says 'Exit'? The one we should be walking right the shit out of? Look at *that* first," complained the frightfully pale woman named Nina, wearing a T-shirt that read "I Am A Delicate Fucking Flower" and leaning against the far wall, pushing her sunglasses back up onto the bridge of her zinc-covered nose.

Toni's manager Bree, aka the most vapid twenty-year-old in the world and younger than Toni by twelve years, cocked her head at Nina, assessing her long, slender limbs. "You know, there's a dress over there that would change your life!"

She pointed to the far left side of the store, where racks and racks of discounted designer dresses in multiple colors hung, as though she had some huge fabric lottery win she'd chosen to share with the lucky pale woman.

Nina rolled her tongue in her cheek, lifting her sunglasses just a hair to glower down at Bree. "I'd have to have a life to change to wear a dress—or actually give a shit."

Right on, Colorless One, Toni silently cheered, fighting a chuckle while trying to make it appear as though she was deeply immersed in arranging the stack of leggings just delivered this morning.

"Nina!" Marty scampered across the store's floor, as quick in a pair of heels as any athlete in high tops. She grabbed onto Nina's arm and smiled with one-hundred-watt charm at the confused Bree. "She just means her life is small and lonely and," Marty made a comical pouty face, "sad. So, so sad because she has no need for a dress. No parties. No chance for a date. No nothing. But do you have any hoodies? Black, of course, like her heart?"

Nina gave the woman named Marty a light nudge and made a face. "Get the eff off me, Crazypants. I don't need a dress. I don't need anything from this overpriced clothes rack. I can get hoodies online. Plenty of

BOGOs to be had if you find a GD Groupon. Now finish whatever you two windbags are doing so we can go to the damn bookstore. Santa's there today, and that's all Carl's talked about since you Skyped him behind my back and told him about this stupid excursion because you knew he was the easiest way to get me to agree to go. Now, Carl deserves a Santa, a nice new book, and some frickin' ice cream for being used like a two-bit hooker, don't ya buddy?" she asked the equally pale young man who was holding her hand and wearing a hoodie that matched hers.

The young man named Carl nodded his covered head, shooting Toni an endearingly shy, crooked smile from beneath the hoodie's material.

Toni nodded her head without realizing she had. Who the hell wanted to shop for clothes when there was Santa and ice cream?

She smiled at Carl on her way to straighten the mussed pile of overpriced designer jeans. "I get it. I'd rather have ice cream, too," she murmured as she passed him.

Bree cocked her head again, her fluffy blonde curls trembling when she stepped in front of Toni, her toe virtually tapping. "Excuse me?"

Toni gave her the infamous Vitali glaring eyeball, followed by the condescending rise of one eyebrow. "Sorry?"

Bree grabbed her by the arm and squeezed. "Don't discourage the customers from shopping, Toni," she hissed, her green eyes blazing. "Now shut up and go, like, fold something."

Toni shrugged her off but Bree held tight, creating an angry spark of electricity along her spine. First, a woman almost young enough to have spewed forth from her vagina was chastising her. Second, she was being chastised—again.

Bree was always chastising her. *Toni, did no one teach you to fold a scarf properly? The fold of the fabric should be on the outside, moron. Toni? How many times do I have to tell you to remind the customers to apply for store credit to receive an in-store discount? Toni, Toni, Toni.*

She'd heard her name more times since she'd gotten this job than she had in her entire life. The sound of Bree's falsely cheerful, squeaky voice had become less appealing than setting herself on fire.

But Bree was the boss.

While she couldn't afford to lose this damn job, Bree couldn't afford to push her around. Because she was going to lose an arm and maybe some of that luscious blonde hair.

Toni sucked in a breath, straightening her stupid pink blazer, a store-employee requirement. "Bree, please take your hand off my arm."

Bree's pouty grape-glossed mouth thinned. "Not until you acknowledge that you've heard me, Toni."

"Heard," she all but growled.

"Nicely, please."

"If you were hoping to have me slap some whipped cream on top of that reply, hope harder. I hear it springs and it's eternal."

Bree's eyes narrowed—but she was interrupted by Marty and Wanda's screams, coming from the changing rooms, at first piercing then growing muted and distant.

"Go find out what those women are doing and check on their creepy boy-toy. He's not right," she ordered, giving Toni a light shove.

Closing her eyes for a brief moment, she repeated her daily mantra. *God. Anywhere but here. I wish I were anywhere but here.*

Under normal circumstances, before she was desperate and needed a job more than she needed her pride, Toni would have taken Bree out with a right hook to her pert little nose, lightly sprinkled with sun-kissed freckles.

But under her current poor-as-dirt, on-the-run circumstance, she couldn't afford to get fired.

Making her way toward the back of the store where the changing rooms were located, she spied the woman named Nina poking her head into the changing room area, still clinging to the young man's hand.

Damn. Was this some kind of scam where these women created a distraction, tied the employees up then robbed the store blind?

But then she heard Nina's raspy yelp, too, forcing Toni to pick up her pace. She blew past the rack of leftover half-off summer maxi dresses and rounded the arched entryway to the changing rooms…

To find nothing but the slatted door of a dressing room ajar.

Toni frowned, her eyes scanning the store again for the women.

Nothing. Not a peep.

They'd disappeared completely, leaving only a pile of clothes they'd planned to try on just outside the changing room on a cushioned bench.

"Um, hello? Are you in there?" She wanted to kick herself for sounding so chickenshit, her voice coming off weak and trembling while she listened for a response.

More silence throbbed.

Her pulse pounded in her ears as she crept closer to the slatted door. Slipping her fingers around the edge, she whipped it open, half expecting the women to charge out, guns blazing while shouting orders for her to stay where they could see her. Which was, her rational mind told her, ridiculous. Three grown women and a pale man-child couldn't all fit in the one changing room.

Yet there was nothing but a small whoosh of air, undoubtedly peculiar in a tiny room with no vent or window, but not nearly as bizarre as those women disappearing.

Her eyes caught sight of the soft beige-and-melon scarf on the floor the woman Wanda had been wearing when she'd entered the store.

Toni knelt down to scoop it up and the entire space shifted, tipping her completely upside down. Her head smacked against the carpeted floor just as weightlessness occurred, leaving her falling fast and furious.

Fear set in with a rapid jolt, her brain reeling as she clawed at nothing but black air. Her eyes watered from the vacuum-like effect of the swirling, downward slide her body had been forced to take.

She clenched her eyes shut and swallowed back bile just before she crash-landed onto what felt like...

Toni let her hand move with caution over whatever was beneath her.

Was that a hand? An arm? A person?

A person?

Aw, hellfire.

Just as she rolled away, her stomach pitching and her head throbbing, Toni heard, "Are you fucking kidding me? This is a fine, fine mess, you two crazyfaces. Look what the hell's happened now! Christ and a GD road trip, Marty! You and all this bullshit girls'-day-out baloney. How many flippin' times have I told you, I don't need to damn well shop with you two to bond? In fact, I don't need to bond at all. I'd rather have my skin peeled off at high noon and have vinegar poured on my seeping wounds on a hot July day under a Texas sun than *bond*. But no. Nah. No one ever listens to the vampire. 'Oh, she loves us and she knows she does'." The gruff, husky voice rose an octave, clearly mocking one of the women's words. "'She doesn't mean it when she says that because we're BFFs and that's what stupid-ass BFFs do!' Well. I'm here to tell you, ass-sniffer, *the fuck* I like to shop! The fuck I want to bond over some lip gloss I'll never wear and hair gel I want to squirt down your throat until those stupid doe eyes of yours swim like little fishies!"

"Nina!" one of the women yelped.

"Don't you damn well 'Nina' me. I have on a *gown*, Wanda Schwartz-effin'- Jefferson. A *yellow* flippin' gown. Yell-the-fuck-oh. And wings. I have *wings*. Hear that?" she asked as a tiny flapping noise flew to Toni's ears. "Those are my motherfluffin' wings! Why do I have wings, Wanda? And why is my hair the size of the Eiffel Tower and as stiff as a ten-day-old corpse? What in the ever-lovin' fuck is going on?"

"Nina!" yet another vaguely familiar voice from the store chastised. "When, I ask you, *when* has all your carrying on ever helped in a situation like this? Now come over here and give me a yank up because in case you haven't noticed, Mouth, I have a gown and wings, too! Everything isn't all about *you*, Selfish Pants. Now, my gown's stuck in something sticky that rather smells of cotton candy and horse puckey. Help me up and shut up!"

Her gown? That made it plural gowns.

Toni's brain told her to open her eyes and explore, but whatever, in Nina's words, GD fine, fine fucking mess these women from the store had gotten into, she was clearly into it, too. And whatever the mess was, it sure didn't sound good. Or feel good, judging from the lumpy pile of whatever was beneath her.

"Holy just-like- Disneyland," one of the women whispered before she whistled.

Disneyland?

Aw, c'mon, Toni. You gotta open your eyes, you big ol' wimp. It's Disneyland! When have you ever closed your eyes? You didn't even close them when Stas had his hand around your throat while he used you like a punching bag at the gym and the barrel of his gun was stuffed clear up in the roof of your mouth. Man up, pantywaist.

She forced her eyes open. Then they opened wider.

And her mouth quickly followed their lead as her jaw dropped and her brain buzzed to life.

Toni rubbed her sockets with her knuckles and reopened her eyes. Just in case she'd been drugged—or was hallucinating due to her recent sleepless nights.

Naturally, it changed nothing.

But she tried again just for good measure, giving her eyeballs one last good scrub with her fist. Forcing them open one more time, she took a good, hard look around.

Yeah. She could see the Disneyland reference making sense.

Maybe it was the enormous gray stone castle and drawbridge off in the snowy distance, or the ornate, carved carriage with white horses. Or maybe even the quaint cottages with thatched roofs and men dressed in roughly sewn breeches and matching vests, all staring down at her from a safe distance as though she'd just dropped out of the sky.

Wait. She sorta *had* just dropped out of the sky.

Oh. My. Hell.

Toni sat up fast, making her head swim. She scurried away from the warm lump beneath her and rose to her haunches, letting her head hang between her knees.

That was when she noted her breasts felt like two freshly popped cans of dinner rolls, squeezed to maximum capacity. Not to mention, her ribs were surely in a vise of some sort.

A vise made of the most beautiful silver taffeta with the prettiest lavender undertones she'd ever seen.

Her hands flew to her chest, feeling for her nametag and the buttons of her pink jacket from the store. But they were gone, replaced with yard after yard of material whispering across the tops of her feet.

"Oh, save us all—she's killed her!" someone shouted.

Someone British—maybe Welsh? Toni's head popped up to find a long, thin finger pointing down at her with accusation. She slammed her eyes shut as small feet scuttled away.

Huh.

"Is she dead?" another voice cried, evoking a round of loud gasps.

"Brenda's not going to like this!"

Toni looked again at the shiny material and gulped. Why did this scenario seem so eerily familiar? And who the hell was Brenda?

Dropping down to the cold earth because her thighs were killing her, she opted out of giving any more credence to the billowing silver tulle beneath the shiny fabric bunched between her thighs.

Then Toni felt a hand at her back, easy yet insistent. "You're the salesgirl from the store, right?"

The voice sounded as though it came from the woman named Wanda. She couldn't be sure because there was no exuberant squeal to her tone like there'd been when she found the scarves for sale.

Toni nodded her head, forcing her eyes back open, but she kept them at ground level, risking only quick glimpses because if she looked up, and allowed her brain to register what she thought she'd just seen, she'd lose her mind.

"I don't know what happened. I heard you all screaming and I went to investigate. The next thing I know, I fell into something. A hole or a vortex...or a vacuum that felt like a *Dyson* was sucking the organs right out of me or...I think—I don't know—and then I landed here on top of...something..."

"I'm Wanda Schwartz-Jefferson. What's your name?" she asked, the beautiful, shiny wings between her shoulder blades softly pumping.

Wings. This woman had wings. Genuine wings.

"Your name? Talk to me so I know you're coherent."

"Antonia Vitali. Toni is fine, though."

"Do you want to know what you landed on?"

She stared hard at the snow beneath her feet. "I want to know a lot of things. Like why you have wings, and hair so big I don't know how you're still holding your head upright. But for the moment, I vote we wait. I'm sure that's cruel and callous, because I'm thinking it's not a stretch to say it was a person I landed on, but I can wait on confirmation if it's okay by you."

"You're in shock. I get it. So for now, give me your hand, Toni. Let me help you up. It's cold down there on the ground and your new outfit, while absolutely stunning, definitely is not suited for this kind of weather."

Wanda's voice was warm and reassuring and tinged with kindness, making Toni suspicious.

No one had ever been this nice to Toni Vitali. Not in a long damn time.

They'd just fallen into Cinderella's lair—was it called a lair? No. It was a forest, wasn't it? Did Cinderella have a forest? She shook her head. *One of* those God-awful princesses, with the lush hair swinging around their waists, trust issues out the wazoo and a lack of fortitude, had a forest. She just couldn't remember which one. Either way, who remained calm and reassuring at a time like this?

Wait. Had Stas sent these women? Had that maniac and his crew finally found her? Had they drugged her back at the store? Given her some kind of hallucinogenic? Was she really in some padded cell back at Stas's House of Horrors and she was just under the influence of drugs?

"Promise I won't hurt you, Toni. Take my hand."

Toni did so, but with great reluctance. Wanda snatched her shaking fingers and yanked her up, gripping her shoulders. "Look at me, Toni."

She did as Wanda demanded, her eyes adjusting to her surroundings in slow increments. Snippets of the big picture flashed to her brain then retreated due to their surreal nature.

No. Effin'. Way.

Then some of it began to sink in. Okay, so thus far she seen a castle far off in the distance and snow-covered trees and a crooked signpost she couldn't read without her glasses with the name of wherever they were, down at the end of a broad, muddy road winding endlessly into the surrounding forest.

There were horses tethered to wagons, cottages with thatched rooftops, and people all milling about in a cautiously wide circle around them, dressed in outfits right out of the Renaissance fair.

What the hell?

"Where?" she finally managed to whisper to Wanda. *"H…how?"* It was all she could sputter as she gripped the woman's cool hand.

The woman named Nina popped into her line of vision, making Toni's mouth fall open when she saw what she was wearing, but that didn't stop her from stomping over to Toni and Wanda, the rustle of more yellow chiffon and taffeta than *Joanne's Fabrics* had on an entire store's shelves swirling in the crisp air.

"What in the ever-lovin' fuck is this?" she demanded of Toni, flicking her almost-black hair.

Toni winced. It was a wonder she didn't lose a fingernail with the amount of hairspray it must have taken to keep all that hair in place.

It was piled atop her head in a riot of sausage curls, at least three layers' worth, spilling down her back and dotted randomly with bright yellow bows all around her head. This was the gorgeous woman who'd been wearing a hoodie and jeans just moments ago?

Naw.

But it had to be. She had on the same pair of sunglasses. She had the same scary attack-mode stance.

"What...what happened?" Toni murmured, her fingers covering her mouth to keep from gasping.

"Yeah. I'd like to know that, too," she said, kind of growly and suspicious as she pushed a long, raven sausage curl from her eyes with the back of her hand. "So why don't you tell us, *Toni*? Who the fuck are you and why the fuck am I here? Who sent you? You'd better pony up or you'd better get right with your maker!"

"*Sent me?*" Toni repeated, utterly flabbergasted at the level of uncontained anger this woman was displaying.

Was this snarling, irate woman blaming her for their landing here? She'd taken the blame for a lot of things in her time—laundered money, snitching, even murder—but time travel to a place that looked like an amusement park set in a storybook? That was too damn far.

Nina, her pale skin like a soft glow against the buttercup yellow of her elaborate gown, now seethed. Like, opened her mouth and flashed her teeth.

"You heard me—who the fuck sent you, and what the fuck do you want with us? Did that crazy bitch Hildegard escape from Hell again? If you don't start talkin', I'm gonna start swingin'. Now warm that tongue of yours up with some answers before I snatch it from your pretty head, girlie."

Wow. This woman was as scary as Stas had ever been, if not scarier. But Toni stood up to him once, gun to her throat and all.

And then she remembered something.

Crazy. Stas had once told her, always be the craziest fucker in the room and everyone would back down—which was how she'd managed to escape him three years ago.

So she let her eyes go wild as she stuck her face right back in Nina's, her finger finding its way just beneath her nose. "Blow me, you crazy bitch! Don't you threaten me! You have no idea who you're screwing with. Got that? I'm gonna tell you once, back the fuck off or I'll rip your throat out! We clear, *girlie?*" she bellowed.

Silence fell over the group of women and the small crowd of villagers backed up, clinging to one another.

And then Nina exploded.

Maybe Stas's advice had been a mistake.

Clearly, Nina held the reigning title of Craziest Bitch In The Room.

Oh dear.

Chapter 2

Nina let out a hiss just before she lunged for Toni's throat, her wings fluttering angrily behind her.

But her friend Marty soared through the air in a leap to rival that of a pole-vaulter, her enormous ball gown in a lovely shade of sky blue twisting around her legs.

She landed in front of Nina so fast, she rammed into her, making them tumble to the ground, the two women tangling up in each other's elaborate dresses. Nina reached around her and yanked one of Marty's wings.

"Ow! That's my wing, Nina! I swear, I'll poke your eyeballs out with my hair if you don't knock it off!" Marty yelped and managed to wrestle Nina to her back, securing her by mounting her hips and pulling her glasses from her face.

Gripping Nina's wrists, Marty planted them above her head as a small crowd of villagers gathered, passing a bag of coins and placing bets. "Knock it the hell off, Vampire! Why in all of the universe would you think this woman's responsible for us falling through that hole in the dressing room, you violent, un-trainable, testy beast?"

Vampire? Had she said vampire?

No. This day wasn't happening. It was not.

"Get the hell off me, Blondie, and give me back my damn shades or I'm gonna eat your face off!" Nina screeched with her closed eyes.

But Marty shook her head, the mile-high hair on the top of her skull never budging. "Nope. Not until you promise to use your manners. I absolutely will not have your chaos erupting all over the place like so much vomit until we know what's going on and where we are. And I won't have you threatening to beat anyone up until we need you to."

Wanda leaned into Toni, smoothing one of her long white gloves over her elbow as though it had always been there while her friends continued to bicker. "Very impressive show there. I can't remember the last person who stood up to Nina, other than one of us or her husband, Greg. Clearly, your fear factor is high, Kimosabe. I like that in a girl," she said on a chuckle.

Toni turned to look at her, still visually trying to block out Candyland while people peeked out from behind trees and stood at the doorways of their charming, snow-covered cottages. "Question?"

"Certainly."

"Did that woman—um, Marty, is it?—just call the angry pale lady a vampire?"

Wanda nodded, her hair equally as unmoving as Marty's. "Marty it is, and she did call Nina a vampire. I fear we'll have some explaining to do. Your world's going to be rocked in more ways than one today, I'm afraid. But bear with me until we work out this little kink?" She waved an elegant hand at the ball of limbs and taffeta dresses Nina and Marty had become.

Toni nodded, also refusing to acknowledge that her own hair was now swinging at her waist. "Let's table that for a little while and focus on," she swept her hand around at the landscape, "um, this. You seem really reasonable compared to your friend, so I'm going to appeal to you. I swear I don't know how this happened. Swear it on my life. I'm just a salesclerk at a stupid designer outlet mall store, making just above minimum wage. I don't know anyone who'd do this. I don't even know what's been done, but if at all possible, I say we blame my boss Bree. She's a horrible human being."

Wanda nodded again and patted Toni's arm, her long fingers giving her flesh a squeeze. "You know, I noticed that. Kind of pushy and power-hungry for someone so young, huh? You'd think she was ruling a kingdom, not an outlet store." Then she giggled, like they weren't in the middle of some whacked fairytale. "Sorry. Pardon the pun."

"You heard Bree say those things to me?"

Wanda pulled at her earlobe with the shiny cascade earring attached to it. "Half vampire, half werewolf. Good hearing is one of the tricks of the trade. Though sometimes, it's a curse."

Werewolf… Toni gulped more air into her lungs while her heart raced. "Not ready to acknowledge that just yet either, if that's okay."

"Oh, of course, Toni. I understand. You have bigger fish to fry right now. We can talk later about that part of this—whatever *this* is. For now, I have to wrangle the twins. So if you'll excuse me?"

Now Toni nodded, unable to do much else. "Of course."

Wanda lifted the hem of her gorgeous champagne-colored gown and hopped over a patch of ice as though she always wore ball gowns and stopped to assess the two quarreling women as they tussled.

Looking down, she said, "Marty, I'm going to suggest you get off Nina and hand her back her glasses before she explodes into a pile of ashes. I know she makes you want to choke her out, but you'd regret the loss of her black soul. I know you would. You'd cry, and quite frankly, you're a messy crier. Nina? Shut your big fat flapping lips until further notice, or it won't be Marty you have to worry about.

"Now, the two of you will get up off this ground because you're ruining your magnificent gowns in the dirty snow; you will introduce yourselves to Toni, who is as freaked-out and in as much a state of shock as we are; and you will do it with your manners intact and your indoor voices. Are we all in agreement?"

Nina's jaw clenched tight, her face a mask of anger. "Wanda, the fuck—"

Wanda's fingers snaked out and clamped Nina's lips together. "Shhh! Now. Don't speak. Wag that razor-sharp tongue of yours again, lose your sunscreen."

Marty let go of Nina's wrists and rasped a sigh, shoving off from her friend's lean torso to sit upright. "Fine. But one wrong move in Toni's direction and it's curtains for you, Dark One. Oh, and nice ball gown, Cinder-Nightmare. Very, very bright and *sunny*, just like your sparkling personality," she taunted, letting her head fall back on her shoulders to laugh out loud.

Nina growled and with a flat palm to Marty's chest, knocked her on her back. Scooping up her glasses to prop them crookedly on her nose with an aggravated hand, she shoved the stems of them into the nest of her triple-tier, wedding-cake-like hair.

"You watch yourself, Werewolf, or I'm gonna spin that color wheel of yours until you puke."

Marty took Wanda's hand and allowed her to help her up, but Nina dismissed the offer, slapping at the yards and yards of constricting yellow material around her legs when she rose.

Marty approached Toni as she brushed the wet snow from her gown, heavily embroidered with dark-blue and gold thread along the bodice. "I'm Marty Flaherty, by the way. So nice to meet you."

Toni stuck out her frozen hand and offered it to the pretty blonde. "Toni Vitali. I'm really sorry about this. I'm as confused as you are—"

"No apologies necessary," Marty cut in on a smile as warm as Wanda's voice. "If you had any idea what we've seen... Well, let's just say, we've seen a lot. We've also kicked some ass while we've seen a lot. So we'll figure this out and kick some ass if the situation deems necessary."

Wanda jammed a finger into the spot between Nina's shoulder blades. "Speak, Cavewoman. Talk pretty. Make words."

Nina popped her lips, crossing her arms over her chest, her stance defensive. "Nina   If-You-Ever-Stick-Your-Face-in-Mine-Again-I'll-Rip-it-Off Statleon."

Wanda's lips thinned as she drove two knuckles into Nina's back. "Can it, Bruiser."

"Well, all right then," Marty said, a bright smile wreathing her face when she looked to Toni and tucked her clasped hands under her chin. "Let's figure this out, huh, girls?"

Was it just her, or were these women behaving as though they'd landed on some movie set and a stagehand was going to come along at any second and whisk them off to their dressing rooms? Because they didn't appear at all phased by this utterly implausible, completely insane turn of events.

Simply saying they'd *seen* things, as Marty had, could imply a wealth of scenarios, most of which were probably nothing like what was happening right now. But who'd ever seen something even close to this?

Toni finally looked down at her clothes and really absorbed her garb, her worst fears confirmed as she plucked at her incredibly tight, unbelievably itchy gown and held up the flouncy-trouncy skirt for the women to see. "Are you seeing what I'm seeing? I mean, we really are...um, we have on...we were just in the outlet mall and now we're in..."

"Shamalot. You're in Shamalot. Welcome, welcome!" said a tiny, tinkling voice full of cheer.

If that voice was attached to tiny wings of gossamer, Toni was headed for the nearest whatever they called a bar in these parts and drinking until she passed out cold. And if she was still here tomorrow, she was going to do it all over again.

She'd faced far worse than this in her time—a gun brawl over a borscht dinner…her brother's finger sent to her doorstep via UPS…the death of her neighbor—this should be cake. Yet, her reluctance to find out whom the voice belonged to was almost bigger than she was.

She didn't want any more upheaval and surprises. She just wanted quiet. She wanted to get up every morning at six sharp, drink a cup of shitty coffee from her half-dead coffeemaker, take a dribbling, lukewarm shower in her pathetic, rundown apartment, put on her ugly pink salesclerk jacket, catch no less than three busses to the outlet mall, and hand over her pride at the door to Queen Bree.

She'd adjusted to the everyday aches and pains of normalcy and almost-poverty. They were startlingly different from her old life, but they were now like macaroni and cheese, comforting if nothing else. Even if her life unequivocally sucked in so many ways, she was still *free*. Free of most of her fear. Free of the constant tension. Free of Stas Vasilyev.

It had been that way for three years now, and she didn't want to give it up.

Wanda gripped her arm as the ground beneath their feet suddenly boomed with footsteps. "Stay near me, Toni. No matter what, stay close," she whispered urgently.

She totally planned to cling to Wanda as ordered for fear of what might come next. Robin Hood and his band of merry men?

Inhaling deeply, Toni turned around with Wanda's direction just as a light snow began to fall, the flakes soft and strangely fluffier than the ones in Jersey. They fluttered in glittering, actually defined shapes to the ground, landing one after the other, forming neat piles.

"'Tis so lovely to meet ye!" the same tiny voice said with a slight brogue attached.

Through the veil of shimmering white, a creature emerged, hulking and blue—oh yes, he was blue, wearing gold shorts with red piping, attached to suspenders over a naked barrel chest.

The crowd of stunned onlookers began to back up as he made his way toward them with lumbering steps that rattled the earth, knocking snow from trees and leaving a deep path in his wake.

He held out a very blue hand and grinned, flashing white teeth the size of small tombstones. "Dannan The Ogre, if yer wonderin'. Nice to meet ye," he said, his helium-like voice a gross, almost comical understatement to his size.

Ogres. Didn't ogres eat people?

"Holeee shitballs," Nina uttered, shoving Marty behind her. Which, had Toni time to think about it, was in stark contrast to the way she'd nearly bitten Marty's head off just moments ago.

"No need to fear," Dannan said affably, as though he wasn't easily ten feet tall with feet the size of fishing boats. Leaning down, he peered at Toni. "Whass yer name, lass?"

"Inedible?" she asked with a wince, nipping at her lower lip.

He chuckled, light and airy and remarkably like he'd sucked a balloon full of helium. "You're frightened, are ye, maiden?"

Toni shivered, not just because she was scared, but because he'd used the word "maiden" in conjunction with her—which was utterly laughable. "Should I speak the truth?"

"Please do."

"Ye is petrified."

With one finger, he patted her shoulder, the heavy weight of it not unpleasant. In fact, it was soothing and gentle. "I understand completely."

"Absolutely no insult intended."

He bounced his round head covered in spikes of snow-white, bushy hair. "Duly noted."

Nina was the first to approach him, and even *she* did so with caution. "So, where are we again, Papa Smurf?"

"It's—"

"Yeah, yeah. I heard you, Dannan The Ogre. Now where the hell are we?"

"Shamalot, o' course. Ye be deep in the heart of the Not So Sherwood Forest."

Duh.

Nina rolled her tongue along the inside of her cheek. "And we got here how, Blue Man Crew?"

"Again, I remind ye, pale lady, 'tis Dannan The Ogre. And I know not how ye came to be, but I think one of ye merry wenches wished yerself here. That's usually how it works. In the process, ye have managed to effectively end the drunken adventures of the Mildly Irritated Witch of the East."

Toni's finger shot up in the air as she stared skyward, still unable to look at the body Dannan pointed to. "Are there any flying monkeys in this scenario?"

Dannan cocked his enormously round head, the trumpet-like ears on either side of his face fluttering. "Flying what, lass?"

Wanda The Soother, as Toni was secretly beginning to refer to her, smiled up at Dannan. "Can you explain the 'wishing ourselves' here you mentioned? Because I can't remember ever wishing myself to a place like this. A quiet, padded cell sans my friends Nina and Marty? Yes. A warm, tropical beach—just me and my man all alone with nothing but the sound of the surf? Absolutely. But a place called Shamalot in a dress so tight my eyeballs are bulging and my ribs have realigned themselves to fuse with my spine? Never."

Wished yourself here. Dannan's words plucked a memory in Toni's brain.

The one where she wished she were anywhere but the outlet mall?

No. Nuh-uh.

Crap, crap, crap. She really *was* responsible for them landing here.

But there was no time to dwell on how horrible she was for the boom of thunder and the sharp crack of lightning.

"Aye, lass, ye've done it now," Dannan mumbled at Toni as a streak of pink and white light crisscrossed through the sky.

Panic raced up Toni's spine. "Done *what?*"

Dannan's blue face was somber with a hint of irritation. "Brought upon us the annoyingly cheerful hospitality, sprinkled with pecan dust and just a hint of fried goose, of Bren—"

"Haaay, gurls, hay!" A southern drawl, lilting and sticky-sweet, touched Toni's ears just as a beautiful woman floated to the ground—right from the sky. From. The. *Sky.*

She landed lighter than a feather, gliding to a full stop, her white, bell-shaped skirt wafting down around her in a cloud of dreamy glitter. She, too, had wings, just like the trio of women, but hers were enormous and gorgeously complex, as though they'd been embroidered with silk threads.

With a wand of glowing silver in her hand, her platinum locks blowing behind her and teased to a mind-blowing mound at the back of her head, she grinned and winked at them.

Toni fought a hysterical scream and moved in closer to Wanda—who still remained outwardly unfazed. Even though, compared to Dannan anyway, this new addition looked harmless, the pile of oddities was finally ganging up on her.

"Howdee and welcome to Shamalot, y'all! I'm Brenda, the Good Witch of the South, and I'da baked a pie had I known you were payin' a visit to my neck o' the woods! So, let me be the first to welcome you ladies as honorary members of the League of Fairy Godmothers! We're an esteemed group of women hell-bent on spreadin' love and happily-ever-afters like soft butter on a pecan muffin!"

Now Marty tilted her head as the snow pelted her face and the cold left her cheeks rosy. "League of Fairy Godmothers? Is that like a bowling team? Do we get matching shirts?"

She didn't know how to bowl. Shit. She was sunk. Toni's breathing shuddered as her panic rose again, but Wanda gripped her fingers tighter and patted her arm.

Nina was the first to actually approach Brenda, and this time, unlike meeting Dannan, she wasn't even a little hesitant.

Planting her hands on her hips, she sauntered toward the ethereal woman and spat, "Screw your pies and your league fairies and your HEA. Tell me how the hell we get out of here—"

"What Nina means to say is, thank you for the lovely welcome. Fab dress. Thumbs up on the big, big hair. Now, how the hell do we get out of here?" Marty asked pleasantly, looping her arm through Nina's and smiling.

The beautiful woman tucked her wand under her armpit then clasped her hands together just under her chin and chuckled, her laughter echoing all around them in shards of muted sound.

"Well, bless your hearts! Feelin' a little out of sorts after your trip, are ya, Puddin'?"

Nina popped her lips and rolled her shoulders. With a crack of her knuckles, she said, "I'm feeling ridiculous in this GD ball gown. Not to mention I can hardly hold my head up with this frickin' hairdo, and I have wings. *Wings*. Now ante up, Princess Puffy. Because I wanna go home."

Brenda shot Nina a smile that was not only stunning but meant to pacify. "Aw, darlin', you do know what they say about big hair, don't ya? The higher the hair, the closer to your maker." She used her wand to punctuate her point by tipping it skyward.

"You know what they say about vampires, don't ya? The angrier you make me, the closer I come to sending your lifeless carcass to your maker," Nina mocked in a ridiculous imitation of Brenda's drawl.

Marty instantly yanked one of the massive curls falling from the top of Nina's head and down along her back. "Shut up," she ordered from stiff lips. "We don't know what we're dealing with here, Elvira. This isn't Jersey anymore. Now, zip it!"

Wanda again intervened, dragging a stiff, reluctant Toni with her. "Brenda, it's lovely to meet you. Truly. However, we have families to return to back…back in our homeland—or whatever. We have people who'll miss us, is what I'm saying. So while this visit has been absolutely incredible and your village is delightful, we really do need to get home. So, if you'd kindly tell us what the fairy godmother league means in relation to us and how we get home, Brenda, we'd be very grateful."

Brenda used her silvery wand with the big ball on the end to point at each of the women, a serene smile on her face. "In order to leave this realm, y'all each have a job, and with that job you have to complete a task."

"A task?" Wanda repeated, her eyes blank.

Brenda nodded, her smile still glowing. "Uh-huh."

Nina snorted, her defensive stance returning. "Lay off the coy games and get to the frickin' point. Tell us what we have to do to leave your theme park in clear, concise terms without all the pomp and bullshit, or I'm going to deflate that big, poofy hairdo of yours. Go. *Now*."

Brenda literally floated toward Nina, capturing her eyes with a hard stare. "I'm doin' my best to be hospitable to you, bein' a stranger in a strange land and all, Buttahcup, but you're makin' my goodwill as shaky as a newborn thoroughbred. Just so's ya know, I can turn you into a toad just like that." She snapped her fingers in Nina's face.

Nina growled, flashing those freaky teeth once more.

And again, Wanda intervened, stepping between the two women, Toni still latched onto her arm while she watched in silent fascination.

"Please, forgive Nina's crass, pseudo-sociopathic behavior and deal directly with me from here on out. What's our task, Brenda, and what does being an honorary member of the League of Fairy Godmothers have to do with it?"

Brenda's face changed, going from dark to light. "Everyone who enters the realm of Shamalot has to give back, and I'm in charge of assignin' y'all a job according to your aura's mental state, if you will. Then you have to complete your assignment before you can go before King Dick and ask him to grant your wish to leave."

"Our auras?" Toni squeaked. What kind of mumbo jumbo crazy business was this?

"Yep! So here's what ya gotta do, Red," she said, winking at Toni. "You have a journey to go on with a pair of to-die-for shoes. They belong to the king, and he's gonna spit bricks when he realizes they're gone from Castle Beckett."

"*Shoes?*" everyone repeated in unison, their heads swiveling on their necks.

Shoes. Toni gulped some cold air. There were going to be flying monkeys, she just knew it.

Brenda bobbed her head before anyone had time to process her words and swirled her wand in the air, creating a puff of pink and white smoke just before she pointed in the direction of the body Toni had landed on.

And then she aimed that glittery stick of mayhem at Toni's feet.

The atmosphere stilled for a moment, growing thick with the scent of gladiolas, the white haze of snowflakes slowing to almost a stop. Quite suddenly, Toni's feet felt heavy, as though they were weighted down by cement, forcing her to stumble forward.

Wanda grabbed for her, righting her by throwing an arm around her waist and encouraging Toni to lean against her.

But then Wanda gasped. In fact, everyone gasped.

"PleasesayIdon'thavetheshoesonpleasesayIdon'thavetheshoeson!" Toni squeaked out, too afraid to confirm her deduction.

"Okay, so you have the shoes, but look on the bright side," Marty chirped, rubbing Toni's arm, her sky-blue wings thumping swiftly. "They're fabulous. I mean, they match your dress like a dream, all purple and sparkly. Love!"

The day's events welled up inside Toni, sitting square in her chest, overwhelming her, constricting her breathing. Enough crazy was enough.

She pushed off Wanda, stumbling toward Brenda as her ankles bowed and her legs wobbled.

Blowing a stray piece of hair from her eyes, she planted her hands on her hips to come off as authoritative as possible and said, "Let's just cut to the chase, y'all. I have to take the shoes to Oz to see the wizard or a variation thereof. The guy you call King Dick, right? And along the way, shitty stuff's gonna happen to me. A psychotic witch, on a bender to frighten even the best sociopath, is going to terrorize me, too, correct? Because all she really wants is the shoes on *my* feet. There'll be fire, and rain, and psychedelic flowers, and flying monkeys. But the whole time, all I ever had to do in order to avoid the shitty stuff and the sociopathic witch was click my heels three times and say the words 'there's no place like home', yes? So why don't I just do that now and we can all part ways and be home lickety-split."

Brenda's face went utterly blank. She stared at Toni for a moment. But then her lips returned to that annoyingly happy grin. "What kinda crazy are you blowin' out your piehole, girl? Didja hit your head on the way in? Who in tarnation's the wizard? Never mind. No time for explanations. Your job is to take the shoes back to their rightful owner, King Dick. Because he's the only one who can remove 'em from your feet now."

"*She* stole them. Why can't she take the shoes back?" Toni asked, pointing to the prone body with a cringe. Why had she had the shoes to begin with? What did the shoes mean?

Brenda rolled her eyes as though the answer was obvious. "Well, duh. Because she's drunker than a coon who fell in a barrel o' hootch, that's why. The effects'll last for days. Maybe even a whole month."

Some of her old spirit returned, the fighter in her rearing its ugly head. The one she'd tried desperately to muffle for three years now. "Okay, then who says *I* have to be the one to take them back?"

Brenda's next words were petulant, as though Toni had dared defy her edict and she wasn't going to stand for it. "Said *me*, Sugar."

Toni shook her head and might have followed up with a stomp of her feet, but the heels were at least four inches and the ground was icy. "No. That's not good enough. I want an explanation."

"Tough cream puffs. You want out, you gotta do your time in the realm," Brenda said, that beautiful smile still wreathing her pink lips. Then she turned to Nina, Marty and Wanda. "Now, y'alls? Your job is like findin' a John Deere in your garage after your lawnmower just sputtered its last breath! You have to help Toni get to the castle and return the shoes, because that's where she'll find her happiness. Which is what we fairy godmothers do best. Shower folks with happiness. So, your job as honorary members is to get your girl here to Castle Beckett by Christmas Eve. And you three will have limited use of those special powers you got. Otherwise it's cheatin', ya hear?"

Toni closed her eyes. Special powers? She wasn't ready to hear what their special powers entailed.

"Got any other jobs available? Like a Brenda the Good Witch of the South flayer?" Nina asked, her mouth turned downward in a sneer.

"How does honorary troll grab ya?" Brenda asked, her hand on her hip, her expression haughty.

Nina didn't answer but she growled again, snapping at the witch.

Brenda assessed Nina for a moment, clearly unafraid before she said, "Listen, the realm assigns jobs according to your aura, and somehow, Cranky Pants, the realm thinks *you* should be a fairy godmother, one who helps a nice girl who needs some happiness in her life get to the castle. I don't make up the jobs, I just assign 'em, Sugar."

"Why can't I just take the shoes off and give them to you to take to this King Dick? You two seem tight." Toni planted a hand on Wanda's bare shoulder to steady herself and rubbed her toes along the back of one shoe to push it off, only to find it wouldn't budge.

"Because you need a J-O-B, Sugarlumps. You can't be a fairy godmother; your aura's all wrong for that at this point in your life. They stay on until you get to the castle, and that's just that," she said with another infuriatingly radiant smile.

Because of course it couldn't be that simple, more panic seized her as she struggled to remove the shoes again, to no avail.

"And the woman who was wearing them? Uh, the Mad and Irate Witch of Whatserville? What's her gig?" Wanda asked with a frown.

"The Mildly Irritated Witch of the East, darlin'," Brenda corrected. "She's my big sister, by the by. Got downright snockered on some thistleberry wine at the winter ball last week and stole the daggone shoes. Can you even imagine the hootin' and hollerin' over that scandal?"

"The horror," Nina groused, brushing her many layers of yellow skirt out of the way of her long legs.

"Exactly!" Brenda agreed, punctuating her point with her wand. "Any ol' way, she put 'em on and took off. Couldn't find her anywhere! Musta been holed up with that cute blacksmith she was chattin' up at the ball. Knew I should have checked there first."

"Again, I ask, why me? What in my aura says I can't be a fairy godmother, too?"

Brenda's shoulders, covered in poofy material, collapsed. "Because your aura's plain miserable, Red. Getting to the castle is the key to your happiness. Ya gotta trust ol' Brenda on this. You need a happily-ever-after like a good southern girl needs her pearls and pumps."

Perfect. She was so pathetic, so pitiable, even some shoes thought she needed a happily-ever-after.

Speaking of sisters and shoes, Toni gathered the courage to ask the question she dreaded the most as she finally looked to her left at the woman who lie in a lump under a snow-topped bush with red berries. Her body was tucked into a loose ball, the red and gold skirt of her ball gown flowing behind her.

Horror and shame washed over her that she'd waited this long into her conversation with Brenda before she'd asked after her sister.

"I'm sorry about your mediocre sister. Or whatever her name is. I would never hurt someone. Did I…kill her?" She gulped, holding her breath and crossing her fingers.

Brenda reached out a perfectly manicured hand and tweaked the tip of Toni's nose. "Don't be silly, Punkin'. She's just passed out cold. I'll give her some hair of the troll and she'll be fresh as a little ol' daisy in the time it takes you to say goober, and then she's hittin' fairy godmother rehab. On that you can count."

Toni inhaled a shuddering breath. *Thank God.* "Okay, so let's address this happily-ever-after then. I don't care what my aura says, I'm good, really. I'm about as happy as I've ever been. So if you could just use your magicthingamajiggy and poof us to the castle, I'll give the king his shoes and we'll ask him to send us home and roll on outta here. That work?"

She used to be a pretty good negotiator in her old life in Jersey. Ask anyone at the flea market. She was infamous for talking the sock guy down on his prices. There was no reason she couldn't be one here in Shamalot.

Brenda's eyes, ringed by blue eye shadow and curly lashes, widened in reproach. "I can't do that. It's against the cotton-pickin' rules, and it's all kinda bad manners to ask me to just zap you on outta here. That's an abuse of power I ain't willin' to touch, sister. The realm has rules, and if I break 'em, I'll upset the balance of order. You have to make the journey to happiness on foot, and your gal-pals here are your guides."

"Point of contention?"

Brenda looked confused as she cocked her head, her hair cascading over her shoulder. "A *what*? Speak English at me, Red."

"Why is it just me who needs a happily-ever-after and none of them? I don't want to throw anyone under the bus, but how did I get the kewpie doll? And I hate to be petty, but why does everyone get wings but me?"

"The answer's simple—because you're not a fairy godmother and they're already happy."

Toni's shoulders slumped as her head throbbed. "But I'm telling you, I *am* happy."

Mostly. Sometimes. Happiness was subjective, and if she wasn't exactly skipping through fields of sunflowers, at least she wasn't being held someone's terrified hostage. It was as close to happy as she'd been in a long time.

"Now, now, Red," she chastised. "No one gets to the realm if they're shootin' rays o' sunshine outta their butts. It was you who wished you were anywhere but that outlet mall, wasn't it? Somethin' ain't right in your life, and it's gotta be fixed or you can't ever leave Shamalot. You wished for it, you got it. The realm knows your heart, and there ain't no foolin' it. This is your journey."

Her stubborn streak, the one that had saved Stas killing from her, kicked in. "Okay then, what if I refuse to go on the journey?"

"Then I guess you'd better see a man about rentin' yourself one of those cute little cottages over yonder and settin' up housekeepin' for life. Oh, I know just the person, too! Sweet as peach pie on a summer day. You want his card?"

Toni didn't have the chance to say one way or the other before Nina was in attack mode.

She circled Brenda and made a fist. "Hold the bloody fuck on!" Nina yelped, stomping her foot in the snow. "I'm no GD fairy godmother. I hate people. I hate *all* people, and the hell I'm wearin' this stupid—"

But Brenda was no longer listening. With a wave of her wand, the tip of the silvery stick emitting a glistening silver dust, she said, "There's nothing more I can do for ya, Dumplins. The realm has spoken. But here's to you, Toni! Go on and get ya some of the good stuff. Bye, y'all!"

And then she and her unconscious sister were gone.

When the silence of Brenda's departure became painfully awkward, when their mouths could no longer hang open without freezing in position, suddenly Nina became animated, her eyes darting around the clearing.

"Aw, for fuckity-fuck's sake! Has anyone seen Carl? *Where's Carl?*"

Chapter 3

"Carl?" Nina hollered, frightening the villagers who'd begun to disperse and go back to doing whatever it was villagers did when they were done gawking at the realm-jumpers.

Nina lifted her skirts with an angry growl and began searching the perimeter of the village in a blur of motion Toni still couldn't believe she was witnessing.

"Carl! If you don't come back here right now, I'm taking away your broccoli cupcakes for snack for a solid week, and you're gonna get coal in your stocking, mister!"

Carl had looked pretty pale back at the store. Maybe he was sick. Fear struck a chord in Toni's belly, spurring her to action. *Fear* she understood. Fear had been her fuel for three years. This was her fault. She'd done this. She had to get her shit together and help find him.

"Is Carl the young man who was with Nina in the store?" Toni asked Marty with trepidation.

Marty nodded, her blue eyes full of worry. "That's our Carl. He's a zombie and the sweetest thing ever. He's not used to being alone. We need to find him right now or—"

"Carl!" Dannan yelled, his tiny voice whipping in the blustering wind as he headed into the woods, selflessly helping to search for someone he didn't even know. "Come to us, lad!"

"How about we split up into small groups? We'll cover more ground that way," Toni suggested, forgetting everything but finding Carl.

The tall pines to the left of them, separating the village from the path, rustled and parted as yet another tall figure emerged, and everyone stopped all motion.

Dear Realm, please don't let this be Maleficent.

For a brief moment, the skies, their dark-purple clouds spewing snow, brightened. Magically so. The heavens opened, and shafts of light mimicking rainbow prisms shone down upon a head of shiny ebony hair.

Birds chirped, frogs ribbited, and just shy of angels singing, Toni was sure she heard the strains of a gentle harp playing somewhere in the distance.

And from the tall trees, out stepped a man. A man so perfect, so magnificent, so chiseled and hard, each of the women, Nina included, stopped and stared as though he'd cast a real live spell on the lot of them.

His thighs bulged beneath the rust-colored pants he wore, the laces pulled tight in a crisscross pattern, ending at his tapered waist; his chest wide and muscled beneath his green shirt and dark brown vest.

Eyes of the bluest sapphire, fringed by a thick down of dark lashes, stared at her. His hair was wet from the snow but it gleamed in all its ebony-ness, slicked back from his face, the ends falling to his jawline.

His cheekbones were high, sharp, and his jaw square and lean. And his arms—oh, those arms. Just thick enough from heavy labor, but not so thick he couldn't put them down at his sides.

There was a collective breathy sigh as everyone's eyes glazed over. He was the most beautiful specimen of man she'd ever seen and it took all she had to keep from letting a breathy sigh escape her throat, too.

As he tromped from the woods, the snow swirling around him, he had his arm around the neck of a reindeer—a very pale and green-around-the-gills reindeer. "Milady?" he called, his voice like liquid warmth, washing over Toni, bathing her soul, and leaving her weak in the knees. "Would this be your Carl?"

Nina approached the newcomer slow and steady, lifting her glasses as the prisms of light above his head faded and the clouds returned.

The reindeer covered the distance between them, running toward Nina with a slow, crooked gait. The animal stopped in front of her and patted his hoof on the snow before tucking his head, antlers and all, into her hip.

Nina's long fingers lifted his muzzle as she looked down into his eyes. "Carl?"

The reindeer reared his head up and tapped his hoof on the ground again.

"Aw, for Jesus's sake, Carl! What happened, little buddy?" She ran her hands over his back and head, checking him thoroughly.

Toni stood off to the side as the women gathered around "Carl" and stroked him, and she wondered...what the hell?

Some inventory was necessary if she was going to go any further. Her brain was a jumbled mess of what was real and what was make-believe.

So far today, she'd been pitched down a rabbit hole in a dressing room, dumped in a strange land, knocked a drunken, kind-of-irritated witch out cold, heard talk of vampires, werewolves and zombies, nabbed a pair of cute shoes she couldn't take off, met a blue ogre and a good witch with a magic wand, discovered she was going to be forced to have some happily-ever-after she'd never asked for, and now the sweet, shy man-child she'd met in the outlet mall was a zombie turned reindeer.

And none of it—*none of it* appeared to make these women question a single second of what was happening to them.

"Milady?" the devastatingly handsome man said, bowing regally before her. "Jon Doe The Stable Boy, at your service."

And then there was this. Jon Doe. The stable boy. Seriously? A man of this ilk deserved a much bigger name than Jon. Maybe something like Perfect or Granite or Flawless, perhaps. But Jon seemed much too simple.

"Milady?"

She licked her chapped lips and swallowed, holding out her trembling hand. "Toni. Toni Vitali."

He nodded his perfect head and smiled, pressing his warm, yummy lips briefly to the back of her hand. "A lovely name for a lovely maiden."

Her eyes would've rolled if they weren't now frozen in their sockets. *Maiden.* Hah. But there was something else. Something new and unfamiliar to Toni. Her heart literally fluttered in her chest as though it, too, had wings just like these women, and her stomach gurgled. Not unpleasantly, but with an excited skip.

"Milady?" he asked, his eyes curious.

"Thank you for finding, um, Carl."

"No trouble at all," he offered gallantly. "He was just grazing in the woods, and his unusual coloring made me stop and ponder his breed—it's like no other. He looks nothing like my stable of deer. It was then he began to whimper, and I worried he'd lost his mother. I see I was right. Odd as that seems."

Toni snorted, condensation escaping her lips in a puff of white. "Odd? You don't know the half of it."

He pointed to her shoes, sparkling in the twilight. "I see you have the king's shoes. How did you manage that?"

"The king's shoes are pretty popular around these parts, huh?"

Jon ignored her question and instead asked, "Speaking of parts, what land is yours?"

"Land?"

"Yes, from whence you hail."

"I hail from the land of designer outlet malls with wormholes. Better known as Jersey," she said as she shivered, her teeth beginning to chatter.

Jon tilted his head, his blue-blue eyes twinkling. "Jersey? I've not heard of this place. Is it far?"

Toni shivered again, crossing her arms over her chest. "Far is a subjective term at this point. But you best believe, it's a long way from Shamalot."

Pulling off his vest, he wrapped it around Toni's shoulders, his fingers brushing her exposed skin and evoking another shiver as a ripple of awareness shot along her spine.

"Have you sought lodging? The eve is upon us, my lady Toni, and the weather will sour quickly."

Now, homeless and penniless, she knew. She had this. Rubbing her hands together, she asked, "Got a match?"

"A what?"

"Never mind. Listen, do you know how to get to the castle? Because according to Brenda the Good Witch of the South, I have to give these babies back." She pointed to her shoes—shoes that were killing her frozen feet right now.

Jon's face darkened for a moment and then it was as though an idea formed, because he smiled wide, his ultra-white teeth as perfect as the rest of him. "I do know the way to the castle. Do you need an escort?"

"She don't need nothin' from you, Hot Breeches," Nina crowed, Carl nestled close to her side.

Marty and Wanda joined Toni, their eyes on Jon. Because really, whose eyes could will themselves away from a long hard stare at all that man?

Toni unglued her own gawking stare from his hulking physique and made introductions. "Jon The Stable Boy, this is Marty, Wanda, and Nina. All fair maidens dumped in your backyard." *Because of me.*

Jon bowed once more, his thick, dark hair gleaming as the last of the day faded. "Miladies, the pleasure is mine. How can I be of assistance?"

Marty whistled and fanned herself with her hand, looking to Wanda, whose wings had taken up a mad whir. "Are you warm? Is anyone else warm?"

"On fire here," Wanda croaked then swallowed, the light-blue veins in her neck working when she nodded. She grabbed the hand Marty was using to fan herself and pointed it at her own face as she lifted the back of her fancy hairdo.

Before she spoke, Nina eyed Jon, a little longer than Toni suspected was the norm for someone as gruff and indifferent as her. "You can assist us by telling us how to get the fuck out of here, *Jon.*"

He looked directly into Nina's eyes, his expression one of confusion. "This word—fuck—means what? Is that from your land?"

Wanda groaned a sigh as she rolled her head on her neck while rubbing at her temples. "That's just Nina behaving badly. My blanket apologies in advance for every word that comes out of her mouth until we part ways. Now, Jon, how do we get out of here?"

Now he smiled again in understanding, as though they were speaking his language. "Have you paid passage on a ship? I can be your guide to the ocean in less than seven days. What is the name of the ship you plan to sail upon?"

Nina brushed her hands together, her full lips going thin. "Yep. We're fucked, folks."

Marty poked Nina in the shoulder. "You don't know that." Then she turned to Jon, her blue eyes widening in a flirtatious manner. "Here's our dilemma, Jon. We don't know how we got here in the first place, but we're not from your...your..."

"Realm," Toni offered as she burrowed under Jon's vest, her tone dry.

"Well lookit you, all speaking the native tongue," Nina said sarcastically, giving Toni's shoulder a thump of her hand. "If it wasn't for you, I'd be at home on the Island right now reading my kid a Christmas story and putting her to bed so I could hunker down on the couch with my man in my very own castle. You heard what that nutbag Brenda The Sticky Sweet Witch said, *you* wished us here to medieval hell. This is on you."

"Brenda?" Jon asked, his spine suddenly rigid, his tone aware. "You've encountered the Good Witch of the South?"

"Yeah, with all her big hair and whistles. The biscuits-and-gravy lady says we can't leave here unless we take this one to the castle for her happily-ever-after."

Jon's face cleared again, his head bobbing at Nina. "Of course, of course. You were summoned to the realm of Shamalot because you were unhappy with your life?"

Toni wondered if this kind of thing happened often.

"Has this happened before?" Marty asked, tilting her head and asking the question Toni wasn't able to put into a proper sentence.

"Often people visit the realm to see the king and ask that their wishes be granted," Jon provided. "But no one from your land of Jersey, as I recollect. So is this why you have come to Shamalot—because you are unhappy?"

Why she cared if Jon knew she was unhappy or otherwise was unsettling, but somehow, it left her uneasy. "I'm not unhappy!" She felt like she needed to say as much again for Jon's benefit—all out in the open.

"You work at an outlet mall. No one's happy makin' minimum wage and working for that yippy blonde with her dresses that'll change your life," Nina remarked, flicking her hard curls from her face.

Finally, she couldn't take the guilt anymore. It rose up like a swell of remorse and overflowed all over the women. "Okay fine, lady. It's true. I wished I were anywhere but there today. I didn't even say it out loud, for hell's sake. I only thought it. But haven't you ever done that? Like 'Wow, I wish I was watching paint dry instead of sitting through this movie'?"

Nina nodded, her curls beginning to fall flat from the heavy snow. "You mean like right frickin' now?"

Toni let her hands drop to her sides with a slap against the lavish material of her dress. "It was metaphoric, for the love of Cheetos! I didn't mean dump me and every person within twenty feet into a land with no running water!"

Jon placed a light hand on Toni's arm, a hand that wrought all sorts of chills and dirty, dirty visuals. "What is a movie and Cheetos?"

Nina tapped his broad shoulder with a frown. "Oh, Jesus and a Renaissance fair—forget the damn movie, Flawless. Just tell us how to get the hell out of here!"

"I am *Jon*, for future reference. And I don't know how you do that, My Lady of Discontent," he shot back, towering over Nina, his jaw rigid. "I only know the rules of the realm, and they are, you must do as Brenda The Good Witch says. I can assist, of course, but I can't detour and keep you from your happiness. As a member of the League of Fairy Godmothers, surely you know that."

"How in the fresh hell do you know I'm a fairy godmother?" Nina growled at him, flashing her teeth.

He twirled his finger in the air around his head with an impish grin that made Toni melt. "The wings are a dead giveaway, but if not for them, then the hair. It's all about the very large hair."

"Okay, everyone just stop!" Wanda ordered, hiking up her skirts and squaring her shoulders. "We're getting nowhere like this. Obviously, the realm or whatever wants us to take Toni to the castle and leaving isn't an option. Now, it's not like we're strangers to an odd crisis or…what is it, now…eleven crises? We're just not usually a party to them in quite this way. That said, we're going to do what we do on every other case we've ever had—help the client. So buckle up, biotches, quit complaining, and let's get Toni to the castle."

The client? Cases? Toni held up a frozen red hand. "Well, hold on. Who says Brenda's the final word on what's what? Again I ask, what if I don't want to go to the castle?"

"What if I drag you and your boogie shoes the entire way?"

Jon stepped between Nina and Toni, his hand going to his hip, where a silver sword sat. "I cannot allow you to harm the fair maiden."

Nina snorted in Jon's face and looked up at him, her eyes gleaming as she yanked her sunglasses off. "Here's the score, Pretty Boy, *no one* tells me what's allowed."

Jon placed a hand at Toni's waist and pushed her behind him. "I warn you, milady, I'm trained in the art of the sword. You do not want to do battle with me."

Nina rocked back on her heels with a sly smile. "Oh really? Well, I'm trained in the art of carnage, buddy. You don't want to see your innards wrapped around a tree, do you?"

Jon lifted his chin, the glimpse she caught of his eyes as she tried to get between them dark and stormy. "That would be heartily unpleasant, but no woman has come to harm while on my watch, and *none* ever will."

Toni removed Jon's hand from her waist—and if she were honest, reluctantly so—then stepped between he and Nina. "Look, this is my fault. I did this to all of us, I'll fix it. You three and Carl go on about your business, and I'll find my way to the castle myself. I'm no stranger to hoofing it alone."

Wanda yanked a glove off and tapped Nina in the head with it. "She most certainly will not. This was an accident, Nina. You know, that thing we specialize in? Besides, you heard what Brenda said—it has to be us who takes her to the castle in order for us to all leave, and besides that, when was the last time we abandoned someone in their hour of need? *Never.* That's when. Now you take Carl and go scout us out a place to stay for the night. Marty can find us some wheels; I'll look for the nearest food court. We ride at dawn!"

Jon held up a broad hand tipped with lean, sun-browned fingers. "I can provide you with all those things, if you'll allow me. And I can certainly be your guide to Castle Beckett."

"You know the way to the castle?" Marty asked. "Smart *and* delicious. Phew. Ice pack, please!" she chirped on a giddy chuckle, her wings picking up their thumping pace.

"If you'll all follow me through the woods, I'd be happy to shelter you for the night and we'll begin our journey in the morning, yes?"

Nina stopped him with a flat palm to his shoulder. "What's the going rate for shelter 'round Fairyland, Jon Doe?"

"Rate?" he asked, his gorgeous face confused.

Nina rubbed her fingers together. "Yeah, you know, like sheckles or rupies or a cow, or whatever the fuck it is you Robin Hoods want as a fee for using your facilities. Name your price, because I'm not going anywhere with you until we have some clear rules."

Jon's face went from confused to horrified in seconds. "I would never require a single pence as compensation for sheltering members of the League of Fairy Godmothers. It's against the rules of the realm and punishable by death."

"Oh, thank God," Marty murmured, her body visibly relaxing. "Because I have no idea where my purse is. Not to mention my cell phone. How are we going to call the boys and tell them we won't be home for dinner, Wanda?"

Jon turned to look down at them all, ignoring Marty's chatter. "Are we in agreement?"

Nina eyed him for a brief, uncomfortable moment before she said, "I'm givin' you fair warning, buddy. One wrong move, one shady shift of your eyes, and I'll kill you. You won't have time to use your sword if your Motel Six turns out to be Motel Hell. Got it?"

"What is a Motel Six?"

Jeez, he was cute when he was confused.

Wanda rolled her eyes and patted Jon's arm. "Ignore her and just take us somewhere warm, please."

But Jon didn't budge. He placed a hand over his heart. "I would never soil my reputation. Rest assured, you're safe with me. Now, shall we?"

He gallantly held out his arm to Toni who took it with little reluctance. She was damn cold and her feet were like blocks of ice. The sun had set, casting a purple haze over the clearing in the village, making her shiver again. She almost didn't care if they stayed in a pup tent.

They met back up with Dannan The Ogre who clearly knew Jon and offered to aide them in their quest to the castle.

As she hung on to Jon Doe The Stable Boy, his broad back her marker through the thickening haze of snow, she stumbled and tripped her way toward wherever they were going.

And still, even with the wind and snow lashing their faces, the bitter cold making her eyes water, this was a cakewalk compared to closing the store with Bree breathing down her neck, demanding she move faster so she could go home and play with her friends on Facebook.

For that much, she was grateful.

* * *

Jon forced himself to remain calm, yet his heart crashed in his chest so loudly, he worried the others would hear its harsh thump. As he held Toni's hand, helping her over logs, pushing the brush from their path, he stole glances at her.

Good realms, she was beautiful. Her hair was like fire, dancing over her slender back and resting on her rounded hips, her eyes the color of the green gemstones he and his brother once dove for during summers at the lake.

She possessed lips he wished to press his fingers to in order to discover if they were as soft and plump as he imagined.

She smelled of the breeze in the summer, a hint of honeysuckle on the vine mingling with the lavender his mother used to grow.

This Toni was intoxicating, leaving him with a tight chest and a heady heart, and he didn't understand this feeling. One he'd never felt before.

He'd never heard of this land she claimed to hail from, but he reminded himself to consult a map the moment he could get his hands on one.

In the meantime, he had to return her to the castle—a treacherous journey to be sure. Though, possibly not for the pale goddess whose title was Nina. She'd almost made him cringe as she'd glared at him and threatened his very life, her pale skin a pretty canvass for her darkly disturbing almond-shaped eyes.

And how was it she was mother to a reindeer? It was absurd. Did this land called Jersey have a new species of reindeer he'd not encountered?

And how odd that Toni had the king's shoes. He vaguely remembered some sort of scandal at the last ball the king held, but he paid no mind to the matters of Castle Beckett these days.

As they approached his modest cottage and stables, the glow of the warm fire inside beckoning, these were the things he pondered.

But what he pondered most heavily upon was Toni—and how he was going to simply hand over this beautiful creature to the king when the time came and why, after only just meeting her, was he left with an emotion so strong?

Chapter 4

When last I left you, dear readers, the three fair maidens and a zombie named Carl were all shopping for Christmas, full of joy and goodwill.

Okay, so not everyone was joyful over half-off scarves and maxi dresses, but you get the picture, right?

As you've witnessed firsthand, tragedy has struck our trio and their newfound fair maiden friend Toni. Well, mostly the tragedy centers around poor Toni, who's never encountered a paranormal event and is now stuck in a land with no running water, shoes that are killing her arches, and the thoroughly impossible Nina, who's being held captive by a yellow dress, poofy hair, fledgling wings and, soon to come—singing bluebirds, circling above her head in a joyous wreath of feathers and song.

Of course, you'd never know Toni was the fair maiden in crisis, for all the caterwauling Nina's doing. But she'll rally—this I promise.

As the group begins their journey through the Not So Sherwood Forest toward destination Castle Beckett after a long, restless night in an unknown land, treachery and deceit await them deep in the thick of the woods.

And again, I stress, some really bad dudes will continue to come their way.

For the wrathful Queen Angria from a neighboring land, is a queen so malevolent, so cruel she'd sell her own mother's organs at a lemonade stand, is displeased—like, spitting mad.

Just this very moment, she's been informed that the beautiful Toni is headed toward the castle, and while she has no flying monkeys to carry out her evil bidding, she's got a buttload of ammunition up her sleeve. And Queen Angria will stop at nothing to prevent Toni from meeting King

Dick's son, Prince Iver Daring, hottie medieval bachelor and all-round winner-winner-chicken-dinner.

In other words, major husband material for the queen's daughter, Resplendant.

The merging of the two rulers' kingdoms would have created the ultimate in not just prime real estate, but power, the one thing Queen Angria craves above all else.

Resplendant was promised to Prince Iver at birth. But King Dick, in all his flukey-kooky notions, has decided Resplendant isn't the maiden for his precious firstborn. This according to his soothsayer, the Great and Wonderful Roz. For as Roz peered into her mirror guide, she saw Prince Iver's truest love, and well…her face wasn't Resplendant's.

During a session of esteemed counsel, Roz suggested King Dick wait for the Christmas Eve ball, when the prince's true love will be revealed and Iver's fate sealed.

Of course, King Dick, wanting nothing more than true, everlasting happiness for his son, sent word he was breaking his pact with the queen. On a scroll with an official seal and everything. Which means it's a really important message, for those of you who aren't from the realm.

King Dick shipped Resplendant out like so much cargo. I mean, lock, stock and easily a hundred pieces of luggage right back to her furious mother's arms.

Wow. That went over big.

Not.

Who knew the queen had so much shit to throw at the wall? It's gonna take a team of people from *Got Junk?* to clean that mess up.

Anyway, Queen Angria's grown suspicious about our newcomer Toni and her coincidental appearance in Shamalot. Could it be that hers is the visage of the fair maiden the Great and Wonderful Roz saw in her stupid mirror guide (her words, not this storytellers)? Could it be she is the true intended for the dashing prince?

Queen Angria's decided to take no chances, and she's handed down an edict of her own.

To her henchman.

Bring Toni to her or lose your 401K—oh and your life.

Cue evil music.

* * *

"What the flying fuck gives, Flawless?" Nina barked, pointing upward with one hand while the other held the tattered hem of her yellow skirt. Her wings fluttered with erratic motion on her back as her lips formed a thin line.

Jon's laughter rang through the forest, bouncing off the thick trees, their branches bowing from the heavy snow from the night before. "Bluebirds, of course, milady Nina," he called with cheer as he saddled his horse Oliver and arranged for a village boy to tend his deer. "They help guide our way, milady."

Nina stopped dead in her tracks and swatted at the circle of fluttering blue wings surrounding her head. They chirped a happy tune, occasionally sitting atop her hair, which, in the bluebirds' defense, did rather resemble a nest.

"Dudes! Knock it the shit off. I can't think with all this damn hair, the wings, and your racket!"

Toni, despite her lack of sleep, her uncomfortable shoes, and her Starbucks deficit, openly laughed. She'd woken up in Jon's cottage at dawn and watched him as he'd gathered items for their journey to the castle, his large body moving in precise, fluid rhythm, captivating her.

Her heart had begun that wild fluttering again and her stomach had fairly tingled just looking at him.

As she'd hunkered down on the mattress made of straw he'd fashioned for her the night before, she'd tried to make sense of what was happening.

But she came up dry. Yes, she'd wished to be anywhere but the store, but why hadn't the realm of Shamalot been listening when she'd wished for a million bucks? Or that Stas would die a heinous, painful death after what he'd done to her brother?

Was the realm like a random generator, granting requests with slipshod aim?

Stas… He was one person she didn't have to worry about here, and waking up with that knowledge had brought her great peace this morning. It almost beat that question in Jon's eyes when he'd informed them he didn't know what this "coffee" they mourned was, and he didn't have any anyway.

She could find a way to live without coffee if it meant Stas would never darken her doorstep ever again. Everything was a trade-off as far as she was concerned.

But still, the happiness part of this boggled her. How could a realm and some king know what would make her happy? And why was she being forced to collect this happiness?

Now, as they made their way through the thick forest, the muted orange of the sun poking out over the vast mountain ranges surrounding Shamalot, she wasn't feeling as peaceful.

"So this vampire affliction you speak of," Jon asked Nina as they traipsed deeper into the forest through thick snow and chilling winds. "I'm afraid we have none of your breed here in our land. Do tell me more, won't you?"

Toni bit the inside of her cheek. They weren't supposed to have vampire afflictions where she came from either.

When the three women had explained whom—or rather *what*—they were and this crisis hotline they ran back in New York for the accidentally paranormal called OOPS, Toni had almost fallen face first into her bowl of gruel, or broth, or whatever Jon was titling that greasy mess he'd given them for dinner.

In fact, her mind had railed fiercely against what they'd proclaimed until they'd shown both she and Jon exactly what they were capable of doing with their paranormal abilities.

Jon hadn't blinked a gorgeous eye while she'd shivered in a corner with Carl at her feet, nuzzling her hand to soothe her. Fur flew, teeth flashed, the corner of Jon's cottage was lifted without even a grunt. Yet, he'd taken it all in stride, and she supposed if you grew up with ogres in your midst, vampires and werewolves weren't such a stretch.

But for her? A plain old human? It was like watching a TV show come to life—special effects and all.

But then hello. She was in a place called Shamalot with the hottest guy to walk the planet, no phones, no electricity, no Internet, wearing a pair of purple shoes she'd inherited from some sloshed witch, and now she was on her merry way to a castle to find a happy ending.

The absurd really exists, Scully.

Yet, that wasn't what she took away from their dinner conversations as Jon had blown out candles nestled in lanterns and they'd all settled in for the night.

What had stuck—or maybe the better description would be impressed her—was how much these women cared for each other. It went deep. You'd never know it by the way Marty and Nina bickered, but there'd been no denying Nina would have taken on Dannan for her friend, had he proven a foe.

While she stared in utter awe like some lovesick teenager at him, they'd shared tales of their crisis hotline adventures with Jon, who had some equally outlandish tales of dragon chasing and fairy catching, and what had stood out the most were the women's enduring friendships. This bond they and their immediate families shared.

They were all fused together in one way or another by their paranormal accidents, but that they'd chosen to stay together, that they laughed about their alleged trips to Hell and genies in bottles as though they were nothing more than road trips to Vegas, made Toni feel very alone in the world.

She realized it didn't matter where she was. Jersey or Shamalot, she was entirely alone. That stung just a little this bright morning.

"So, how are we this cold but lovely day, fair maiden Toni?" Wanda asked, looping her arm through hers. "You've had a lot to digest."

Remorse pained her heart and guilt ate at her gut. "I'm really sorry about this, Wanda. Taking you from your families, especially at Christmas. They'll be worried sick, and it's not like we can call them or send a message to let them know you're all right. Who'd have ever guessed throwing a random thought like that into the universe would produce this?"

Wanda patted her arm, her pretty smile clear and bright, her wings especially festive this morning. "I told you, we specialize in situations of this nature. It's why we come off so unaffected. Marty wasn't lying when she said we've seen some things."

"How do you guys feel? I mean, okay, maybe you've had a crisis or ten, but usually the crisis is about someone else. Not you. You have *wings* because of me." *Wings. Wanda had wings.* She instantly apologized again. "I'm sorry. So, so sorry."

"Oh c'mon. I have wings! I also have an amazing gown and hair so big I could probably joust with it. It's every childhood wish come true. They make me a little giddy, to be honest. And this isn't your fault, Toni. But I'm a firm believer everything happens for a reason. Care to share your reason?"

She swallowed hard, forcing one foot in front of the other as Dannan cleared a path for them with his large feet. "I can't think of any offhand. I was just having a bad day at the store is all."

"Ahh. You're not ready yet. I understand, but I want you to know, when you are, we'll listen."

Wanda's warmth and compassion were almost more than she could bear.

"Why are you being so nice to me? You should be pretty angry—and even though it was an accident, resentment is still up for grabs."

"Because I get the feeling you haven't had nice in your life for a long time, Toni. Everyone should have some nice to offset the unpleasant."

No truer words. But she wanted the focus *off* of her and the lack of nice in her life. She didn't know these people, and for all their goodwill—well, except for Nina—she wasn't a sharer. She kept things close to her vest for a reason. Because you never knew who was listening.

She'd learned that the hard way.

"What do you think's going on back home right now? Are your families calling the police, sending out search parties? They sound like a pretty tight bunch."

Wanda grimaced, tucking her chin into a pelt of fur Jon had given each of them to keep them warm. "That's the one thing that pains me most. Not being able to let my husband Heath kno\w I'm all right. But I can't fret over what I can't change, honey. He knows me well enough to know I'm pretty tough. Besides, who's to say the passage of time is the same here in Shamalot as it is in Jersey? Isn't it always topsy-turvy in a fairytale? Anyway, enough about me. What about you? Any family who'll be worried for your safety?"

A tear stung her eye, and she'd like to think it was the harsh wind that had picked up as they curved along the snow-covered path and entered a small patch of what looked like toadstools straight out of a cartoon. But it wasn't the wind.

Still, she shook her head. "Nope. No one will know I'm gone. Except Bree, and my landlord when rent time rolls around. Wow, am I ever going to get my ass handed to me for this. I'm guessing a pink slip will be waiting for me when I get back."

"Bree can stuff those damn scarves and her power trip up her tight, perky ass," Wanda said on a demonic chuckle. "If your happily-ever-after involves going back to Jersey, I think Marty might be able to help you with a job if you'd be willing to relocate to Buffalo."

Something lodged deep in her heart shifted a centimeter or two. Just enough to be noticeable. "You're doing that nice thing again. You don't even know me. Why would you consider me worthy of a job?"

Wanda shrugged her shoulders and smiled again. "It's just a vibe I get. No one's fooled me yet."

"So what's your vibe on Jon?" And she didn't mean the sexy-smexy one. He had more than enough of that to go around. God, he was so delicious she'd considered reconsidering her vow never to become even remotely involved with a man again.

Wanda expelled a long breath, her eyelashes fluttering. "Oh, that man. He's enough to make me reset my moral compass. If there was no Heath in the picture, I just might feign virginity and throw myself as tribute at his feet. Phew, he's pretty phenomenal to look at, huh? But I haven't figured him out yet, to be honest. Something's just not jiving for me."

A shiver of fear slithered along Toni's spine. "Do you think he's a bad guy?"

"Nope. Not necessarily bad. Not bad at all, in fact. His intentions all outwardly appear to be good. He's a good host, if you could call whatever it was he cooked up in that big cauldron being a good host. He's well-mannered and his cottage was adorbs…there's just *something*. But don't worry," she said on a confident wink. "I'll figure it out."

"I have ears, milady Wanda," Jon joked, slowing his pace to fall in step with them, his strong thighs eating up the distance they traveled. "I'm saddened you didn't enjoy the toadstool soup. I let it simmer all day, too. I do not know where I'm going wrong."

"Crow's feet, lad. Ye must always use a healthy batch if ye wish to impart a hearty, savory flavor," Dannan offered helpfully, brushing away snow like a plow as they continued to press onward.

Jon nodded his dark head, playfully knocking Dannan in the stomach with a light rap of his knuckles. "Of course, my friend. I should just hire you as my chef."

Dannan's tiny chuckle trickled to her ears. "Ah, lad, that would require roots. I'm footloose and fancy free, as ye well know. No ties bind ol' Dannan."

But Jon and Dannan's good-natured chatter became muffled as a low voice calling her name caught Toni's ear. She fell behind the group as they continued to talk, stopping in the middle of the clearing they were passing through.

Tree stumps sprouted everywhere, a light film of snow covering them. The trees surrounding the perimeter sparkled in the sun, ice dripping from the branches like glassy talons.

Colorful toadstools bowed in the wind, their multicolored, broad tops bending forward then back, as though waving her toward an enormous tree with a hole carved in the center of its base.

Now *here's* where she should seriously rethink letting everyone else get so far ahead of her, but come on. Since she'd long passed fear and was well on her way to curious, she wanted to see all these amazing wonders that were things she'd only seen in movies.

If she stopped to think about this, really think about it, being here in Shamalot was every childhood fantasy fulfilled. Magical and serene. So she decided to take a quick peek and then she'd catch up with the others.

As she made her way to the snow-covered base, the scent of something familiar tweaked her cerebral cortex. Toni squinted at the tree, with its long, craggy limbs, and then she squinted again.

Was that a tendril of steam wafting from the tree?

It damn well was. And the scent drifting toward her nose, filling it with caffeinated bliss?

It was the scent of the nectar of the gods. The scent of a Starbucks white-chocolate mocha, extra whipped cream, please.

No. That couldn't be real.

But a hand, supple and smooth, slithered from behind the tree, holding something. Something in a white paper cup with a label Toni knew well.

As she got closer, she saw a name in bold, black print on the cup. Just like the nice Starbucks barista Anthony would write on her cup every week when she treated herself to a grande on payday.

Shut the front door. What sorcery was this?

She almost couldn't contain her joy when a weak voice said, "Toni?"

Oh my God, the voice even sounded like Anthony's!

You'd think that should have been her first clue. But no. She wasn't into clues or ominous warnings, like that gut feeling briefly reminding her this was too good to be true.

She tamped that bitch back down where it belonged with all the other warnings and fairly skipped the remainder of the way to the hand—because it held the fruit of the gods.

The moment she reached for the cup, a full body appeared, popping out from behind the tree. The torso belonging to the body had on a pink jacket just like the one she was forced to wear at the outlet mall.

Toni snatched her hand away and looked upward.

"Bree?" Wait. Why did Bree sound like Anthony?

Worse, had she followed them down that crazy rabbit hole, too? Leave it to her to screw up a perfectly legit free pass from that hellhole by showing up just so Bree could hound her about improperly folding the new batch of winter scarves—in another realm, no less.

Goddammit.

Maybe Bree could take the shoes to the castle. If anyone needed some happiness in her life, it was shallow, self-centered Bree. Where was Brenda when you needed her pearls and life lessons?

Toni stopped dead in her tracks, forcing the hand that desperately wanted to snatch that coffee cup away to her side. "Bree? What are you doing here? *How* did you get here?"

Bree smiled her aggravatingly phony smile and straightened the hem of her jacket with her fingers. "The same way you did. I was going along, minding my business on my coffee break and checking the dressing rooms for leftover clothes from the customers, and wham! I fell down that hole just like you and those other ladies and the creepy kid did. Where are we, Toni?" she asked, her eyes wide, her lower lip trembling.

Bree's shivering got the best of her softer side. She yanked off her pelt and wrapped it around Bree's slender shoulders. "We're in Shamalot. It's a long story best told by the people who live here. I bet Brenda's going to be here any second to give you your job and read your aura—or however that works. Suffice it to say, you're going to have to do something you probably won't want to do."

Toni hoped that involved folding millions of stupid scarves with the folded edge facing outside.

"Like what?" Bree asked, giving her Thumper eyes as she pulled the pelt over her nose to warm its red, pert tip.

"I don't know. But if it sucks as much as my job, you're in for a real treat."

"I'm sorry I was so mean to you, Toni. But I'm really scared. Please take me with you. I'll share my coffee if you do."

And again, Toni heard warning bells. When had Bree ever spoken to her as though she was anything more than her peon? Never. That's when. But those bells weren't loud enough to talk her out of a cup of steaming paradise.

Once more, Toni reached for the coffee, her frozen hands grateful for the warmth of the paper cup. Bree was just a kid. How could she say no to her when Toni had people helping her and Bree had no one? "That's really nice of you, Bree. Thanks."

Putting the tips of her fingers under the cup, she encouraged, "Drink up, Toni. It's freezing here. Much colder than Chersey."

Just as the tab opening was positioned at her mouth, Toni paused and frowned. *Chersey?* She moved the cup from her lips and looked hard at Bree. Really hard. Maybe she'd just heard her wrong?

So she decided to test her. "Shamalot's nothing like Chersey."

Bree nodded her blonde head, the curls as bouncy as ever. "So I see."

Damn. Damn. Damn. This wasn't Bree. Which was crazy and creepy, but likely no less nutty than the fact that Nina was a vampire and Marty was a werewolf and she was in a magical kingdom. But, dear God, why couldn't the warning bells have been about anything else but the coffee?

Just as she was about to confront faux Bree, Jon's big frame flew into view and he roared, "Drop that, milady!"

All Toni saw was the shiny blade of his sword as he sliced it through the air and knocked the cup from her hand. Landing in front of her, he pushed her behind him in a protective manner and demanded, "Reveal yourself or feel the sharp tip of my sword through your gullet! Who sent you, miscreant?"

Goosebumps swept along her arms. Wow, he was dreamy. Chivalrous to a fault, handsome, hot. Just his hand at her waist was enough to steal her breath. And she'd love to linger and enjoy his chivalry.

But something strange was going on.

Toni's feet began to tingle and twitch in her shoes. Suddenly, her feet didn't hurt quite the way they had as they'd walked through the forest in the cold snow, with her toes mashed together in shoes that were like medieval torture devices.

No, in fact, they felt like a part of her, as if they were made specifically for *her* feet. They were no longer clunky and awkward...almost as if they weren't there at all.

She was so busy focusing on her feet, she almost forgot Jon and Bree.

"*Who* sent you? Answer me or die!" Jon demanded once more, waving the sword under Bree's nose, its sharp tip poised at her nostril.

Faux Bree didn't appear to like that at all. She wrinkled her nose before she pushed the sword out of the way with a forefinger—and then began to melt right before their eyes.

Toni gasped when, without warning, her feet forced her to move, propelling her forward toward Bree with an alarming speed.

But Bree's body was no more. The puddle of pink and blonde colors blended and shifted like gel then began to slither upward, the image distorting, twisting, changing.

Green scales began to form all along Bree's ever-growing arms and legs, and then this thing she was becoming fell forward onto four legs, making the earth quake and crack, sending fissures throughout the forest floor. It sprouted loudly flapping wings in shades of emerald and blue, whirring them in mad thumps.

As Toni slammed into the belly of the beast and fell backward, it lifted its mammoth head, rearing its long neck upward and opening its mouth wide to reveal a forked tongue, slithering directly toward her.

A dragon. She was staring a bona fide dragon right in the face. This was really happening.

Toni scurried backward in a crabwalk as fast as her hands thrust deeply in the snow would allow. Panic seized her chest, fear and disbelief immobilizing her.

Jon's sword rose high, arcing in the dwindling sun as he rushed at the beast, but just as he bellowed a rebel cry, Toni's feet virtually lobbed her upward, thrusting her full throttle toward the stream of fire faux Bree spewed.

But in that moment—a slow, painful moment, where she was literally looking down the throat of a dragon—her body began to react in ways her mind disagreed with two million percent.

As her mind screamed, *are you fucking kidding me? You can't take out a dragon with the thump of your fist, Toni Vitali! You can't even make it through an entire Zumba class without clinging to the ballet bar, begging that sadistic instructor Dominic to end your life*, her body did just that as she landed on the dragon's back and it took flight.

Midair, she raised her fist high and brought it down on the dragon's snout, making him rear backward and howl his displeasure so loudly, snow fell from the trees in clumps.

"Milady Toni, no!" Jon hollered, waving from the ground just as the tail end of the dragon thwacked her like a tennis ball.

Her mind said, *drop like you're hot, dumbass! Curl up in the fetal position and pray for death!*

Alas, her body entirely disagreed again as she grabbed on to the dragon's thorny tail and clenched her jaw while, hand over hand, she climbed her way back atop its body, headed for its Mothra-like wings.

Again, her mind interfered. *You're a certifiable nutbag if you try this, Toni. If you do, I'm done with you. You're dead to me. But before I write you off, look down below. This thing's eyeballin' that huge hole in the ground.*

Her eyes briefly caught the image below, a hole, probably the size of the alleged hole in the ozone with nothing but blackness along the interior. But her body pressed forward and latched on to a wing, fighting the cutting wind and the almost ear-shattering screech of the incensed faux Bree.

The dragon began to weave frantically, waffling in and out of trees like a stunt aerialist until it soared higher. From her position at the tip of his neck, Toni saw Nina, Marty, and Wanda below, screaming something she couldn't hear and waving their arms.

Marty began to literally climb up the side of the tree where Toni met faux Bree, using her arms and legs in rapid motion, with Wanda hot on her heels, their fairy godmother wings swatting the air.

Nina flashed into her vision briefly, the bluebirds still circling her head though more anxiously now, chirping above her as she used her long legs to launch herself into the air, wobbling slightly.

However, Toni was already where she needed to be.

She knew she was, and she didn't even stop to think that was odd. It just was.

Pressing one of her heeled feet to the middle of the dragon's wing, she latched on with both hands, her eyes stinging with tears from the cold, and yanked backward with everything she had in her.

Once more, her mind revolted. *What the hell do you think you're doing, Crouching Tiger? Have you suddenly become some mythology slayer? You're on the back of a dragon, twit!*

Ah, but her body fought back as she broke the dragon's wing and he began to nosedive toward the ground, screeching and blowing a stream of orange-and-blue-tinted fire.

Her mind was back again, and this time, her body mostly agreed with its assessment. *Knock-knock. Brains here! You do realize you'll be a grease spot when this bad boy hits the ground, right? With the speed this dragon is racing toward that hole, you're stewed, Vitali. Nice knowin' ya.*

"Milady! Jump!" Jon yelled as he ran alongside the dragon, his hands cupped over his mouth, his long legs pumping. "I'll catch youuu!"

Fingers grabbed her newly acquired length of hair, shoring the strands upward and effectively plucking her from the back of the dragon as it careened in a spiral down to the pitted depths of the hole below them.

Toni heard a grunt in her ear as she slammed into a drift of snow with a bone-crunching smack.

"Ugh!" Nina yelped, keeping her arm securely around Toni's waist and rolling with her down a bumpy hill. They tumbled and sputtered like a half-human, half-undead snowball, kicking up snow and dead leaves in their path until they came to a full stop.

Toni groaned, flopping to her right side, forcing air into her lungs with loud rasps.

There was the thunderous sound of Dannan's footsteps and the cries of Wanda and Marty off in the distance, but she was too dizzy to lift her head. Instead, she let it loll to the side, ignoring the brittle, wet snow.

"What the fuck just happened?" Nina muttered, pushing the soaking-wet hair from Toni's forehead.

Nina's hands were oddly soothing as she ran them over Toni's shoulders and face, checking her eyes and nose, her cheekbones and arms. "Jesus and a snow cone, why the hell did you wander off?"

"Starbucks," she muttered. It was all she was capable of saying.

Nina bracketed Toni's head with her hands and stared down at her, sunglasses concealing her eyes. "Really, Looney-Tunes? Are there barista's aplenty out here in One Hundred Acre Woods?"

She didn't have time to answer as Jon plowed through the snow and dropped down beside her, pulling her from Nina's gentle hands and lifting her in his arms. "My lady, you're freezing. We must warm you or you'll catch your death."

Maybe on the outside she was freezing, but her insides would beg to differ as Jon carried her, tucked to his wide chest, toward the very tree that had started all her trouble.

His chest heaved against her left breast as he huffed for breath, creating all sorts of imagery in her head—images she had no business dreaming up when she was in such a pickle. Still, they assaulted her, making her skin tingle and her heart race, and if she had an ounce of energy left, she'd wrap her arm around his shoulders just to see what it felt like. But she was depleted.

"Dannan," he barked, "a blanket for the lady, please. You'll find one in my pack atop Oliver."

Marty and Wanda rushed up to her as Dannan spread a rough blanket on the ground and Jon set her on it like a helpless child. He leaned down as he settled her, their lips inches apart.

As her eyes began to gain better focus, all she could see was his luscious mouth and the hear the erratic crash of her heart trying its best to get out of her chest—and the shafts of light over his head while a distant harp plucked a soft tune.

Aw, for the love of Cheetos. Enough already!

But then she realized—Jon saw something, too. In that brief, sweet moment, everything stopped. Their eyes met and held, their breath mingled, the cold air turned balmy.

"Milady?" he husked out, but she didn't have the chance to explore what had just passed between them because Wanda shoved him out of the way.

Both Marty and Wanda were on their knees in front of her in seconds, their big hairdos flopping to either side of their heads, their dresses torn from climbing the tree.

Wanda reached for her first, grabbing her hand. "Toni! Are you all right? We tried to help but our powers are weaker today than they were just last night. Poor Marty couldn't even totally shift. What were you doing up there? You could have been killed!"

Toni stared up at the two women who'd been so nice to her and shrugged her shoulders. "Good point. And I can't explain what was going on. First, my feet got all tingly and warm. Then my mind was telling me I was just shy of certifiable to get on that dragon's back, but my body wouldn't take no for an answer."

Marty peered into her eyes, the intensity of the stare almost frightening. "*What?* Did you hit your head? She hit her head on impact, didn't she?" she asked Nina, who'd followed them toward the tree.

Carl nuzzled Toni's cheek, pressing as close to her as he could without spiking her clean through with his fuzzy antlers. She lifted a weak hand and rubbed his muzzle with a smile.

"I didn't hit my head when we landed. I can't explain what just happened because I'm still wrapping my brain around the word 'dragon'. I was on the back of a dragon. A *dragon*. You know, wings and fire—so much fire—forked-tongues and scales?"

The three women nodded their heads, but again, no one batted an eye. Not even a twitch.

Toni's mouth fell open. "Aw, c'mon. You guys have *seen* dragons?"

"I'd show you pictures of a baby dragon, but I don't have my damn phone." Nina grinned then, and with that, everything about her changed. Her face was no longer pinched and scowling, it was alight and beautiful with something that was obviously near and dear to her heart.

This gruff, foul-mouthed woman likely loved as hard as she fought. And that struck Toni somewhere far deeper than she was willing to go. For right now, there was the issue of a baby dragon.

Closing her eyes, Toni shook her head. "I don't believe you. I've listened to you talk about genies and bottles and demons and—and—a dragon's just too far!"

The vampire clucked her tongue. "Really? A dragon's what sets you over the edge? I'd have thought the genie shit woulda been your end game—maybe even the cougar. So a dragon's your emotional limit? Noted," Nina said on a cackle.

Marty and Wanda shook their sodden heads and looked at Toni as if she were the one who'd lost all her marbles.

Marty straightened Toni's bodice and smoothed out her rumpled skirt. "You just sat on the back of one, didn't you? I'm telling you, it's true. She's precious and really just getting her wings under her. We love her to itsy-bitsy bits. See her every chance we get. Skype with her all the time. Her name's Noa."

Jon brought over a flask and knelt beside her, holding it to her mouth as she gratefully drank, her throat dry and sore.

His chiseled face was a mask of concern as he cupped her chin. "You must never speak with strangers, Toni. The woods are dangerous and fraught with enemies. Not everything is as it appears."

Toni nodded her head in agreement. No shit. Pressing her back into the hard bark of the tree after another long gulp of water, she burped, fully intending to excuse herself.

But that would be difficult, considering courteous words weren't the thing coming out of her mouth. No. Instead, a hot stream of acrid fire flew from her lips.

Jon yelled to Dannan to grab another flask as he grabbed the edge of the blanket from the ground and wrapped it around Marty's head, knocking her to the ground and patting her big hair.

Which was, of course, on fire thanks to Toni.

Maybe dragon *was* her emotional limit...

Chapter 5

"So, you gonna get the fire going for the troll roast, or am I?" Nina quipped, cackling as she slapped Toni on the back.

"Only if you fan it, Sunshine Wings," she quipped back.

This time, Nina didn't appear to take offense. Instead she snickered and said, "Touché."

She'd breathed fire. Real fire. From her mouth. Still unable to address that, she asked Nina with a sheepish glance, "I'm really sorry. It was the last thing I expected. Is Marty okay? Does she want to eat me for dinner?"

Nina flapped a hand and hiked up the front of her torn and tattered yellow dress. The bluebirds scattered momentarily then returned to their rightful place above her head, chirping their happy tune. "Nah. Her hair grows back because she self-heals. She'll be right back to her gelled-up, sprayed-to-within-an-inch-of-the-ozone-layers life in no time flat. I think. I dunno. Our powers seem to be doing weird shit here. It's like we're all off or something. But don't you worry your pretty little fire-breathing head about it."

They'd stopped for the night in a place Jon thought was safe enough, as long as there was always someone on guard. While he set up their camp, she and Nina were doing their part by making a fire as Marty and Wanda looked for the sugared winterberries Jon had told them about.

Carl and Dannan huddled close together as the ogre told Carl stories and they pitched tents made of a fabric Toni couldn't identify.

The wind howled a desolate cry and though the snow had stopped, when the sun dipped, the temperatures had, too.

"What did Brenda mean when she said you couldn't use your special powers to get to the castle?"

"I'm bettin' that nutty *Hee-Haw* honey meant I couldn't throw your ass on my back and fly you there. Which is some kinda stupid bullshit, if you ask me."

Toni gulped and tried to act unfazed. "You f...fly?"

"I do. And as you saw, Marty shifts into a hairy ass-sniffer and looks like she popped right off a damn movie set, and Wanda has fangs and she's pretty strong, but she shifts, too."

"Because Wanda's a halfsie, right?" She couldn't even believe she was having this conversation when just a day or so ago she was asking Bree what she wanted her to do with the new shipment of ponchos.

"Yep. Half vampire, half were. But she can't fly. Sucks hairy donkey balls at it."

"So you guys are all friends? You really did meet because you used to sell makeup before Marty was turned into a werewolf?"

Nina threw some stray branches into the pit they'd made in the ground and nodded. "Yep. It's been almost eight years since that shit went down."

"That's nice," she whispered.

If only Nina knew *how* nice. As they'd walked, Marty had told her stories about how they'd all met via her cosmetics company, about their children and baby dragon's incredible birth, and hearing her talk about their families and barbecues and birthday parties and Christmases past brought back the empty ache of loneliness Toni had fought so hard to keep from eating her alive.

"What about you, Dragon Slayer. You have family back home?"

Turning her back to Nina, she pretended to search for more branches. "Nope. Just me."

"Friends?"

"Nope."

"So you wanna tell me what the fuck made you latch on to that dragon the way you did? It was damn impressive, but risky as all hell, considering you're a *human*. Do you have a death wish or some shit? Because if that's the case, that makes you dangerous, and I won't have you risking everyone else's lives just because you don't feel like you have anything worth dropping your feet on the floor for every morning."

Toni swatted at a stray tear with her thumb and inhaled, stooping to grab a thin limb. Did she have a death wish? Had she been that reckless because she was alone in the world and there was nothing left anywhere for her? Was she unconsciously looking to end it all?

Toni fought that notion even as she denied it, trying to keep her voice light. "No death wish, promise. I can't explain what happened. It just happened. I just instinctively knew what to do to disarm the dragon. And I guess I'm not so human anymore if I'm breathing fire, huh? Does that make me one of you?"

Nina grunted and yanked up one of her ripped sleeves. "I don't know what the hell it makes you, but I'd sure like some answers. Usually when we have a client, we have a source that's bigger than just making a random wish in your lady brain."

"A source?"

"Yeah, like the person who ends up accidentally turned had tangled with someone or something to get in the fix they're in. Case in point, Wanda's yappy, rambling bookworm sister, Casey. She had demon blood spilled on her at a bar when she was chasing after her out-of-control twin charges. Poof. Instant demon. But you have an entire realm doing this to you, an unseen entity. How the fuck do you fight that?"

Yeah. Good question. How the fuck?

Pushing her tangled hair from her face, Toni nodded and turned around. "I'd like to know, too. Listen, I don't know if I thanked you properly for saving me today. I would have been a grease spot if not for you. I guess I didn't think the whole thing through, but it was like not being in control of all my faculties. Brawn over brain or something... Anyway, thank you. I'd have never survived without you."

Nina stopped gathering limbs for the fire and looked her directly in the eye. "The best way to thank me is to not wander off by yourself. There's obviously some crazy shit out there, and I don't know if it was luck or what that saved your sparkly ass, but we might not be so lucky next time."

"Who'da thunk a Starbucks could cause so much trouble?"

"You do realize the Starbucks was basically Snow White's apple, don't you, Boogie Shoes? A metaphor or some such shiz?" Nina asked, her gaze hard and unflinching as her wings pumped softly.

She'd thought long and hard about it as they'd continued their walk to the campsite earlier today. "I do now. I guess at the time, because I was desperate for coffee, my impulse control got the better of me."

"From now on, just stay close. I can't protect you if I can't see you, dipshit."

Toni chuckled, bending at the waist to arrange the limbs. "Is that what you're doing? Protecting me? You're not such a bitch after all, huh?"

Nina cracked a branch in half, the sound harsh in the silence, reverberating off the trees. "I'ma say this once. Respect for having the balloon-size clangers to stand your ground with me. I like a chick who can handle her own shit. You're in a small class of people who've lived to tell the tale. But do it again? Die. And it'll hurt. Oh, Jesus and your lady brains spattered from here to kingdom come, it'll hurt."

Toni shivered, wrapping the blanket Jon had given her from his pack tighter around her. She didn't doubt Nina meant what she said. She also didn't doubt there was much more to Nina than met the eye.

Nina came around to her side of the fire and plopped down on a fallen tree trunk next to her. Pointing to the pit they'd made together, she said, "Breathe, Fire Starter."

Tension coiled in her stomach. "What if I can't do it again? Or worse, what if I can?" What if, for the rest of her life, she was going to set things on fire? Like Marty's hair again? Or a house?

Not one to mince words, Nina looked right at her, her pale face sharply contrasted by the dark night. "Then you'll deal. We'll help you."

Help. No one had given her much of that in a long time. Not the police. Not the people she'd once worked with. No one. "Why would you help me? You don't even like me. I'm the one who's responsible for this whole mess. You should hate my guts."

"It's just what I do. It's what we all do. I bitch about it plenty. I complain. I swear. But I do it because the other two windbags need me to do it. We're ride-or-die partners for life."

She did it, whether willingly or not, because their friendship meant something deep, something she cherished far more than she'd ever let on. "Would you do this OOPS thing if it wasn't for Marty and Wanda?"

Nina paused for a long moment as she looked off into the depths of the forest before she said, low and husky. "I dunno. We've come really close to losing each other, and even a client or two. That fucking sucks some harsh ass—to always be so damn freaked about the safety of the people you love. Not that I'd take any of it back, because we found some awesome shit and some awesome people along the way. And that's not to say if somebody needed help, I wouldn't help. Because nine times outta ten, I would. Injustice pisses me off. And it's unjust to land in a place called vampire or werewolf or whatever with no one to hold your goddamn hand and help you through it. But sometimes I wonder…"

"Wonder what?" Toni asked softly, placing a hand on the vampire's arm.

There was turmoil in Nina's tone, in her body language. It was almost as though she was at a fork in the road of her pending eternity despite what Brenda had said about her happiness. Something was troubling her, and right now, it was far easier to try to figure out Nina than it was to delve into her own problems.

But then she clammed up and the old crusty Nina returned, front and center. "Nothing, Designer Duds. Just breathe and it'll all be fine. We'll get Mick and Tess to show you how to control your fire breathing when we get back to Jersey."

Mick and Tess were the parents of the baby dragon they'd spoken about with such love, something she was still digesting along with everything else.

Sighing, Toni looked down at her gleaming shoes, unmarred from the day's events. "Jersey seems pretty far away right now. I feel like I'll never get back there."

"You won't if you freeze your sissy ass off. Now breathe and stop yammering with the girl talk. I suck at squishy feelings."

Inhaling deeply, Toni closed her eyes and blew, the heat rising in her throat as she expelled a long breath and coughed from the burnt taste filling the interior of her mouth and settling on her tongue. An acrid puff of air fell from between her lips and then voila.

Fire.

Holy Hannah, she was really breathing fire.

Nina slapped her on the back with approval. "Good job, Puff."

For some reason, maybe because she suspected it was likely hard to win, Nina's approval made Toni grin.

Dakota Cassidy | Accidentally Ever After

* * *

"And then, the big bad wolf ate the Three Little Bears' porridge. All of it. Nom-nom," she said as she rubbed her stomach for Carl, who leaned against her. "But then Papa Bear comes home and he sees the wolf has eaten all his porridge and he says, 'I'll huff and I'll puff and I'll blow your house down!'"

Carl stomped his hoof on the ground in gleeful approval.

Nina's sigh rasped in the air. "Southey would fuck you up if he could hear you trashing his shit. It's *Goldilocks* and the Three Bears, knucklehead. No wolf. No huffing and puffing. Yer killin me, Smalls." She quoted *The Sandlot* with a roll of her eyes. "I'm outtie for guard duty. Try not to hack up any more fairytales, huh?"

Reaching down, she rubbed Carl's antlers with a smile. "Okay, so maybe it was Goldilocks. But seriously, who wanders into someone's house and eats their porridge right off their table? It's rude."

"Milady, you shouldn't be out here without escort. The hour is late and many creatures roam the forest."

Toni's eyes flew upward to Jon's, who'd just finished his patrol of the perimeter of their makeshift camp, with Nina taking over so he could rest before they headed out again at dawn. His hulking figure cast shadows against the forest walls with the fire as his backdrop.

He stepped forward toward her, and the usual happened. Prisms of light shone on his head and that infernal harp twanged its usual introduction of his arrival.

She let her eyes rise skyward and lifted her hands. *"Seriously?"*

"Milady?"

Toni sighed with a slump of her shoulders. "Sorry. It got a little cold in the tent. Plus, Marty snores something fierce and I couldn't sleep."

Jon chuckled, sitting beside her on the log in front of the fire, their thighs just touching. "She has hearty lungs, that lass."

Toni nodded, twisting the ends of her hair to avoid looking at Jon. Suddenly she felt awkward, as if she were at her first high school dance, sitting on the bleachers while the Backstreet Boys played and everyone had coupled up, instead of the grown-ass woman she was today.

64

"She does." Carl stirred at her feet, and she reached down to stroke his head, settling him back in.

Jon poked the fire with a stray branch, making a rush of embers soar upward. "These maidens, have you known them long?"

"Just over a day now." But it seemed like much longer. So much had happened in just a day.

"They're fierce, these women who assist you. I admire that."

"You're not at all afraid of them, are you?"

"What's there to fear?"

"Oh, I dunno. Maybe having every ounce of blood sucked from your body—or being torn limb from limb and your liver used as pâté on a cracker?"

Jon chuckled, the sound deep and rich in her ears. "Bah. They are no worse than Queen Angria and her henchmen. In fact, they are quite likeable in comparison. I rather enjoy their banter."

This time, she listened to the warning bells. "Queen Angria? Does she have flying monkeys?"

"Flying what?"

"Forget it. I just knew there was an evil queen in here somewhere."

Jon nodded his head, the smile leaving his eyes. "Evil is a kind word where Queen Angria is concerned. She rules her land with an iron fist."

Now that she'd processed the day, she was finally able to ask, "Who was that back in the forest? The dragon? Why did she or *it* offer me a Starbucks?"

"She offered you a ship?"

"A ship?"

"I assumed Starbucks was the name of a ship."

Toni giggled, clamping her hand over her mouth to keep from waking everyone. "No. Starbucks is a place to get coffee. Like you'd get some ale here at a pub in Shamalot."

"This coffee you speak so highly of, it troubles you to do without? Three of you have mentioned it more than once on our journey, and the tone you use suggests death is more desirable."

"Troubles isn't the word I'd use. It's more like a craving. You know what that is, right?"

Jon turned to look at her, his sapphire-blue eyes intense. "I do, milady," he answered gruffly.

Her heart throbbed in her chest, matched by the rhythm of her pulse pounding in her ears. "So who was that back there? She looked just like my boss from the store until she wasn't."

"There are many evils in the forest, Toni. I've warned you of such not to frighten you, but because the land of Jersey sounds quite different than my Shamalot. What you encountered was one of the queen's henchmen, a shapeshifter. They will do whatever it takes to tempt you into doing their bidding. Things are not always as they appear."

Toni barked a laugh, making Carl's head pop up. "That's not so different than Jersey." Or Stas, who was nothing like he'd appeared.

Jon remained silent, letting his elbows settle on his knees as he stared off into the fire, and she tried not to ogle his thick thighs.

"So why was the queen sending in one of her henchmen? Clearly he was tailored to me because he tried to entice me with my favorite coffee. What could she want with me?" Because that would fall right in line with what Nina had said about their prior OOPS clients.

The shoes. She probably wanted the shoes. All the bitches wanted the shoes.

"I don't know, but I intend to find out as we head toward the bridge tomorrow midday."

Looking down at her heels, Toni lifted her muddy, wet skirt and pointed to them. "Do you think it's the king's shoes she wants? I mean, my feet did tingle just before I attempted a suicide mission."

"They tingled? Describe, please."

Toni shrugged her shoulders. "They just got all warm and then my brain and my body were in full-on war. My brain said 'Don't do it, dummy', but my body seemed to know exactly what to do."

"The shoes..." he muttered as perplexed as she was.

"Yeah. The shoes. Because where I come from, chicks die because of a sweet pair of heels."

"They kill chickens for shoes in Jersey? This land is hostile, your home, yes?"

Toni giggled into her hand again. "No, chick means girl or woman, and there's a story about a girl whose name is Dorothy and she falls into a place called Oz and—" She stopped talking when Jon's face went from concerned to perplexed.

Toni shook her head and patted his arm—his strong, hard, awesome arm. "Never mind, the point is, are these shoes important in some way?"

Jon shook his head, cupping his jaw and rubbing the dark stubble. "In all of Shamalot's vast history, that I can remember anyway, have the books ever involved a story about a pair of shoes. I have lived here all my life and never heard of their existence. As such, I don't understand the queen's ire."

"Maybe this was just a random drive-by temptation? Henchmen need to let off steam, too. Maybe he was just practicing his henchmen-ness and he chose me as his target for lack of anyone else. I mean, I'm not from Shamalot, so it was easy to catch me off guard and fool me, right?"

She liked that explanation much better than the idea that some rabid queen was looking to kill her.

"I don't know Angria's intent. Though, this much I promise, no harm will come to you or yours. Not while I watch over you," he whispered, the words tight and fierce.

Toni fidgeted, uncomfortable with having so many people on her side. Which was about as stupid as stupid got, but she was so used to being alone, she didn't know what to do with so much support. It was time for some lighter fare.

Placing her chin on top of her fist, she asked, "So you run a reindeer stable? How unusual. Very cool, but unusual."

Now Jon looked away and toward the fire, his gleaming hair falling from the tie he used to hold it in a ponytail. Hair she fought the impulse to tuck back behind his ear.

"'Tis not so unusual here in Shamalot. We have more snow days in the calendar year than not, our reindeer are useful."

God, he was sexy. "You like working with animals?"

"I love my work and the animals. It brings me great peace."

Jon reached down and ruffled Carl's back with a genuine smile. He'd spent hours with Carl on their trek, talking to him and telling him stories about his adventures as a youth in the forest.

Carl looked at him with admiration in his soft brown eyes, and it made Toni's heart hitch every time.

"Does your family live here in Shamalot with you? Got any brothers or sisters you're looking forward to having Christmas dinner with?"

His wide back stiffened without warning, the vibe between them totally changing from discovery to intrusion. "My family is in another land, one I do not wish to live in."

That sounded a lot like "end subject". But then he asked, "And you, Toni? What is this Jersey like? Is your family there?"

"Jersey is Jersey. Land of some of the best diners in the world and where we all use exits off the turnpike to define where we live. And no family. It's just me." *Liar* that voice inside her head whispered.

"What about your mother and father?"

"What about yours?" What was with all the questions about her family today? Couldn't she just be an orphan in peace?

Jon sat back, planting his broad hands on his thighs. "You're displeased."

"I'm not." She was just edgy and nervous. Who else from her past could show up and reveal her secrets? If the queen had in fact sent Bree—or faux Bree—how had the queen found out about her existence? Her crystal ball?

How did the queen know Bree was a surefire foil in a plan of attack? Who else was lurking out there that looked like someone from home, just waiting to fool her? Whoever this Queen Angria was, she didn't want anything to do with her.

Now he looked offended. "Your tone suggests otherwise."

"Well, maybe you don't read tones very well."

"I know discontent when I hear it, milady. What about your life back in Jersey are you hiding?"

Now she bristled. That was none of his business. "What about being a guide means you get to ask personal questions, Julie The Cruise Director? Did we hire you to pry or did we hire you to get us to this crazy castle everyone's so up in arms over?"

Now his eyes narrowed in her direction. Gone was the cheerful Jon Doe of this afternoon, replaced with a scowling—albeit, damn him, still super-hot—annoyed Jon.

"What is this nonsense you speak? I'm no cruise director, whatever that is. I'm a stable owner."

Toni rolled her eyes as she rose, tugging Carl's reins. "Never mind, Lancelot. We clearly have an issue with our land-to-land connections. It's just a figure of speech, sort of. Forget it. I'm suddenly tired. Good night, Jon."

He rose like the gentleman he was as she swept off, the rustle of her skirt crisp in her ears. She crunched her way awkwardly to the tent, pulling Carl in with her then dropping down on the nest of blankets.

As Carl settled against her, Toni stretched her feet, her mind racing at warp speed with questions and worries.

But one thing was for sure, no one needed to know about her family, alive or dead, or why she was hiding away in an outlet mall in Jersey.

Because it wasn't just dangerous for *her* to tell someone her pathetic plight—it was just as dangerous for anyone else to have the information.

* * *

"Aye, ye've done it now, lad," Dannan said on an amused chuckle, his small voice taunting as Jon leaned against a large tree and whittled a stick.

"Done what?"

"Ye've angered the saucy maiden. My guess is ye didn't wish to do such."

No. He had not wished to do such. He found Toni intoxicating, beautiful with her hair the color of the sunset, brave, intriguing with her coffee and her talk of this land called Jersey.

He wanted to absorb everything about her, learn from her, discover her depths. She was nothing like the maidens here in Shamalot. But she was as prickly as the sugared pears his mother grew in her garden. Yet he knew not why.

He tightened his jaw, clenching his teeth. "I asked a simple question. A simple answer was all that was needed."

Dannan sighed, the breath whistling from his lungs as he crossed his arms over his massive chest. "If only lasses were simple creatures. But alas, they are not. They are complex, and opinionated, and infuriating as only lasses can be."

"But she is surely easy on the eye, aye?" he said on an ironic chuckle.

"Indeed she is. That is the crux of the problem. Temptresses they all be. If only they could tempt with their mouths closed."

Jon laughed, slipping his knife into his boot. "I don't mind the chatter as long as it's about anything other than their gowns or the dramatic choice of whether to serve marbled bread or rye at their next tea. There need be substance to the conversation."

"And milady Toni is anything but mindless," Dannan agreed. "She was quite fierce on the back of the queen's minion, was she not, lad? How do ye account for such bravery from a maiden who claims she's nothing more than a shop girl?"

Jon heard the respect in his friend's voice. True, Toni hadn't made a single complaint as they'd trudged through ankle-deep snow—none of them had. But what she'd done with that dragon went beyond bravery.

'Twas damn foolhardy. Yet, how had she known to break his wing? Instincts like that didn't come from selling gowns—or "leggings", as he'd heard her call them.

Something was afoot. Something he didn't have figured out.

"I don't know, friend. But she's dangerous to us if she has no plan when she goes into battle."

"Aye," Dannan said on a nod of his blue head.

"And she hides something from her land—something personal and quite possibly painful. I cannot pinpoint what."

"As do ye, Jon Doe," Dannan all too easily reminded him.

His jaw tightened again, but then he relaxed. He wasn't in any immediate danger from the queen or anyone else. Toni was. "But I'm not the one in need here, ogre. Toni is."

"Oh, lad. Ye need far more than ye think. But for the moment, this is neither here nor there, as they say. In this moment, we must worry about the queen. What does she wish from our newly acquired maiden, and should we warn the other she-warriors about Angria?"

That was indeed a puzzle that needed solving. The shapeshifter in the clearing had been sent by Angria, he didn't doubt that. He'd tracked enough in his lifetime to know their scents, their patterns.

Yet, what could Toni possibly have that Angria wanted? Was it truly a pair of shoes he'd never heard of? Toni had said her feet had tingled just before she'd jumped on top of the dragon. But for shoes to give her such courage? It was preposterous.

But worse than these shoes, who would Angria send in next?

It was obvious she'd put a pretty pence on Toni's head. The henchman's appearance was no random act. This worried him far more than whatever Toni herself was hiding from everyone.

Dannan yawned, his mouth opening wide enough to fit two people inside. "We must sleep now, lad. The morrow comes swiftly and we need be alert for the sake of Toni and her bonny friends."

Sleep. Hah. He'd hardly slept since meeting Toni. The prior night before their journey began, as he lay before the fire, hearing her soft intakes of breath, his stomach had tightened…as had other places on his body.

He'd watched the sweet rise and fall of her breasts, wished to touch the curve of her hip, the outline of her full lips.

But to do so would only complicate matters. She was from another land—one he'd decided was quite far away, and she'd want to return to it once she'd been granted her happiness by King Dick.

Still, he railed against the idea she'd leave, and it left him uncomfortable and out of his element.

It was all just silly nonsense best left for those who believed in true love's kiss.

Of which he did not. He'd kissed maidens aplenty in his time, and none of them did to him what the legend told. He was not a believer in the tale his mother regaled him with at bedtime when he was a child.

Pushing off the tree, he fought to ignore the soft outline of Toni's sleeping body in the tent just beyond his and followed Dannan toward their beds.

Sleep would fix all his ills, and tomorrow, he'd find out what Angria wanted with Toni, finish their journey to the castle, happily drop her off, wish her well, and go back to his quiet life at the cottage with his reindeer and his crops.

That settled, he hunkered down beneath the rough blanket and closed his eyes.

Only to find Toni's face lurking behind his eyelids.

His sigh was grating and irritated as he turned over restlessly.

Dannan chuckled from just outside the tent. "Count sheep, lad. It helps pass the time when a lass weighs heavy on yer mind."

"Quiet now, ogre." Jon growled his words. "Or I'll see your head roll then mounted at the cottage!"

His response only made Dannan laugh harder, the squeak of its tinkling lilt still, after years of friendship, leaving Jon amazed. For a man so large, his voice was sprinkled with fairy dust.

"I bid ye goodnight, Jon Doe. May yer dreams be maiden free!"

Chapter 6

The next morning, as they rose to pack up and begin the next leg of their journey, Jon informed them that he was certain the attack yesterday was personal and aimed at Toni. He warned each of the women about the existence of Queen Angria and her evil and the possibility she wanted Toni's shoes.

"So you think the shoes had something to do with that crazy stunt she pulled yesterday?" Marty had asked.

Jon had shaken his head. "I know not of these shoes, but there is a distinct possibility Angria desires them if they have some sort of rare gift now bestowed upon Toni simply because she wears them."

Nina had nodded her head as though she thoroughly understood, while Marty and Wanda followed suit. "I fucking knew it. It always boils down to some shit like this. *This* kinda crazy I get. So don't fret your pretty face about it, Reindeer Whisperer—we get batshit bitches. We got Red's back all the way."

Now, as they moved deeper into the forest, Nina snaked a hand upward and captured one of the bluebirds who'd spun around her head since they'd begun this trek and brought him down to eye level. She'd been out of sorts all morning long and picking up speed with each step they took.

The bluebird continued to chirp happily, his head bobbing just above her fingers. "Dude, cut it the hell out. I can't take it anymore, man. I haven't slept in two days, and this flippy-flappy, yippy-skippy song you winged anomalies keep chirping is old. It ends now. Your time to come in for a landing has arrived. So here's the skinny. Shut those damn beaks and you can rest those feathers by riding on my boy Carl's back the rest of the way to the castle. Keep it up, despite the fact that I love animals more than I love people, and I roast your little blue asses for dinner, tiny buddy. *Capisce?*"

She set him on Carl's back and, ironically, the others followed suit, lining up along the blanket covering his spine, their puffed-up chests swelling further.

Toni tweaked the edge of one of Nina's wings, hoping to turn her bad mood around. "Did I tell you how nice you are today? You sure have purty wings. I'm sick with jealousy."

"Did I tell if you say one more thing I'm gonna snatch your tongue from your face?"

"Oooo, did someone have a bad night?" Toni teased with a grin, rubbing Carl's antler as they walked.

"Someone is a fucking vampire who should be sleeping right now, not taking the diva king his shoes while some power-trippin' queen chases you. Someone hasn't slept or fed for two damn days. Someone's about to flip a nut if all the other someones don't shut it."

"Fed?" What an odd word to use for food.

"Yeah, fed."

She hadn't noticed until Nina mentioned it, but the vampire hadn't shared in their meal of winterberries or roasted chestnuts—nor had she drunk a drop of water. But the word "fed" in relation to eating a meal was a rather strange choice. "Why haven't you, um, eaten…or fed. I mean, why didn't you have some berries with us last night? We had plenty. I would have shared, too."

"Because Crustypants can't eat food anymore," Marty teased, yanking the length of Nina's dirty yellow skirt.

Toni fought an astonished gasp as they climbed yet another hill. "Then what do you eat to live?"

"I don't live, numbnuts. I'm dead, remember?"

Then something registered. Maybe it was a fact from a movie or a TV show or whatever, but it would be another of her worst fears realized since she'd first learned Nina was a vampire. But no. She didn't really drink… Did she?

Toni stopped for a moment, putting her hand on Nina's arm. "So then you really eat—"

"Blood. More specifically, I *drink* blood, and I'm gonna need some soon. Any particular spot on your neck you want me to tap first?" Nina lifted her cracked sunglasses and glared down at Toni.

Yep. Worst fear realized. But she was determined to take this new information in stride, too, right along with everything else. "So how do we get you blood?"

Her face changed again, darkening with worry. "I don't know. I don't do human or animal blood. We drink this synthetic shit my husband's clan provides. One taste of the wrong blood and it could fuck everything up."

"So you're an eco-conscious vampire?"

"No. I'm one who doesn't want to turn into a raving lunatic and commit mass homicide. Real blood does weird shit to a vampire. It can make you lust for the genuine article all the time, and that's how you lose control and start taking bitches out—or innocents, as we call them. My clan is determined to live with humans—which is a good thing for you. Now quit yakking and go make nice with Flawless. He's all pouty after your argument last night."

Toni looked down at the ground, her next words not a question but a statement. "You heard us."

"The Adirondacks heard you two. I'm a vampire. Super-speed, super-strength, super-*hearing*."

Guilt washed over her. Could Nina die if she didn't do this feed thing? She was still learning the particulars of this undead stuff, but the more she heard, the more it was becoming just like a movie.

Toni latched on to her arm, trying to slow her. "You're out here because of me. I want to help. Tell me what I can do, Nina."

"Got a spare vein?"

Toni blanched, looking helplessly to Marty. "Is that what it takes?"

Marty patted Toni on the back with one hand, using the other to tuck a long lock of her blonde hair back into the massive cone it had become. "It's going to be all right. Jon says he knows a fairy who can turn water into wine—maybe she can do the same with blood. We'll figure it out. Promise."

Everyone was always so calm, so "oh, it'll all be fine. We got this". But now, this woman could die or turn to ashes or whatever vampires did when their undead lives were over and it was all because of Toni's mistake. She couldn't live with that. Not after everything else she already lived with. No more death.

As they traveled north toward the castle, the terrain had become hillier, rougher; her feet ached and her back was killing her. It was a stark reminder to do more cardio when she got back to Jersey.

Dannan again took the front, with Jon a mere two strides behind him, leading his horse Oliver on foot. Nina chatted with Dannan like they were old friends. She said he reminded her of her demon friend Darnell back in Staten Island.

As opposed to she and Jon who had spoken nary a word this morning as they'd packed up their camp and began the next leg of their journey. His jaw was rigid, his eyes focused on the road ahead, totally avoiding her.

Toni had stayed as far back in the lineup as she could, forcing her eyes to look anywhere but at his tight butt and his broad back. In all fairness, she'd overreacted to his question about her parents. She wanted to say as much and apologize, but maybe it was better if he was angry with her rather than his usual friendly self.

If they didn't speak, he couldn't ask any more questions she wasn't willing to answer.

As morning turned to mid-afternoon and they approached this bridge Jon had spoken of, set far off in the distance beyond a tangle of vines, he held up a long arm and waved them toward him.

As they gathered around, he pointed to a thicker portion of the woods, the entry clotted with dark trees making the shape of an oval. Jon's skin was ruddy from the cold, his eyes stoic as he spoke. "This is the Garden of Wings, fairies dwell here. We must forge through their playground in order to reach the bridge before late afternoon. Be warned, maidens, fairies are known for their playful though harmless pranks, but the queen's henchmen are my true worry. They often hide in the thick of the gardens, attempting to snatch the winged goblins and wring their powers from them or force them to guide their black souls to the mines, where gold is allegedly hidden. You must beware. If there's a price on Toni's head, they'll be especially keen today."

Nina rolled her shoulders and lifted her chin. "Just might get that blood sooner than we thought."

"Aye, maiden. Shall I carry ye? I am happy to do so," Dannan asked.

Nina shook her head with a slow smile. "Nah, Papa Smurf, I got this."

Jon planted a hand on Nina's shoulder. "Do not tax yourself, maiden. This portion of our journey can't be avoided if we're to find what you need and the proper nourishment you require from the Blue Fairy, Elessandra. I would ask that you all stay close and ignore the whispers of the trees the henchman hide in. Their voices can grow loud and drive you to madness, but they seek only to steal your mind and cannot be trusted."

Why talking trees surprised her after riding on the back of a dragon was a mystery, but it was like an aftershock now rather than a full-on earthquake of crazy. Still, Toni was determined to see that Nina got what she needed. She wouldn't be here if not for her random wish. She'd keep that in the forefront of all future endeavors.

Rolling up the long sleeves of her gown, Toni merely nodded and began to follow Dannan and the others into the garden, only to have Jon stop her by capturing her wrist.

"I mean what I say, Toni. You, especially, must take great care."

"Is this because of yesterday? Are you going to remind me how easily I was roped in by a cup of coffee forever? I told *you* just like I told everyone else—I don't know why I got on the dragon. It was instinct or something I can't explain. I can promise you, if I'd had all my wits about me, I would have never climbed on the back of a dragon. I'm not an idiot."

"Then you must curb your foolish impulses."

Foolish? The nerve. But she knew how to shut up when there were more pressing matters.

So Toni gave him the blankest stare she could summon and pulled her wrist from his grasp. "I get it. You're in charge. No dragon-slaying for the foolish salesgirl today."

The corner of his luscious mouth lifted ever so slightly in time with one raven eyebrow. "The fair maiden doth have ears."

"She also doth have a fist, which she'll gladly shove down your throat if you don't lay off thee, or ye, or me, or whatever. Now let's go ignore some henchman and trees." With that, she turned and marched toward the entry to the Garden of Wings, hopping over the scratchy sting of the thorny tangled vines at the opening with Jon's soft chuckle ringing in her ears.

* * *

"Oh dear," Wanda murmured, her eyes scanning the landscape of the garden.

Yeahhh. Toni nodded without realizing it as they took their first glance around the Garden of Wings.

"My God, girls. It's magical. Like every childhood dream realized. Imagine the selfies to be had here," Marty whispered on a breathy sigh as a blinking blue light whizzed past her head.

All around them multicolored lights dotted the interior of the garden, buzzing and zipping in and out of the foliage of the woods.

"Fairies?" she whispered to Jon in utter awe.

He leaned into her, pressing his lips to her ear and making her shiver. "Indeed, milady. Beautiful, yes?"

Toni nodded, feeling suddenly serene as she allowed her body to lean into Jon's harder one. "So beautiful," she murmured, her stomach doing somersaults at Jon's touch.

These trees, while covered in snow like the rest of the forest, still had leaves on them—leaves in the shape of hearts in ice blue, stringing across the long, bent branches and spilling from the tops of their tall peaks like fountains shooting water. The ice forming on each heart-shaped leaf was crystallized and shimmering as though they'd been dunked in white sugar.

Stumps covered in the greenest moss she'd ever seen were grouped together like small tables, and miniature tea sets sat upon them, the tiny teacups half full. Purple wisteria wound around tree trunks in a riot of endless flowers, draping and swaying in the suddenly very humid air.

Cottages with thatched roofs and circular doors hung like small Chinese lanterns throughout tall oaks with pink and purple leaves, threading their way around the perimeter of the path they took.

And all along the path as they walked, tiny voices much like Dannan's twittered, the staccato cadence fluttering and quick.

That was when she heard her name, a rhythmic, almost tribal beat, *"Toni, Toni, Toni!"*

"Keep walking, Dragon Slayer," Nina coaxed from behind, poking a knuckle between Toni's shoulder blades.

"You hear it, too?" she asked as sweat beaded her upper lip.

"I hear it. I hear everything these fucks are saying because—*vampire.*"

Toni nodded, forcing herself to keep her feet moving, trying with every last ounce of will to ignore the merciless chant of her name. But the throb in her head grew, almost hurting.

Carl came up from the rear and nudged her with his antlers, nudging her to keep her feet moving, rubbing his nose against her hand as a reminder to push past this.

"You *can* do this, Toni!" Jon whisper-yelled in her ear, wrapping his arm around her waist and pulling her close. "You must, or succumb to the madness. We're almost at Elessandra's."

Briefly, she wondered why no one else appeared affected by the buzz of the fairies or the whisper of the trees, but the maddening hum of their voices distracted her.

Sweat began to pool between her breasts as the fairies circled her head, calling to her, singing her name, inviting her to partake in their mayhem.

But it was the whispers of the trees that haunted her. *"Everyone knows, Toni. They know. They know what you've done. They know!"*

Still, she fought to press forward, the shoes like weights at the end of her ankles, her head light and heavy at the same time. Dannan's feet plodded forward, the thump of their heavy slaps against the earth now mingling with the taunts, becoming a drumbeat, a canvass for the whispers.

Each step became like a walk in quicksand until Marty pulled up from the rear and took her other arm. "Sing with me, honey. It's the most wonderful time of the year. We should be singing carols! Wanda, you start."

"Rudolph the red-nosed reindeer, had a very shiny nose!" Wanda crooned, her voice cracking.

"Who is this Rudolph? Reindeer most certainly do not have shiny noses," Jon protested, looking at Marty as though she'd sprouted another head.

Toni's breathing became ragged as the humid air stuck in her throat, but she was determined to focus on anything but the suggestions being whispered in her ear.

"He's a kids' story back in my land. He's an outcast. The other reindeer make fun of him because of his nose. They're mean assholes. He leaves Santa's camp—or something, and then he runs into Bigfoot—"

"The Abominable Snowman," Nina corrected on an amused chuckle.

"Right and then...shit happens. A lot of shit..." She gritted her teeth because she couldn't remember the rest of the damn story for the noise in her head.

The bluebirds hopped on her shoulders, all six of them, chirping the tune right along with Marty.

Now Nina came up behind her and gripped her shoulder, her long fingers pressing into Toni's skin. "Then one foggy Christmas Eve..." she belted out directly in Toni's ear. "Sing, kiddo. Sing with me. Focus and we'll do this together."

The landscape became a blur of muted lights and fuzzy shades of haunting limbs, all looking to snatch her up with crystallized talons.

"Just hear those sleigh bells ring-a-ling, ring-ting-ting-a-ling too..." Marty's cheerful voice faded, the grip of her hand on Toni's arm feeling farther and farther away.

Until she was entirely alone.

The world around her began to spin, twisting and turning even as she stood stock still.

And then as quickly as it began, it stopped.

Abruptly, she was standing in a meadow, tall stalks of lavender and sunflowers rocked to the rhythm of a warm breeze. Toni lifted her face and inhaled. It was just like the meadow behind her grandmother's back in Idaho.

No. No it wasn't. It couldn't be. Remember the words of warning Jon spoke, Toni. Things are not always as they appear.

Right. So she wasn't really at her grandmother's house with the porch swing and her old beagle, Tootsie, lying at Toni's feet. She was in a fairy garden with bad, bad dudes who wanted to trick her so they could drag her off to this queen to get something from her she didn't understand.

Shaking her head, she tried to dispel the image in front of her, but there was no purging it. The sky grew a brighter blue, the clouds somehow puffier, the breeze warmer, the flowers more colorful. As though someone was using a lens to bring everything into focus. And then her brother Cormac was there, waving her toward him, smiling, happy to see her—above all, safe.

God, he looked so good. So handsome and tall, his strong features serene.

It was then her heart constricted. It had been three long years since they'd said goodbye, and she missed him so much she almost dropped to her knees.

He waved again, the sun catching the glint of the ring on his finger.

No, Toni. That's not your brother. Remember what Stas did to his ring finger? This illusion has all its fingers.

Run, Toni! Run far, as fast as you can! her instincts screamed.

But run to where? She swirled around, almost tripping on the length of her dress. Dropping the pelt from around her shoulders, she grabbed the ends of her skirt and raced away from the image of her brother, ran until her feet were bloody and the shoes pinched her bridges so hard she had to bite the inside of her cheek to keep from yelping her pain.

Tears stung her eyes as the scenery whizzed past her and then the voices returned, but they were no longer courting her like a lover, they were screaming her name.

Toni! Toni! Toni! We know what you did! You ruined your brother's life!

The wind began to howl once again, tearing at her dress, whistling through the length of her hair, and still she ran harder.

As she flew from the pounding in her head, the panic racing through her veins, she stumbled and tripped over a stump, hidden in the meadow's floor, tumbling end over end until she slammed into something hard.

A grunt of pain ripped from her throat, now raw as she gasped for breath, and she forced herself up on the palms of her hands and looked around to assess where she'd landed.

A fluttery, soft hand reached out and caressed her cheek, comforting and gentle. "Poor Toni. Are you lost again? Come with me, I'll take you to your friends," the small voice murmured, light and airy.

A fairy. She was staring at an honest-to-goodness fairy, her gossamer eggshell-colored wings twittering in the air. Her dress was made of the tiniest of feathers in green and blue, just brushing the tops of her thighs, and a halo of gold surrounded her head.

Her tiny hands held out to Toni, she said again, "Come. I'll take you to your friends, but we have to hurry!"

Aw, hell no. She wasn't going to end up fooled again. She'd never live down the Great Starbucks Incident of 2015, but by God, there'd be no more stupid on her behalf.

So she decided to take Jon's tact—the fearless, angry-warrior one.

Driving herself to her feet, Toni stomped her foot and demanded, "Reveal yourself or face the wrath of my…"

Her what? She didn't have a sword like Jon—or even a weapon, for that matter. This had gone much better when Jon made the threats.

"Forget I said that. Just tell me who you are and what you want!"

The fairy laughed, twitching her miniature toes in time with her wings. "Nothing more than your safety, Toni. Now hurry, come with me!"

"Um, no. Not gonna happen. You crazy bunch of Shamalotians have fooled me once. That won't happen again. I nearly ended up flatter than a pancake the last time I gave in to temptation. I'll just wait right here, thanks."

The fairy looked confused, her ethereal face strained. "But your friends are waiting. They're just over there. See?" She looked over her shoulder and pointed with a sweet smile.

Yep. They sure were. With an exception: This particular manifestation of Nina lacked one thing—the bluebirds who'd been her constant companions since they'd started. They weren't on Carl's back either.

Toni sauntered close to the fairy and snatched her up by her wings, holding her with thumb and forefinger. "Liar. If you guys are going to conjure up hallucinations, at least pay attention to the details and get it right. So, who are you and what does your boss want from me?" Toni demanded, giving the fairy a light shake.

The fairy pouted up at her, her wee features distorting. "I'm just trying to help you, Toni," she said as though she were hurt, her voice rising.

Toni made a face at the fairy. "Enough with the bullshit stories? *Who are you and what do you want?*"

Just as she asked the question, her fingers exploded apart, the fairy escaping her grasp and flitting off to the distance, where she morphed, shedding her small body in favor of a much larger mirror image, growing, rippling back and forth in the wind that had now turned bitterly cold.

With the swift prowess of a ninja, the fairy made a fist, creating a ball of fire she made dance in her palm. Then she lobbed it forward, the screaming orange-and-blue flame coming straight for Toni.

In that moment, Toni's body responded in much the way it had when the dragon had appeared. Her feet began to tingle, growing warmer by the second, and her hands arced upward, effectively catching the flame and hurling it back at the fairy with a harsh grunt.

And again, for the briefest moment, her mind said, *shut the front door! You just caught a fireball, dude.*

But her body wasn't satisfied with just catching the fireball, her body wanted to catch this menace and make her talk—make her admit she'd been sent by this effed-up queen.

And then she remembered something. Something important.

She could breathe fire.

Hah!

Closing her eyes, Toni inhaled deeply, summoning up the visual of the night before when she'd started the campfire, and then she recalled Nina's words—*just breathe.*

That familiar acrid taste in her throat returned, rising up in a wave of bile just before she blew a hot stream of fire in the direction of the fairy, swishing her head left to right to spray her foe.

The fairy screeched her outrage, rising high in the air like an enormous half human, half butterfly, her wings pounding out a throbbing beat. Pushing her legs together, she made an arrow of her body and shot forward at Toni, the wind whistling like a missile launching as she raced forward.

Toni! She's headed right for your damn head. Duck, you idiot!

But her body was all like, *Fuck that. Why not just jump up and catch a bitch midair like you've suddenly been drafted in the NBA?*

Her legs didn't falter; her feet no longer ached with that dull throb. Instead, they felt as if someone had injected them with adrenaline as she fell to her haunches and pushed off, leaping upward and looping her arm around the torpedoing fairy's neck.

"Gotcha!" she roared, launching her to the ground, throwing her with such strength, the fairy's body left an imprint on the meadow's floor.

Landing solidly on her feet, Toni wasted no time in jumping on top of her and pinning her to the cold earth, straddling her hips.

Victorious, she grabbed hold of the fairy's feathery bodice and yanked her upward. "Who the fuck are you and what do you want?" she roared in her perfectly proportioned face.

"Toni!" A voice from far, far away, laced in frantic tones, yelled, "Let go of her, for shit's sake!"

Nina? What was Nina doing in the meadow? No. It was another trick. It wasn't really Nina.

Hands slipped under her armpits and began dragging her from the fairy, but Toni fought the notion she might not get the answers she needed. So she struggled, but the arms were stronger, pulling her, tugging her, and all the while yelling, "Toni! Wake up!"

"Milady! Come back!" Jon bellowed, his strong hand cupping her cheek.

Come back? From?

Cold water from out of nowhere splashed her in the face. Toni sputtered and coughed, fighting to open her eyes as she swiped at them with her fingers.

"Toni, honey? Wake up! It's me, Wanda. Look at me!"

Her eyes flew open to find herself back in the Garden of Wings with everyone staring down at her, worry marring their expressions.

"What happened?"

"One minute ye were here with us, the next ye disappeared into thin air, lass," Dannan said, his blue face concerned. "We followed the sound of the crash yer body made when ye landed on the ground. Where did ye go?"

Toni shook her head. "I don't know! It's like you said, I was here and you all were singing Christmas carols and then I was in my grandmother's meadow…"

So now someone was just snatching her up?

Jon's face came into her line of vision next, his eyes troubled, his hand cupping her jaw. "Toni, are you all right?"

She didn't have time to waste lingering on the fact that his hand felt pretty damn good on her skin. She was out for blood. The blood of a lying fairy.

"Where's the damn fairy?"

Jon pointed over his shoulder with clear hesitance. "I'm afraid you've maimed the Truth Fairy, milady."

"The Truth Fairy? Seriously?" she asked, spitting at the water dribbling down her face and over the front of her gown.

"Of course, lass," Dannan responded, kneeling down to place his hulking frame in front of her. "The king uses her oft to parse the liars from the truth sayers. 'Tis important when creating armies to keep our lands safe."

"Oh yeah? Well, the Truth Fairy just tried to kill me with her ninja fireballs."

"That's not true!" a diminutive, weak voice protested from behind Jon.

"Liar, liar, wings on fire!" Toni croaked, her throat raw.

And then Marty and Wanda gasped.

Toni's eyes flew to the fairy lying on the ground as she began to return to her normally petite size—well, except for her nose. Her nose sprouted from her face like the pointy end of a carrot.

Jon pulled Toni upward, tucking her close to his chest in a possessive gesture she wasn't up to fighting. "What say you, fairy? Does the maiden speak the truth?"

Flitting upward, her head rolled on her neck as she warred with the weight of her nose. Pressing her tiny hands to each cheeks, she held her head upright to keep it from lolling. "Look what you've done!" she screeched in outrage.

Toni was astonished, her eyes going wide. The nerve. The damn nerve. "What *I've* done?"

"You've stolen my powers!" the fairy squeaked. "I can feel it! Disgusting humans! The lot of you!"

Dannan plucked her from the air and eyeballed her. "Did the queen send ye?" he growled.

Her legs dangled as she tried to shake her head. "No!"

Dannan looked to Toni, his blue face stoic. "She speaks the truth, maiden."

Regaining some of her energy, Toni planted her hands on her hips. "You know this how?"

"Look at her nose—it hasn't grown again. She speaks no falsehoods," he said, as though they should already know that bit of information.

Toni's brain raced through her vast array of fairytales and she suddenly remembered. "*Pinocchio?*" she asked on a shout.

Dannan's brow furrowed, his head cocked as his fluted ears wagged. "Whom?"

Toni narrowed her gaze at the fairy. "Is that how you tell if the king's army is lying? By making their noses grow?" she asked.

Jon looked down at her with what she thought might be a hint of pride, secretly making her a little giddy. "'Tis exactly the way, Toni. How did you know this?"

Toni rolled her eyes, forgetting everything was upside down here. "Same old song. It's similar to a fairytale back in my land. But I'm telling you, this fire-slinging winged nut launched a fireball at me! It's not *my* nose that's bigger than my head, now is it, you teeny-tiny winged terror? No. It's yours, which means you're lying. I didn't steal anything from you!"

The fairy struggled against Dannan's grip, her little body swinging to and fro like a festive pendulum. "But you did! Now *you* have the power to prove falsehoods. What will I dooo?" she cried.

Toni cocked her head to the right and paused to put this new revelation together. Yesterday, she'd fought a dragon. Today a fairy. She'd come away from the first battle with the ability to breathe fire. Now she had the ability to find out when people were lying by making their noses grow?

Where was this bag o' tricks when she'd tried to prove Stas was lying about being a killer?

"So you're telling me I'm the new Truth Fairy?"

"Arghhhhh!" the fairy screamed, writhing and twisting to no avail.

Toni didn't have time to focus on the particulars; what she needed was to get to the root of the problem. This Angria and her grudge. "So why would you try to trick me into going with you if you don't work for the queen and weren't planning to take me to her? What's the dealio here, Truth Fairy? What's your motivation?"

"Greed!" a voice boomed, shaking the snow and leaves from the trees as a long staff crashed to the ground in front of their feet.

Ding-dong, fairytale character number three calling...

Chapter 7

The Truth Fairy shrunk in Dannan's fingers, her eyes wide and full of terror. "Ellesandra, my queen!" she gasped.

"Silence!" the woman ordered, stomping her staff once more.

So this must be the Blue Fairy? Interesting.

Her hair was the color of the rainbow, falling to the ground to sweep at her feet in swaths of curls. Long robes in every shade of blue imaginable fell in graceful folds about her rounded body, and on her back, magnificent wings of gold throbbed.

Her eyes were a beautiful shade of violet, full of liquid warmth and concern, her round face soft and plump. She wasn't at all small like the Truth Fairy, in fact, she was quite life-size.

Instantly Jon and Dannan knelt before her, bowing their heads, right arms resting across their hearts in reverence.

The Blue Fairy tapped the tops of their skulls with the edge of her gold staff, elaborately adorned with carved snakes winding about the length, the work so intricate, each scale was visible. "Rise, boys," she murmured, smiling fondly down at them.

Jon plucked her hand up and planted a kiss on the back of it, giving her one of his devastatingly handsome smiles. "Ellesandra, my queen. So good to see you."

She gave him a mischievous grin. "Are you chasing after my fairies again, lad? Like in the days of old? Some things never change," she teased, her chuckle light and easy. "And Dannan, have you given up picking clean the bones of humans yet? All that protein will kill your cholesterol."

Dannan's head fell back on his shoulders and he laughed, his helium-filled giggle making Toni smile despite this new predicament.

"Ah, Ellesandra, I gave those up centuries ago, which ye well know. Shame on ye for trying to frighten our otherwordly friends. But alas, 'tis good to see yer beautiful face once more."

Ellesandra chuckled until her gaze fell on Toni. She cocked her head, her eyes curious. "You're not from this world."

Toni licked her dry lips and curtsied—because it seemed like the thing to do—her ankles bowing inward awkwardly. "No, ma'am. Jersey. I'm from, um, the land we call Jersey. Toni. I'm Toni Vitali."

Ellesandra's nostrils flared and her lips pursed. "And you three? You're not like her."

Marty and Wanda were the first to react, but Nina was slow and sluggish as she trailed behind them. "I'm Marty Flaherty and these are my friends, Wanda Jefferson and Nina Statleon, a vampire, and a werewolf, and a halfsie. And this," she reached out and rubbed Carl's muzzle affectionately, "is Carl. A zombie in our world."

Ellessandra's smile beamed when her soft eyes landed on Carl. She reached a hand out to cup his muzzle. "Ahhh, a gentle soul, your Carl is?" she asked, though Toni suspected the fairy knew the answer.

"The gentlest ever," Nina whispered, her lips now alarmingly pale as she reached for Wanda's and Marty's shoulders, her knuckles white.

"You're a good lad, aren't you, Carl? I can see it in your eyes. Good blessings be yours always, my lamb," she said, blowing a kiss toward him. A kiss that turned into rainbow-colored dust as it clouded over Carl's head, falling around him in glittery sprinkles of powdery light.

"And you…" She pointed to Nina, her eyes critical as she scanned the vampire's slumped form. "You suffer?"

Nina's head hung low on her long, graceful neck, but her eyes remained fierce. "I'm just hungry and tired," she said, her teeth tightly clenched.

Toni slipped between Marty and Wanda and looped Nina's arm around her neck in order to hold her up. She pulled her to a stump, brushing it free of snow with the fabric of her dress before setting Nina on its surface. "Rest," she whispered, placing a hand on the vampire's shoulder and squeezing.

"Ellesandra," Jon cut in, his tone urgent. "Our apologies for taking you from far more important matters, but your assistance is needed. As you can see, a guest of Shamalot is in desperate need, and we have an unusual request…"

"Say no more, dear friend," Ellesandra said, holding up a hand covered in rings. "But first, I must deal with my errant fairy."

"Please, please, please, my queen!" the Truth Fairy begged as she squirmed in Dannan's grasp. "I was tempted by gold. It will never happen again!"

"*Whose* gold called upon your recklessness?" Ellesandra demanded, her sweet face no longer so sweet.

"Queen Angria! She's put a price on the red one's head. Endless riches be had if we bring her to the queen!"

"Why? What does she want from me?" Toni spat.

The fairy's head shook rapidly as her frightened eyes captured Toni's. "I know not! I know only she has handed down orders to bring you in alive!"

Ellesandra shook her head and tsked her displeasure. "You have betrayed your title, fairy! You shall pay!"

"But she stole my power, my queen! She made my nose grow three times its size!"

Toni's finger whipped up in the air as she left Nina's side, her eyes narrowed as she confronted the fairy. "Hold up there, Tinkerbell. You tried to trick me into going with you. Then you tried to set me on fire. I just returned the favor. I didn't steal anything from you on purpose. It just happened."

Which had become the story of her life these last few days.

Ellesandra's eyes went wide. "You defeated the Truth Fairy? A *human?*"

Toni nodded, brushing her tangled mess of hair from her cheek. "Believe me. No one's as surprised as me. Look, this is a long story, but a couple of days ago I worked in an outlet mall for a boss I could have spat from my vagina if I were just a few years older. Now I'm breathing fire and making liars' noses grow. Color me as shocked as you. But it wasn't on purpose. *She* started it. Which I think is obvious from the state of her nose."

"This is a startling turn of events," Ellesandra said, whisking her vast robes over the snowy ground as she headed down the path. "Follow me, darling ones, and I shall make all things right!"

* * *

Toni's mouth fell open when they entered Ellesandra's cottage, which wasn't really a cottage at all, but a mini-castle. The outside was deceptive—it looked like all the other cottages in the Garden of Wings, covered by the colorful sugared vines and trees so prevalent, but the inside was nothing short of spectacular.

A spiral staircase in the middle of the vast entryway led to places unknown, winding upward into what looked like swollen pink clouds the consistency of cotton candy. Vases in creamy ice cream colors held ferns and ivy, spilling from their tops in lush green. Candleholders as tall as Toni supported fat, squat candles, their scents filling the house with pears and lavender.

Rough stone fountains sculpted into fairies riding swans spewed forth champagne-colored water, the bubbles dissipating as they hit the air.

Windows as high as the ceiling with oyster-colored drapes falling to the ground in graceful sweeps spanned the room, the view to the world of the Garden of Wings in all its pink-and-purple twilight almost incandescent.

Ellesandra waved them to the back of her home, past room after room filled with books, fairies dotting the interiors with their bright hues and cheerful buzzing. She took them to her kitchen, where tables and chairs sat off to the left, vases of flowers centered upon them.

A cauldron bubbled beneath a warm fire in a stone fireplace, misty tendrils of green and blue rising from its depths. She motioned them to puffy chairs around the hearth as she gave orders to an elderly man who stirred the cauldron.

"Nourish our guests, please, Hamish. Their journey has had pitfalls," she said as she swept out of the room, taking Dannan and Jon with her.

Toni helped Nina to a long couch, the armrests gilded in gold and blue scrolls, setting her gently on the cushiony edge. "Lean back, Nina." She pressed a light hand to Nina's shoulder and instead of biting it off, she actually did as Toni commanded without a single word of protest, making Toni's heart constrict.

Hamish, his stout body attached to short legs and even shorter feet, produced steaming teacups. As he bent forward, the thin wisp of graying hair atop his round head wafted upward.

He peered over round spectacles and smiled warmly. "The coffee you so desire, miladies," he said, setting a tray on a table with a bronzed sculpture of a fairy beneath it, the hands of the statue holding the glass tabletop aloft. "Milk and sugar as well."

"God, he sounds like Arch, huh, Marty?" Nina asked, her voice so weak Toni was beginning to really worry.

Marty brushed one of the vampire's soggy curls from her milk-white face with a tender hand and nodded. "Yeah, he does, friend." She patted her lap. "Here, put your head on my lap and rest."

Nina did so without protest, letting Marty stroke her raven hair as Wanda slipped in next to her friend and inched over so Nina's upper torso sprawled across both the women's laps. Wanda patted Nina's sagging wings, her face lined with worry.

She looked so small and helpless, Toni had to fight tears. This was not the woman who'd threatened her with endless harm. This wasn't the woman who cussed like a sailor and stomped around in a dress like an Army sergeant.

This was a woman who's emotions ran deeper than most. Who lobbed angry insults and taunts, but who'd die protecting the people she loved.

She decided right then and there, she didn't care what Angria did to her, but Nina had to go home now—or she'd die. Screw Brenda and screw her tasks, but especially screw getting her to the castle. She'd find a way to get there without jeopardizing Nina's life.

"We'll figure this out, Nina. Swear we will," Wanda whispered, her breath shuddering in and out of her lungs as she bit her trembling lower lip.

"You think Charlie's okay?" Nina asked, her words thick, yanking hard on Toni's heart.

"Aw, you know it, Elvira. If the boys know we're gone, Arch is in full maternal mode by now. He's buying stuffed unicorns and more *Teletubby* DVDs than even your drafty castle can hold."

"I'll kick his stodgy British ass if he gets her one more stuffed animal," Nina groused, her eyes half-closed.

"Aw, you don't mean that, Snookums," Marty said with a hitch in her voice, her wings sagging.

"I damn well do. And listen, if I don't make... You know what the fuck I mean. Any bitches come sniffin' around my man, you better take 'em out.

91

Hard. I will haunt you from the afterlife if you screw it up, Blondie. But mostly," she said, her words beginning to slur, "take care of Charlie. I don't want some damn stranger muckin' my kid's head up. You two know what I want for her. Keep her close. Promise me, *please*."

Marty and Wanda looked at each other. The fear for their friend was clear and sharp, almost palpable, falling over the room with a heavy hand.

Wanda pressed her fingers to her lips. "You just hush, Dark One. Charlie's just fine, and so are Greg and Arch and Darnell, and our men, and Hollis, and you will be, too because we don't leave each other—ever. We'll be home before you know it. Trust me, Vampire."

Nina nodded and closed her eyes, depleted, her body limp as she sagged into her friends. Carl whimpered, driving his nose under her body and hiding his eyes.

On quiet feet, Toni began handing out coffee to the women while she silently prayed Ellesandra would have something in her magical arsenal to save Nina.

Hamish brought dainty sandwiches with fat sausages in them, slathered in mustard, the delicious scent almost making Toni's eyes roll to the back of her head.

She made plates for Marty and Wanda, filling the delicate China to the brim with food because she had to do something or she'd lose her mind.

What if Nina died because she was trying to help her? It didn't matter that if you took the rational path, no one in a million years could have predicted the fate of Toni's words. What mattered was these people were helping her, and their support had become invaluable, and now someone was in danger of losing her life.

"Sit, Toni," Wanda ordered, pointing to a chair, her eyes glassy. "You need to eat, too. You've had another rough day and I won't have you collapsing."

Toni stuffed a knuckle in her mouth to keep from screaming her fears for Nina out loud. Instead she whispered hoarsely, "There has to be something we can do. Maybe Ellesandra can zap you guys back home. I'm fine. I really am. I can get to the castle without you. I'll explain to the king when I get there. He doesn't sound like a bad guy. No way would he let someone die just because of some stupid rule. We can get a sick note or something from the big boss Ellessandra. She'll explain. Surely he'll listen to her. I just can't let this go on—"

The clunk of Jon's boots interrupted her as he came back into the room and knelt down in front of Nina, his handsome face pained. "I shall carry you, milady. Fear not, 'tis just I, at your service." He looked to Marty and Wanda then. "May I?"

"Ellesandra can help?" Marty whispered, a tear falling from her eyes as she stroked Nina's cheek with the back of her hand.

His nod was curt, his strong jaw tight. "We think so. Though we must do so apace." He scooped up Nina's limp form in his big arms and turned to take her from the room, his muscled thighs carrying him toward the back of Ellesandra's home, where he disappeared again.

Toni gulped as she stared down at her coffee, unable to even consider drinking it. What had seemed so appealing yesterday, what she'd likely have given her left lung and a kidney for one sip of, felt stupid and vapid now.

She leaned forward, her elbows on her knees, and let her head rest in her hands, tears slipping from her lashes and falling to the mosaic-tiled floor as she closed her eyes and made another bargain with the universe to save Nina.

Take me. If this involves the "you scratch my back, I'll scratch yours" theory of the realm, then take me instead. No one will even know I'm gone back in Jersey. Please, just take me.

* * *

Jon pushed his way out the back door of Ellesandra's, and Toni's heart began that crazy crashing his appearance always evoked while her stomach did a backflip.

And on cue, shafts of light twinkled over his head and the strains of that stupid harp rang in her ears.

"Shut up, would you?" she hissed to the sky with a roll of her eyes.

"Milady, speak up. I did not hear you."

"I said, how long do we wait to find out if it worked?" she asked Jon as he sat beside her under a portico by a fire pit made of white stone.

She watched the glistening snow fall beneath a pink and deep-purple sky. She was wrapped in a blanket made of the softest cashmere smelling of rose petals, hunkered down on a toadstool made for two, hoping against hope whatever Ellesandra had cooked up for Nina worked.

His handsome face was grim. "Ellesandra said we must wait until the midnight hour."

Toni blew out a shaky breath, tucking her nose into the blanket and closing her eyes. "There has to be another way, Jon. She can't stay here much longer or she'll... I can't let that happen. She has a little girl and a husband. She needs blood."

She realized her hysteria was rising along with her voice, but there was little she could do to stop this new wave of panic.

"Have faith, Toni. Ellesandra is one of the most skilled healers in the land," he said, his voice husky and low.

Faith. She'd had that once, but not anymore. "I'm all out."

"Why? What troubles you so that you cannot hope? I know something darkens your doorstep. What can it hurt to share, here in my world, when yours is so far away?"

Misery welled in the pit of her stomach, tugging at her already knotted gut. "Because what happened was awful, okay? What I did was awful, and I've been running from it ever since."

He captured her hand, stroking her palm, his fingers tender and warm. "Then I urge you to tell me your woes. My ears listen well."

Maybe he was right. What could it hurt? Her world was light-years away. No one would ever know...

"I had a boyfriend—"

"Does this word mean the same thing in your land as it does in mine?"

"Probably not. Let me reword. I was involved for a short time, or maybe betrothed is a word you'll better understand, to a man who was part of a very bad group of people. Kind of like Queen Angria's henchmen. It's called the Russian mafia. I didn't know it until it was too late, but then it was...well, too late." So late. So, so late.

Jon paused, looking into her eyes, his face darkening under the light of the half moon. "So you didn't know he was a henchman?"

"No. I worked in the finance department of a car dealership run and owned by this bad man's father. We'd only dated for a couple of months when what I'm about to tell you happened."

"You handled gold?"

Oh she'd handled it all right. Handled it so well, she didn't even know she was handling it. Closing her eyes, she nodded. "Yes. Lots of gold."

"And what is this car dealership you speak of?"

She sighed, licking her lips. They had some huge otherworld deficits—technology being the biggest. "Cars are like your carriages, only with motors and windows and vroom-vroom— Never mind. They're a means of transportation in my world. Where I worked, we sold them."

"For hefty sums, I imagine? Especially if they vroom-vroom," he teased, his eyes amused.

She chuckled and shook her head. "They're probably the equivalent of ten herds of sheep here in Shamalot."

He waved a dismissive hand and grinned. "Sheep are rather inexpensive. Now *reindeer*—"

"Not the point, Stable Boy."

He sobered, his gorgeous face becoming serious as he straightened and cleared his throat. "Of course. Please continue."

"Anyway, my betrothed, Stas was his name, was laundering money through the dealership."

"He washed the gold, you say? How peculiar."

Toni groaned. "No. Not literally. Suffice it to say, the gold was illegal, and I handled it. Which meant I could go to prison if the police...I mean the people who guard Jersey...ever found out."

"So then what happened?"

"One night, just after I'd figured out what he was doing, that he was using the car dealership as a front to launder money, I decided I'd confront him. I really hoped I was wrong, but I know numbers, Jon, and those numbers didn't add up. Anyway, I asked my supervisor to meet me at the dealership so I could tell him about Stas and what he was doing. I was too afraid to do it over the phone. Little did I know, my supervisor was also a part of the mess."

God, that night. She'd never forget that night—finding out Andre was part of the whole thing, the blood, their laughter at what they'd done.

Jon's beautiful sapphire eyes narrowed to mere slits in his head. "And did you confront this scoundrel? Were I there in your land, I would have beheaded him. No one steals from the king."

"I never got that far, and now, looking back, it was a good thing. When I showed up, for some reason I took the back way through the service entrance instead of the front doors. I don't know why, because it was out of the ordinary for me. But I've thanked my lucky stars every day since I chose that path."

Because it had been the right one. She paused and swallowed hard, tightening her grip on the blanket.

Jon cupped her jaw, letting his thumb run over her lower lip. "This pains you, milady. I cannot bear it. I will not press if you wish for it to remain a secret."

No. She'd come this far; it was time to go all the way. "Stas and Andre, my supervisor, had just kill…killed a man. I don't know who he was or why he was at the dealership, but they were standing over his body, and the body was in a pool of… And Stas had a gun in his hand and they were laughing about it while they waited for *me*."

Toni couldn't contain her sob as her shoulders sagged and her chin dropped to her chest. Her fate would have been the same had she gone in the front door. It just took one little hiccup in her routine to save her, and she wasn't wasting that second chance.

"Toni," Jon whispered, pulling her close, letting his chin rest atop her head. "No more. No more tonight. This stresses your heart and I do not like it."

She buried her face in his shoulder, fighting hot tears. "It's okay. Really. Needless to say, I got the hell out of Dodge as fast as I could, because I knew they'd be looking for me. I'd told Andre when I asked to meet him that something was going on with Stas."

Jon's grip tightened on her arm, his voice low and menacing. "Why do I suspect this Stas found you?"

And then, she'd done the dumbest thing she'd ever done in her life. She told her hothead, overprotective brother. "Because he did. I stupidly confided in my brother, and to this day I can't believe I did something so careless. But at that point, I still didn't know anything about Stas's involvement in the mafia or how widespread his reach was. I just thought he was a bad guy with a hot accent. But I had to tell someone what I saw. So I told my brother Cormac that Stas was cooking the books. I didn't know what else to do. I knew I should have gone to the police, but I panicked."

She'd wanted Cormac to go with her, and that had been the plan, until…

"Forgive my ineptitude. How does one cook a book? Surely there's no culinary value in leather and parchment?"

Her shoulders slumped. "It means to fix them so they look like one thing but are absolutely another. Anyway, I told my brother. We planned to go to the police and tell them everything I'd seen."

She'd never forget Cormac's handsome face when he'd heard her story that night, after she'd left the dealership. His disbelief, his rage.

"I suspect your brother is a fierce knight?"

Toni nodded, her heart tight with sorrow. "He is. It's just the two of us since my mother died six years ago, and we were…*are* very close. He took me to his house and told me to stay put. But Stas showed up and the next thing I know, I'm out cold and Cormac is gone."

Jon lifted her chin, forcing her to look at him. "And this Stas? What did he do to you, Toni? *Tell me.*"

She shook her head as salty tears welled in her eyes. "He tied me up, held a gun to my head, threatened to kill me."

And she'd stuck her face right back in his, dared him to pull the trigger, using the same technique he'd once told her he used when confronted with a heated argument.

Be the crazy, Antonia.

And then he'd laughed at the size of her balls, his deep-brown eyes glinting with maniacal pleasure. But Stas was far more into a good mind game, which he'd played like an expert by telling her all the things they were going to do, not just to her, but to Cormac.

"A gun? This is a weapon?"

"A bad weapon. Maybe even worse than a sword. It's faster, stronger."

"But you escaped his clutches."

"Just by pure luck. Stas might be pretty badass, but he's not exactly a rocket scientist."

Jon's stare was blank.

"It means he's not very smart. I managed to get loose while he was on his cell phone in another room. I know Cormac's house well, so I climbed out a window and slid down a trellis and made a break for it. Somehow I got back to my apartment, and that's when I found…" She sucked in the cold air with a shiver.

Jon stiffened, the sympathetic anguish clear on his face. "Cormac?"

Toni shuddered, rubbing her arms. "No. My neighbor, Woody. I remember seeing him as Cormac and I left. My best guess is that he heard us talking about going to my brother's place. Stas probably used his strong-arm tactics to get him to spill the beans about our location. Woody saw me that night when I got back from the dealership—he knew something was wrong because I was close to hysteria by that point. Stas must have sensed that Woody knew something, because he killed him and left him in the middle of my living room."

Gripping her temple with her forefinger and thumb, she fought that image, the resurrection of the memory of Woody's body, facedown on her hardwood floor, a hole in the back of his head.

"This Stas must die," Jon growled with clear agitation, the muscles of his arms flexing in tension.

"If you ever get to Jersey, I'll give you his address. Bring a sharp sword," she joked.

"This is no laughing matter, Toni. He is vicious and should swing at dawn."

"Don't think for one second I don't want that, but proving it is a whole other story."

Just before she'd taken off, she'd made a phone call to the police. Told them everything she saw at the dealership, about Woody and her brother, and they'd claimed to have taken all that information down—and had done absolutely nothing.

Because Stas was part of a network of cold-blooded killers just like him who were pretty good about cleaning up their messes. No one matched the brief description she'd given to the police of the man at the dealership, and Woody's death wasn't a death with no body to show for it.

He was just a missing person.

Jon brushed the hair from her eyes, tucking it behind her ear. "What happened to your brother, Toni?"

She licked her lips, suddenly dry and stiff, her body tight with unbearable tension. "I don't know. I never saw him again after that. But Stas did leave me one thing back at my apartment to remind me I was better off shutting my mouth."

She'd hidden out at a sleazy motel one town over for a week, with no luck convincing the cops they had two murders on their hands while she'd researched Stas and his family. It was a week spent frantic, afraid, with almost no sleep, until she finally realized Stas probably had connections to the police she'd never get past.

"What happened next?"

That same bile rose in her throat, hot, pungent, almost making her gag at the recollection. "I went back to my apartment in a stupid disguise, hoping to grab some of my things when I realized the police were never going to take me seriously. There was a box waiting outside my door…"

"Don't say anymore, milady. I do not need to know," he murmured against the top of her head.

Her throat was too tight to speak anyway, her stomach hot with that sour acidic roll that hit her every time she thought about the contents of that box.

Cormac's ring finger, and a phone call from Stas with a warning: *Talk and he dies.*

Chapter 8

As the snow fell, her head on Jon's shoulder, his free hand stroking her hair, she bit the inside of her cheek to keep from crying. "I called the police anonymously to report Cormac missing, but they said I had to come in to file a report. I had an appointment with a detective. And I went…"

Jon stroked her arm, his gentle fingers soothing her. "But?"

"But I took a risk, and I went to the police station. I even wore that same ridiculous disguise I wore to my apartment. I asked for the detective I'd spoken to on the phone and the police officer at the desk pointed him out. Thankfully, I wasn't in Stas's line of vision, but I saw him. I saw him rubbing elbows with the same damn detective I was supposed to talk to as if the two of them were old friends. I know he showed up there that day because he'd been given a head's up. I knew it was Stas's way of sending me a message that no one was going to listen because he owned the cops, too. The detective is dirty, maybe they all are. I don't know. I just know in my gut, he was a part of covering up what Stas and Andre did," she whispered fiercely.

"How did you end up at this store you speak of so often?"

"After that, I ran to the farthest part of Jersey I could get to without leaving the state altogether because I wanted to at least be nearby if I found anything out about Cormac. I hate that I ran, but I didn't know what else to do. I was no good to Cormac dead, and no doubt Stas would have killed me if he could find me. So I took every last bit of money I had out of my savings account and I ran as far as I could get with what I had. I ditched my car in case Stas might have it followed."

"And then what did you do, milady?"

Toni sighed, her eyes tearing. "My money ran out pretty quickly, but Cormac and I used to camp a lot as kids, so when I began to run low, I camped in the woods for days. I found odd jobs for a little while, stayed in homeless shelters until the dust settled, and then I got the job at the outlet mall, using my dead mother's social security number, of all things. We share the same name, and it makes me sick to my stomach to do it, but if Stas and his people go looking for me with their connections… Anyway, that's where I've been ever since. But I didn't stop looking for Cormac. I scoured the internet for any mention, an article maybe, *anything* about an unidentified body. I kept calling the police from prepaid cell phones. I—"

"This cell phone you speak of, explain. Also, the intor-net, is it? How does one scour a net?"

Toni placed a hand on his broad chest, trying not to relish the feel of his hard pec beneath her palm. "I promise I'll tell you later all about how much easier it is to live in Jersey in my time. Our forms of communication are superior to the ones here in Shamalot."

Jon chuckled, the soft rumble reaching her ear as he settled her back against his chest. "So you've hidden away all this time with no luck finding your brother?"

Sorrow seeped back into her bones, that ugly helplessness she'd lived with for what felt like forever.

"Not for three years. Nothing. Not a trace of him. I even went back to his house, but there was a new family there. I guess the bank foreclosed…"

She shrugged her shoulders. Cormac had worked so hard for that house. He'd loved every inch, every room. Watching the people who'd moved in from behind a maple tree two houses down, laughing in the sunshine out in his sprawling front yard, playing Frisbee with their children, had almost made her want to run to them and scream the house wasn't theirs to enjoy.

They had no right to laugh when she was so miserable, but it wasn't their fault Cormac was gone.

It was hers.

"I feel like a coward. Like there was just one more thing I could have done to find him that I didn't, you know? Maybe that's why I got on that dragon's back. Maybe all my pent-up aggression over Cormac, my helplessness, is forcing its way to the surface. Maybe I'm metaphorically saving Cormac over and over."

"Might I speak freely, Toni?" Jon asked, ever formal.

She nodded her head, too wrung out from the day's events to protest.

"You're no coward. Never say such. You feel guilt because of your brother. This guilt relates to Nina, too. You fight so fiercely because you want to make up for the loss of your brother. And it all leads back to this bastard Stas, whom, I assure you, should I ever encounter, will leave such encounter with no head."

His possessive tone made her shiver, but his words made complete sense. Her life spinning so far out of control had all begun with Stas and the murders, which had eventually led her to working at the outlet mall for Attila The Bree, which then had led to meeting the ladies from OOPS.

Maybe, in some twisted way, she was trying to keep everyone from harm by taking enormous risks because she hadn't been able to save Cormac. But was it a death wish like Nina had pointed out?

Or did she think each time she defeated one form of a villain or another, she was racking up some sort of points to make up for not finding her brother? As if she could turn them in to the mailman with a self-addressed-stamped envelope and she'd get something in return—like the return of her brother.

Toni shook her head to clear the cobwebs. "I feel like everywhere I turn, I leave disaster in my wake. First it was Cormac, now it's Nina. Would any of this have happened if I hadn't thought a stupid wish up in my head? I've spent a lot of time staying out of any kind of trouble since everything happened. I take a different way home from work every three days. I don't go out, not that I can afford to anyway. I don't date, I don't—"

"Date? I must insist you explain this term in your world's language."

"See men. You know, go to one of those movies I'll tell you about, talk on the phone, go for walks, have dinner," she said on a soft sigh.

"Ah. Then might I tell you, I'm not displeased you don't date men?"

Her heart shuddered in her chest and her toes tingled. "The point is, I stay out of the limelight. The only reason I'm doing something as public as working at a store is because I couldn't find work anywhere else, and I think I'm deep enough into Jersey that Stas would never consider looking for me there. The job stinks, but it gave me a roof over my head." Besides who wanted to hire a woman with an accounting degree and a killer on her ass?

"There is no need to run here in Shamalot. Here, you're safe with me," he said.

She slid forward on the toadstool and gave him a look of utter disbelief. "It's a good thing you're pretty. Have you forgotten Queen Angria?"

He leaned forward, too, cupping her chin. "I said you were safe here with *me*, beautiful maiden. I'm not in your land of Jersey. I would always protect you, should you stay here."

Toni's throat went dry. "I don't know what you're trying to say."

He slid in closer, splaying his hand across her lower back and pulling her tight. "I think you do, milady. I'm saying, stay here with me," he murmured, just before he pressed his lips to Toni's and she melted into him.

The moment his mouth aligned with hers, fireworks went off behind her eyelids. Vivid, colorful sparks, shooting upward as the soft pressure of his lips increased.

Toni leaned into his powerful strength, her back bowing, her heart pounding. She clung to the lapels of his vest, her fingers shaking from the sharp sweetness of his mouth on hers.

Jon slipped his tongue between her lips, the silken rasp making her nipples tighten and press hard against the bodice of her confining dress. The blanket around her shoulders fell to the ground and suddenly it wasn't cold and snowing, it was hot and maddeningly delicious.

Each stroke of his tongue made her weak, made the space between her thighs hot and achy with need. His thickly muscled arms hauled her closer, his breathing strained, matching the heave of her chest.

She drove her fingers into his hair, pushing away the piece of material he used to hold it back and threading her fingers through the soft silken strands, clinging to him.

Jon moaned into her mouth, tightening his hold as he leaned back, pulling her until her hips were pressed to his, the strain of his shaft against his breeches making her squirm.

Her arms went up around his neck as he took her mouth, devoured it, captured it until Toni felt faint. She wanted this man, wanted to know what he looked like naked, wanted to stop wondering what his hands would feel like on her flesh—

"Hey, Flawless! Quit eatin' her face off and get the hell in here before you knock her up. The last thing we need is magical fairytale babies!"

Nina?!

Thank you, thank you, thank you! she mentally shouted as she and Jon pulled apart in guilt.

Jon's eyes instantly found hers and they held self-reproach. "Milady, my apologies. I've risked your honor and good reputation."

Pressing her hands to her hot cheeks, she took in a shaky breath. She'd been kissed before, and at one point or another she was sure she'd been kissed well, but it was *nothing* like Jon's kiss.

"You didn't do anything wrong. Where I come from, we kiss all the time."

His eyes went wide and one eyebrow rose. "Out in the open when public eyes are upon you?"

Toni snorted. "Uh-huh. It's not inappropriate to make out. Maybe not in, like, the *Shop Rite*, but when you're alone in the privacy of your home, no one gets upset."

"You do this in your land without an escort—this dating? It's unheard of here."

"As long as you're an adult and you're both consenting."

"I take back what I said about staying here. I think I like your land better," he said, his chuckle deep and husky.

She shrugged with a smile, her pulse still slowing but her thoughts far away. "I don't know, I think I like Shamalot. It's magical."

"There is plenty of magic to be had, but we do not have phones and nets and dating. We'd do well to learn from your kind."

"Either way, there's nothing to worry about. Besides, who would care if my reputation were soiled anyway? No one. So you're safe."

Jon grabbed her hand and captured her gaze. "I would care, milady. I would care greatly."

She had to look away from his intense stare. "We should get back inside," she whispered.

Toni rose to leave, her hand slipping from Jon's. But it wasn't without reluctance as the warmth of his flesh dissipated.

Making her way inside to where Marty and Wanda sat sipping coffee and eating the sandwiches Hamish had made with a very animated Nina, Toni couldn't help but smile to herself.

Nina was okay.

That was all that mattered right now. Her brother, what she'd told Jon, their kiss…it would all have to wait.

Sneaking up behind Nina, careful not to unsettle the birds curled up in her hair, Toni wrapped her arms around her neck and gave her a hug—a long, hard one just before she planted a wet kiss on the vampire's lean cheek.

"I'm so happy you're better. There'd be no reason to get out of my tent every morning if you weren't around to offend me and call me ugly names."

The quick acknowledgment Nina gave by squeezing her wrist was all Toni needed just before she flicked her hand. "I could tell how happy you were. So happy, you almost sucked Flawless's lips right off his GD perfect face, huh?" she joked on a growl.

Everyone laughed, even Toni.

And in that moment—a moment she was sharing with people she was coming to like—she felt less alone, less like there was no point to getting out of bed each morning.

She liked that. She liked that a lot.

* * *

"Ye like the lass?" Dannan asked just outside of Ellesandra's, both of them leaning on the fence with their elbows, watching the rise of the new day.

"Why do you ask?"

Dannan chuckled and winked. "'Twas evident when ye almost gobbled her face off out here last night. 'Twas more evident by the happy tune ye whistled as ye prepared for today's journey. True love's kiss is grand, aye?"

That made Jon pause. Was that what this was? Love? Nay. So soon? They'd only known each other a mere few days now.

He was intrigued, yes. The very thought that someone might hurt her back in her land incensed him. To the point he wished to travel to her Jersey, hunt this Stas down like he'd hunted so many before him, and chop his thieving head off.

Thinking of Toni helpless, alone, out in the cold while she camped and had no home to call her own, enraged him.

Thinking of her lips over and over, soft, tasting of the sweetest strawberries, before he finally found sleep last night almost drove him to dive into the cold snowdrifts piled up outside Ellesandra's path to the front door.

But love?

"What do you know of true love's kiss, ogre?" he groused, annoyed that he'd been called out. "It's nothing but a silly legend made up by a bunch of maidens who have too much time on their hands."

"Then yer mother is a silly maiden? I think she might box yer ears for sayin' as much, lad."

Jon turned to look at his longtime blue friend. "My mother? What do you know of her romance?"

Dannan grinned, folding his hands together. "I know the courtship she shared with yer father. Ye forget, I've been around more than a hundred years. I was there. Ah, 'twas a thing of beauty. Everyone said as much, and when they talked of yer parents, they talked of yer mother and her story of true love's kiss. She told anyone who had ears the legend was true."

Jon rolled his eyes at his friend. He didn't want to talk of his parents. "You are daft, good sir."

"Nay. I'm observant, and I enjoy the maiden's company. She makes me laugh."

Now he smiled fondly—almost too fondly for his own liking. "Aye, with her talk of phones and cars, she is quite amusing." So amusing, she made his gut tight and his morals questionable.

"Have ye given thought to what awaits her at the castle? This happiness that chattering Brenda speaks of? What could it be?"

"I have given it thought, yes. I know not what it means. Nor do I know what the shoes mean, but they mean something. Mark my words. I believe they're responsible for these powers Toni has acquired. It's as though she's absorbing her foes' strengths. How can that be? Have you ever heard of these shoes?"

Dannan made a face at him, nudging his shoulder. "Why would I know about shoes, lad? What ye think of me? I do not wear fancy garments with ribbons and bows."

Jon shook his head. Those shoes meant something, and he wanted to know what. If not already, it wouldn't be long before Angria knew she had them, and their worth.

"I meant were there any rumors floating about. Something you might have heard in your travels through the kingdom."

Dannan scoffed. "Nay. I have never heard rumors about shoes. The king keeps his secrets well, aye?"

Aye. "Ellesandra knows nothing of them either. 'Tis a quandary, but we must be more alert than ever. The queen would surely like to get her greedy hands on them."

"Again, I wonder, could this be the reason the queen's sent her henchmen for our Toni? I shall go back to the ways of old and pick their bones clean should they try to harm the lass again!"

Jon hopped upon the bottom rung of the fence and reached up to slap his friend's back. "Ease off. There will be no delicate fingers in your soup tonight. You made me a promise long ago. You must not break it."

"Yes, yes," the ogre groused his displeasure. "I was a fool to agree to such nonsense. But it was under duress. Alas, ye had that pointy sword nestled at my nether regions. I regret the day I ran into ye in the forest, Jon Doe. For my stomach yearns all these years for a tasty human thigh."

They'd met when Jon was just thirteen, and he and his friend Theo were out in the forest practicing their swordplay. Theo had tripped over Dannan, who was hidden beneath an enormous pile of brush, napping.

Upon waking, the sleepy ogre had plucked Theo from the ground and threatened to eat him in one bite.

But luckily, Jon had his wits about him that day, and he'd ducked under the ogre's wide stance and offered to take his manhood if he chose not to let Theo go.

And they'd been friends ever since. Now, in his thirty-fifth year, he was grateful. Dannan had taught him everything he knew about the woods and life on his own. He'd been especially invaluable this past year.

Jon barked a laugh. "You would no more have eaten my friend Theo than I would have sliced your man parts to ribbons."

"Now ye tell me this? He was a mighty meaty lad," Dannan joked, his eyes squinting with laughter. Then he sobered. "And what about Toni? How will ye fare once we get to the castle?"

Jon looked away from his friend and off into the distance, where the castle sat high atop a mountain, beautiful and ominous. "I will do as planned. Bring her to the gates and leave her to find her happiness as Brenda requested. I cannot break the rules of the realm. The realm says deliver her to the castle."

"No more than ye already have, lad?" Dannan taunted, his eyes inquisitive.

But Jon ignored him. "Then we shall continue our adventure back at home where we belong."

"Ah, but what if her happiness is with ye here in Shamalot? Will ye still be able to let her go? Will ye risk losing her forever if she goes back to this land called Jersey?"

"Who said her happiness had anything to do with me?"

He'd asked her to consider staying without even thinking about what the castle had in store for her. What if her happiness had absolutely nothing to do with staying here in Shamalot? What if it had to do with going back to Jersey and finding her brother? He couldn't ask her to give up the chance.

So he'd stay away this next leg of their journey, unwilling to become more captivated with her than he already was.

"Just an ogre's hunch. Have ye sent word to the castle we'll be arrivin'?"

Jon shook his head. "Why would I do that? I told you the plan—"

"Bah! Aye, ye told me the plan, but I'm callin' yer bluff. Ye no more wish to drop the lass and run when we get to the castle than ye wish to have yer man parts sliced off. I suggest this—let the important parties at the castle know we're to arrive. No more. No less. Agreed?"

He hated admitting it, but he *had* tried to get word to the castle. But as wretched as the weather had been, no one was willing to take the risk to deliver a message for free. "I have already attempted such, friend. No one wishes to make the journey for little to no pay."

Dannan grinned, his fluted ears wagging. "I knew I could count on ye to at least try. Now answer the question. What will ye do if she chooses to return to her land?"

Jon clenched his jaw, along with his resolve. "I will do as I promised and not look back."

Now Dannan slapped him on the back, almost knocking him over the fence. "Take care, lad, or our fair maiden will have yer nose growing," he teased, his laughter ringing through the crisp morning air.

Indeed. Care he would take. He'd take care not to fall further prey to true love's kiss.

Whether the furious beat of his heart in his chest wanted it that way or not.

Chapter 9

Toni groaned as she hunted for berries. Her ankles ached and her dress was beginning to feel like a pair of psychotic Spanx, squeezing her, pinching her, and generally getting in her way. Wandering along the path as she searched for berries, she eyed their surroundings as night began to fall, the forest still as beautiful as it had been when she'd first opened her eyes almost a week ago.

She could swear she'd heard the ocean as they'd chosen a spot to settle in, the surf lapping at the land, the scent of salt in the cold air.

Shamalot had everything, without the stress of Stas. If this crazy queen didn't have it out for her, it would be the perfect place to reconfigure her life—a new beginning.

She'd decided she really loved it here. Despite the danger they'd encountered, despite the lack of coffee and creature comforts. The woods brought her peace. She could roam them for days, exploring if not for the price on her head—which was why she was teamed up tonight with Marty as her babysitter.

They'd continued their trek onward after leaving Ellesandra's with plenty of supplies and the wish that they return someday under happier circumstances.

Day after day, night after night, they walked. Nina was much stronger after Ellesandra's magic elixir, but she only had enough to last for another few days. Thus, the push to make it to the castle was ramped up. They slept little, walked for what felt like miles, all in an effort to keep Nina alive and return these stupid shoes.

And she'd do it all again—whatever it took, as long as Nina would remain on this side of the grave.

Sometimes as they walked, she relived the most magical kiss she'd ever shared with a man. Remembered his warm embrace, the ease with which she'd opened up to him. Wondered if Jon felt what she felt—*hoped* he'd felt what she felt.

Maybe what she'd told him about how she'd run away from Stas had left her a lot less warrior-ish and much weaker in his eyes. He'd kept to himself since they'd left Ellesandra's, leading the herd of them like the expert he was, avoiding all contact and conversation, with *her* specifically.

Which made no sense, and she planned to call him on his behavior. Because enough was enough. In her land, she'd always been straightforward about her feelings.

Tonight, Jon was about to get a load of her feelings dumped right over his head after dinner. All that talk of staying in Shamalot then giving her the cold shoulder since the night they'd kissed was crap.

Carl trotted toward her, his lopsided muzzle tinted with green. She held out her hand and he came to her, nuzzling her palm. "How about another story tonight, Carl? After we finish up dinner? I say we do *Little Red Riding Hood*? Or *The Three Little Pigs*? I think both have wolves in 'em."

Each night, she sat with Carl by the fire and told him one of her favorite fairytales from her childhood. Nina had said he loved to read, and in her efforts to make up for what she'd put him through, she made sure they never missed what she'd come to consider their special time together.

She sucked at remembering the stories, according to Nina. Apparently, *The Three Little Pigs* didn't have an evil queen or a talking mirror anywhere in their story.

But whatever. She'd fallen in love with Carl, and when the time came to say goodbye, Toni knew he would be one of the hardest to part with.

Carl stomped a hoof on the ground, which she took as a sign he approved. She planted a kiss on his head and chuckled fondly, continuing her search. "You got it, buddy." She moved deeper into the woods to gather more berries for their meal, Marty not far behind her, humming to herself.

But Carl stomped his hoof again, swishing his hindquarter against her thighs and shoving her back.

"We have chores to do first, Carl. You know that. I said I'd tell you another story, and I will. Now go help so we can get you fed, buddy."

But Carl stomped his hoof harder, his soft eyes wide and fraught with something Toni didn't understand. A sliver of fear spiked the back of her neck. "What's wrong, little buddy?" she asked—just as she spied what looked like piles of berries.

Kneeling down, she took a closer look. "Score!" she muttered to herself, scooping up as many as she could hold in the pocket of the warm pelt Ellesandra had gifted each of them with. The pelts she'd placed a spell on that kept them warm no matter how cold the bitter winds blew.

When she lifted her head, she spotted a clearing where an adorable cottage sat smack in the middle of the frosty trees. Lanterns gave a cheerful glow from the inside, the eaves dripping with blue-tinted icicles. A hearth burned bright just beyond the big window in the front, warm and inviting.

Hiding behind a tree, Toni peered closer as Carl began to whinny his discontent. She scratched his ears distractedly, still trying to see if anyone occupied the cottage.

"Marty!" she whisper-yelled in her excitement. "Look!"

Carl whimpered once more and there was a hint of panic in it, one she instantly needed to quell so they didn't get caught, just in case whoever was in the cottage wasn't on the up and up.

"Shhhh, Carl! We don't know who lives here. The way my luck's gone, it'll be some half-whacked Rapunzel who'll try to strangle me with her luscious hair."

Carl whinnied one more, bumping into her to try to turn her back in the other direction—and that was when she felt the sharp edge of a knife at her ribs.

"Looking for something, milady?"

Her eyes flew open as they adjusted and she saw the outline of cloaked, huddled figures. As they came into focus, she caught sight of Marty, her big blonde hair mashed up against another man's chest, his gleaming knife at her throat. She was struggling from behind the hand he had clamped over her mouth.

He began to drag Marty backward, the hood on his coat hiding his face, but his eyes—she caught a glimpse of his eyes, and they glowed an ominous red.

What the hell? Were they wolves?

The Three Little Pigs wolf? No. Maybe the Big Bad Wolf wolf? Or more of the queen's henchmen? Fear struck with a sharp ping in her gut.

The man at her side gripped her arm, pressing the tip of the knife to her waist. "I'll gut ye like a pig if ye don't move yer pretty arse. *Now!*" he roared gruffly in her ear, making her jump.

Carl stood caught between the foursome, his sweet eyes helpless. He'd been trying to warn her. Damn. When would she learn to pay better attention?

"Look at what we have here, Bromley," the man cackled, rounding on Carl and dragging her along with him. "Supper, eh, mate?" He looked to his partner in crime, who nodded back.

"Aye! We'll feast for a week!"

The hell. Toni sprang into action without thinking. With her free hand, she waved Carl away. "Shoo-shoo, small creature of the forest. Go find your *mother* now," she said woodenly, staring hard into his eyes, hoping against hope he'd get the message she was trying to convey. *Get help.*

As the henchman began to drag her away, she dug in her heels. "Wait, wait, waaaait!" Toni yelped, yanking at her imprisoned arm. "Before ye gut me pretty arse like a pig, quick question?"

The man whirled her around, his face confused, but his eyes were the same red as his friend. "Speak!" he demanded, giving her a bone-rattling shake.

"If you huff and puff, can you blow that house down?"

As he pondered her question, she shot Carl another urgent signal with her eyes. Carl obviously wasn't getting the message because he refused to budge.

The henchman gripped her arm harder, digging his grimy nails into her flesh. "What is this nonsense ye speak, lass?"

"What about that nonsense don't you understand?" she asked, as her teeth chattered but her chin lifted in defiance. "Hang on, I'll go slow. If. You. Huff. And. Puff. Can. You. Blow. That. House. Down? Has working for the evil queen stolen your hearing?"

The henchman growled at her, jamming his face into hers and flashing his sharp teeth, dripping with saliva. But she refused to back down as she tried once more to shoo Carl with her hand. "Wow, what dirty teeth you have. You should see a toothbrush about that."

The henchman snarled again, pressing the knife tighter to her waist. He gave her a hard shove—and that was when Carl gave her opportunity to strike.

He reared upward on his hind legs and whinnied long and loud, startling the men and giving Toni the chance she needed to break free.

With a howl, she yanked her arm from the man and barreled toward Marty's captor, her head down, her feet moving like they were on fire. She ran straight for the man with the hood, only to hear Marty scream, "Run, Toni! Get to the cottage!"

Toni lifted her head at the odd demand, slowing her roll to stop just twenty feet from where the hooded man stood with her friend.

Why would she advise her to run to the cottage and not help her escape the clutches of a guy with glowing eyes?

Oh, wait. I know, I know! that little voice inside her screamed. *You, Toni Vitali, have been fucked again! That's not really Marty, Super Genius, and you shouldn't go to the cottage.*

Duh, duh, duh! She wanted to scream.

"I have her now, Stokes!" the man with Marty yelled.

But she had no time to fret over her foolishness as flaming arrows began arcing the sky. Grabbing the harness on Carl's back, she began to run for cover, but he was slow and sluggish, his gait hindered by whatever had happened to him in his human form.

And then she remembered. *Again.* She could damn well breathe fire.

Dragging Carl as fast as she could, she *did* head for the cottage, darting between flaming arrows as though she were wearing a pair of Air Jordans rather than four-inch heels.

"Stay behind me, Carl!" she hollered as an arrow landed directly in front of her. "Don't move!"

Inhaling deeply, she prayed her reach would go far enough into the woods to fry the bastards.

The harsh taste of smoke filled her lungs, forcing her to exhale in a long, shuddering cough. Fire erupted in a molten orange-and-blue stream, thick and wide as she swerved her head and just as she heard the men scream, she heard her name.

"Toni! Over here! Come to me!" Jon bellowed as what sounded like Dannan's footsteps pounded through the forest.

"Toniiiiiii! We're coming!" Nina roared.

Yeah. Right. That wasn't Nina. She wasn't falling for that again. Instead, she exhaled harder, moving her head from side to side until stream after stream of fire flew from her lips.

"Knock it the fuck off!" Nina yelled again as footsteps neared.

Toni hiccupped, stopping the flow of fire as she peered into the night.

As the smoke cleared, Nina stomped forward waving away the smoke, half of her hair and a portion of her gown totally obliterated, the bluebirds, though quiet now, still circling her head, their feathers singed and puffs of smoke spewing from their tiny beaks.

"You got the bad guys. Now cut it the fuck out and listen to me, Fire Starter! It's *me*, nitwit!"

Oh no. No, no, no. Toni backed away, pushing Carl with her. They rounded the corner of the back of the cottage, plowing their way through deep snow to stop on a small patio area with a back door. As footsteps grew closer, so did Toni's panic.

Obviously, these particular bad guys weren't going to give up so easily, and she had to protect Carl or they'd be making reindeer soup out of him—or Nina'd make Toni soup out of *her* if he ended up hurt. But he was too slow to make a break for it.

Think, Toni. Think. What's the one thing they'd never suspect you to do?

Trap herself *inside* the cottage.

Holding her finger to her lips, she looked at Carl to signal him to be quiet, yanking on his harness and dragging him toward the tiny red door.

With a slow turn of the handle, she found it swiveled all the way. Thank God.

Leaning down, she whispered in Carl's ear, "On three, buddy," and pointed to the cottage door. Holding up her fist, she threw up her fingers one at a time and on three, burst through the cottage door, yanking Carl in with her and slamming it shut.

She whirled around, her eyes searching for a lock or a bolt to secure their safety as she heard the rumble of footsteps coming from the other end of the tiny cottage. "Front door's open, dingbat."

Her heart began to pound as Carl pulled away from her, running toward the front of the cottage. "No, Carl!" she hissed. "That's not Nina!"

"Get in here, nutball! Now!"

Okay, maybe that was Nina. How could she be sure?

And then there were gasps.

Then the maybe-not-so-fake-after-all Nina said, "For the love of dolphins. Is there anybody in your fucked-up kingdom who doesn't have more issues than *Playboy*, Flawless?"

Toni snuck to the quaint kitchen's entryway and poked her head around the corner to see everyone was gathered about a big claw-foot tub.

But was it really everyone, or were they just shifters *pretending* to be everyone?

How was she supposed to know? They needed a safe word or something.

"I smell you, Fire Starter," Nina said. "Get the hell in here, and do it now, or I swear on these stupid wings flapping around behind me, I'm going to rip your feet off and take them to the damn castle myself!"

Toni stepped out from the entryway and into the light of the sitting room as the group parted to fully reveal the claw-foot tub.

Toni's mouth fell open, but only after she, too, gasped.

Note to Realm,

Look, I've been introduced to many a wonder here in your magical kingdom. Good times I'll remember for always. A gift, really. But this? Well, you've outdone yourself. Kudos.

She lifted a finger and pointed toward the tub. "Is that a...?"

"Mermaid, honey. I'm a mermaid. You want me to sound it out for you?"

* * *

Squirrels and rabbits and all manner of small forest creatures hovered in a corner by the fireplace, shivering as Nina began scooping them up, stroking their heads while she ordered the bluebirds to explain that they weren't there to harm them.

Seven small men in pointy red-and-white-striped knit caps with festive suspenders attached to their breeches stood to the right inside the cozy cottage, arms crossed over their chests, stout, short legs wide apart, stoic faces in place.

One sneezed, and without thinking, Toni said, "*Gesundheit.*" She approached him with slow steps, taking care not to frighten him. "I'm Toni. You're Sneezy, right?"

"*Who?*" he barked up at her, his face scrunching, making his bulbous red nose almost disappear into his face.

"Sorry. I meant, what's your name?"

"Charming's my name," he growled at her, his face screwing up into a scowl. "We're the Seven Wharfs. And I warn ye, harm one hair on her head, I'll make yer liver my supper!"

"Okay, little man, chill on the death threats," Nina said, patting him on the head with a grin. "We ain't gonna hurt anybody. Sit yourself down over there with your little friends and mind your manners."

Then she turned to Toni, dropping two fuzzy rabbits into her arms. "Make nice. They're freaked-out."

Jon sat beside the tub on his haunches as he listened to Muriel explain to him how she'd ended up in a cottage in the middle of nowhere after a battle with some sea witch named Pricilla, while the real Marty and Wanda rifled around in the kitchen, scavenging for food.

Muriel was simply stunning, her red hair spilling from the bathtub and falling to the floor in pools of color. The sapphire-blue of her clamshell bikini top shimmered, reflecting against the four or five inches of water left in the tub.

But her tail? Her tail was magnificent, regal in its ever-changing color, iridescent against the firelight.

And it was a *tail.*

She was a real mermaid.

O. M. G.

"What happened?" Jon asked, his gorgeous face full of concern.

Yeah, what happened, Perfect Ten?

Muriel's eyes burned with anger, her creamy cheeks flushing red. "It was Pricilla the Sea Bitch! I angered her when I clubbed one of her smarmy pet eels to death after he made a pass at me. She hurled me from the sea and I landed here."

"How long have you been here?" Jon asked, looking around the cozy cottage with its homemade quilts and tiny chairs made out of rough wood.

"Too long," she drawled, fanning her fin, her eyes sad.

"How have you survived like this, Muriel?" Jon asked, leaning into the beautiful woman…er, fish.

She lifted a long, slender finger and pointed to the small, very angry-looking Wharf men with a gentle smile. "These little darlings fill the bathtub to keep my fin alive. But they can't carry me to the ocean and they simply cannot do this forever. I so long for home," she wailed, a tear escaping her emerald-green eye. "Damn that thorn in my side Pricilla! When I get my hands on her, I'm going to dine on her eels for supper!"

"You know each other?" Toni asked, her eyebrow raised. Why it bothered her that Jon knew this luscious creature was a sure sign she needed to take a step back. She had no claims to him. He'd kissed her, and he hadn't been back for more.

Jerk.

Jon nodded affably, his smile fond, his white teeth flashing as he allowed a squirrel to cuddle against his ear, scratching its chin. "Aye, she often swam near my boat with her sisters when I was a child. We've known each other many moons, have we not, Muriel?"

She fairly purred her consent. "Indeed we have, I—um, Jon. Some of my most precious memories are from the days we spent together, when the sun was high and the water warm as a freshly heated bath."

Yeah, yeah. Good times.

"So why don't we just take her to the ocean?" Toni asked. "I heard it as we searched for berries, didn't I? It can't be that far."

"'Tis dangerous, Toni," Jon said, as though she were some kind of dolt. "You have no idea the kind of power Pricilla the Sea Bitch has—she can steal your very voice."

Toni rolled her eyes at him. "Is that all? I can think of a few voices I'd survive without. Don't be such a sissy. We just need to get her to the water's edge, right? Dump her in… I mean, gently place her in the ocean, and we out. What's the big deal?"

"You know nothing of the sea, Toni," he spat, his blue eyes angry, his expression tense.

Was he willing to let Muriel suffer because he was scared of some crabby witch? Clearly, he wasn't so flawless after all.

The long day, her frustration, her aching, pinched-to-within-an-inch-of-their-lives feet, and her stupid, confining dress made her lash out. "No, *you* know nothing, Jon Doe!" she yelled at him, stomping toward the back door, her arms full of shivering bunnies.

She opened the door and stepped outside, sucking in the bitterly cold air.

"Touchy, touchy, Red. Your green's showing," Nina crooned in her ear.

Toni whipped around to face the vampire. "Oh just hush. I'm not jealous. What's to be jealous of? Her gorgeous hair, her perky breasts? Her emerald-green eyes? You'd think being in the water all the time would shrivel her creamy skin to a prune. But no. She's this close to perfection. But am I jealous? Don't be silly. I'm just tired and annoyed. She needs help, Nina. Are we just going to leave her here? She can't live in a bathtub forever."

"You damn well *are* jealous, and I'm all in favor of throwing her back. But Flawless says this bitch Pricilla is badass."

"And we're not?" she asked as she stroked the bunnies' heads.

"Look, kiddo, you're way ahead of yourself. We're weaker here than we are at home. You can breathe fucking fire. Sure, that's pretty damn useful, but not so much in the water. Use your lady brains, would you?"

Point. "Okay, that's fair. But I can't just leave her. I won't. What if you guys had left me?"

"We didn't get a choice, remember?"

Toni's face flushed. "While that's true, would you have left me *given* the choice? If Brenda hadn't threatened you, would you have just washed your hands of me? And don't lie to me because I'll know. Remember, I don't just breathe fire."

Nina scratched a fuzzy brown squirrel under the chin and smiled at him. "Fair enough."

"Did you just agree with me?"

"Yep."

Toni looked to the sky with a cringe. "And there was no thunder? No lightning?"

"Did you just push my last goddamn button?"

"Sorry."

"Now let's address the girly feelings because I know that shit's comin'." She looked at the bunny nestled in her arms. "Cover your ears, fluffy dude, here comes the whine."

"I'm not jealous."

"Yeah? Coulda swore I saw your eyeballs roll to the back of your head when the fish-chick was talking about moons and warm water. But maybe I read that shit wrong."

"You absolutely did."

"Liar."

"Am not."

"Are damn well so. You two have been avoiding each other like the plague since we left Fairy-ville."

She clenched her teeth so hard, she was sure they'd break. "Everything is fine."

Nina held up the bunny and rubbed him against her cheek, her voice raising an octave when she said, "Hear that, little guy—shit's all good."

"Shit's peachy," she said, dropping another bunny into Nina's arms.

"Listen, I'm just gonna say this once and then I'll let it go. The adrenaline in cases like these runs super high. So all those lady feelings get distorted and amped-up a notch or ten in your lady brain. You get all excited over shit that would normally roll off your back. Everything turns into a drama. Flawless is a good guy. He likes you. I can tell. You like him, too. That's nice. So stinkin' nice. But keep some shit in mind, here. You live in another realm, Toni. It's not like you can catch the redeye here from Jersey to visit, yanno? So don't fuck with the dude. I don't know what the castle and all this happiness stuff means, but maybe it has to do with finding your brother, and that would mean going back to Jersey."

Her chest became tight. "You heard about my brother?"

"Because—"

"Vampire," Toni interrupted on a sigh.

"Right. Also, something else I want you to think about. This Stas is a lowdown fuck. If I ever run into him, his head staying on his shoulders is gonna to be the least of his GD worries, cuz I'll eat his intestines for my midnight snack while I make that puke Andre watch. He's a bag o' dicks to be sure. But you didn't do this to your brother, kiddo. You didn't launder money. You didn't hack off someone's finger. You didn't kill anybody. *Stas did.* You didn't do anything but be in the wrong place at the wrong time. You tried to make shit right, and no one would help you. That's not cowardly. Clear?"

Toni remained silent, but Nina nudged her shoulder, her eyes intense as she looked down at her. "Clear?"

Tugging one of Nina's sopping-wet curls, she nodded. "You're all right, vampire," she said, her voice cracking.

"Yeah? Well, you suck as bad as this godforsaken dress," she said with a grin.

Toni laughed, forcing her eyes to her feet to keep Nina from seeing her tears, and then she sucked it up. "Here." She handed Nina the remaining bunnies. "I'm going to convince a stubborn pain in the ass to help me get Muriel to the sea."

"Grrrr," Nina said on a laugh as she set a bunny free to scamper off into the snow. "You get 'em, Red."

Chapter 10

"Milady," Jon said, keeping his eyes focused on tending Oliver when she tapped him on the shoulder.

She'd thought long and hard about what Nina had said and tried to look at it from Jon's point of view. What if her happiness was finding her brother and she had to leave here forever?

Was he protecting himself from that possible fate? While it made her feel giddy and girly, she'd been pretty one-sided about this. But that still didn't excuse him choosing to leave Muriel to suffer.

"I have a bone to pick with you."

"I'm quite sure you do."

"First of all, how can you claim to be Muriel's friend if you're willing to just leave her here? What kind of friend are you, anyway?"

"The kind who thinks of the greater good," he said, the profile of his jaw rigid.

Toni grabbed his arm and forced him to stop brushing Oliver. "Explain."

"I have a choice to make. One I do not make lightly, for Muriel *is* my friend. Nina must get to the castle so she can return to your land or she will die. We've already extend our journey by half a day's walk. Would you have her die in order to bring Muriel to the sea, when I can do such on the way back? She is safe here with the short men. For now, that is good enough."

Suddenly, she felt like a total jackass. He was being a good leader and she was challenging his vast knowledge of his world. She'd snapped at him for no reason. She should have known honorable, chivalrous Jon had a plan, but she was so busy trying to make up for not saving her brother, she was mucking up everything else around her.

Letting her eyes fall to the snow, she whispered, "You're right. I jumped the gun, and it was wrong."

"'Twas indeed," he replied tersely, his spine rigid.

Which made her bristle. "I said I was wrong, now you're supposed to accept my apology and the fact that I'm a total twit and we move on."

"Apology accepted," he said stiffly, returning to his chore.

But Toni couldn't stand the tension anymore. One more long day without him so much as looking at her, and she'd just scream.

She gripped his arm and forced him to look at her again. This time, her words were softer. "I said I'm sorry."

But damn he was good at holding a grudge. His glare was like the icicles hanging from the cottage. "And I said you were heard, milady. Now good night."

When he turned away, all fiery and brooding, it incensed her despite the fact that, even angry, he was hot. She wiggled her way between him and Oliver and waved a finger under his nose.

"Don't you dismiss me, pal! What's up your ass, anyway?"

The corner of his mouth lifted just a little. "My *ass*, milady? One cannot fit anything in a space so snug. Why ever would you assume something was lodged there?"

Now *she* was angry. Angry that they had this language deficit, angry that she'd been a little jealous of Muriel. Okay, a lot. Angry that she'd gotten so angry.

Toni made a face at him. "It's a figure of speech, Smarty Pants. It means something's bugging you. Now out with it so we can finish this journey to Castle Beckett like adults."

"I was not aware we were not behaving as adults. Your journey has been for the most part successful, has it not? Your heart still beats, yes?"

Toni crossed her arms over her chest. "Don't you gaslight me, buddy. You know what I mean."

Jon's jaw clenched. "I know nothing of this gaslighting or phones or intor-nets or cars! I only know you infuriate me, intoxicate me—"

"*Intoxicate you?*" She fought a thrilled smile as their chests pressed together and he leaned in close, the wind lifting his raven hair to blow it across his perfect face.

His eyes narrowed. "Aye!" It was fair to say he spat the word, as though he were irritated by his admission. "You with your talk of Jersey and the sway of your hips in your tattered dress...your long legs as they crunch along the snow in small strides. Your hair brushing your waist in enticing flashes of auburn. Your brave, selfless heart when you're willing to risk yourself for another like small Carl and the maiden Marty. You intoxicate me, and I do not like such. It muddies my thoughts—"

She threw her arms around his neck and laid one on him, stopping all talk when she clamped her lips to his and molded herself to his hard frame.

Jon moaned into her mouth, dragging her hard against him, dropping Oliver's brush and wrapping his arms around her waist.

The rigid line of his shaft pressed at the apex of her thighs and her nipples tightened when he drew her tongue into his mouth. His knuckles brushed the underside of her breast as his hands roamed over her arms before threading through her hair, making her groan in response.

Butterflies fluttered their delicate wings in the pit of her belly as the heat at her core grew. Her leg wound its way around his hip, his hand lifted her skirts, driving under her pantaloons and caressing the bare flesh of her thigh.

And it was heaven. His calloused palms smoothed her skin, making her press herself deeper against him, wanting to absorb the heat of his broad chest, roam her hands over his wide back.

"Ahem. Excuse the interruption, lovebirds," someone said, tapping Jon on the shoulder.

They broke free of one another in guilt, Toni falling back against Oliver's side and Jon jamming his hands behind his back and clearing his throat.

Marty sighed a dreamy sigh. "Aren't you two the cutest ever-ever? We were just discussing the merits of holding you both down and forcing you to kiss and make up, but I see love conquers all. I *love* love. It makes me happy. Now, make yourselves presentable for public consumption because we got trouble, right here in Fairytale Central."

"Have the henchmen returned, milady?" Jon asked, his hand instantly going to the sword at his side.

"Nope. Not that kind of trouble. This kind of trouble involves a dry well and a crack in that tub in the cottage. So finish making up and get to the cottage pronto. Oh, and," she brushed her hand down Toni's skirt, yanking it from her pantaloons, "lemme get that for you," she said on a light chuckle before turning and skipping back toward the cottage.

"Milady, my—"

"Don't you apologize. It ruins the moment," she teased, looking up into his beautiful eyes.

He wrapped an arm around her waist and pulled her close to plant another kiss on her lips. "This conversation isn't over. We shall continue this later," he murmured, taking his leave as he adjusted the front of his breeches.

Toni took a moment to catch her breath, breathing in as much of the freezing air as her lungs would allow before she followed him inside to see what was happening now.

But not before she secretly smiled again.

Wow, he could suck face.

* * *

"We have no choice but to take her to the ocean, Flawless. This shit can't wait. If I let Ariel die on my watch, my kid would kill me," Nina said, glaring at Jon.

"Muriel, darling. It's Mure-ee-ull. Sound it out," the mermaid croaked, her face growing paler by the second.

Nina frowned down at Muriel. "Can it, fish. Let the adults work this out."

The well to the Wharf's cottage had finally run dry, and worse, the heavy weight of Muriel's tail had cracked the chipped porcelain—no amount of heated snow would stay in the bathtub now, and as a result, the beautiful mermaid was suffering, gasping for air.

"*If* we do this," Jon warned, his face tight, "we must be prepared to face Pricilla the Sea Bitch and we'll need all of our resources to battle her, but we must also prepare for the possibility of a delay in our effort to get to the castle—and that puts you in harms way, Nina. I will leave the choice up to you, but as you know, I am reluctant to risk your health."

Nina shrugged as Wanda and Marty squeezed each of her hands. "There's no choice, dude. She's suffocating. Can't happen on my watch."

Jon began unwinding a long piece of rope, holding it up to show them. "A blizzard is brewing; we must stay together at all costs. Tether yourselves to this and hang on tight. We'll walk single file until we make it to the shoreline."

Tears stung Toni's eyes as she rolled up her puffy sleeves in order to help. God, Nina had more courage in her pinky finger than she'd have in a lifetime. "So tell me what we have to do. I'm in."

Jon pointed to Dannan, who peeked in the window. "Will you carry her?"

"Aye, lad," he said, giving them a big blue thumbs up.

"Good deal," Nina said as she picked the tub up and carried Muriel out the front door with the Wharfs hot on her heels, murmuring their goodbyes.

Toni had to fight to keep her jaw from unhinging. Nina's strength was something that took getting used to—even if she claimed it was weakened by the realm, but she was right behind her anyway.

Gripping her arm as Dannan carefully lifted Muriel, she asked, "Are you sure about this, Nina? We need to get you home and the faster we get to the castle, the faster you get the blood you need."

Nina turned to her, pulling the hood of Toni's pelt over her head and tucking her hair into it as more snow began to fall. Then she tightened the tether on her waist. "Don't you worry about me, kiddo. I got this. But make sure you hang on to the rope tied to my waist, okay? If we lose somebody in this snow we got brewing, can't promise even me, with all the vampire shit I have, will be able to find you. You'd freeze to death out here if you stopped moving. The cold doesn't affect me. Got it?"

Toni gulped. "Okay," she whispered before she looped her fingers around Nina's and squeezed.

The vampire squeezed back before scooting around the tub and yanking Toni along with her.

As they set out into the night, a line of road-weary travelers with Dannan in the lead, she fought the ominous shiver creeping along her spine. And when the snow began to blow and the wind began to howl, she sent up another silent prayer to the realm to keep them all safe.

* * *

The wet wind stung her cheeks and made her eyes water, raging in gusts of bitter air as they stood on the sandy beach, preparing to set Muriel free.

Waves crashed against the rocks in frothy splashes of saltwater, lapping at the shoreline in angry slaps to tear at the sand.

The women all huddled together, covering Carl, who shivered violently. The bluebirds tucked themselves into Nina's pelt, their tiny wings quivering.

Muriel managed to lift her head, her smile grateful as she wiggled her fingers. "Thank you, my friends," she whispered, her voice carrying on the wind. "If you ever need me, call my name!"

Dannan prepared to walk into the water, Muriel in his arms, her head flopping weakly. He looked to Jon. "She's so weak, lad!" he yelled over the wind. "Can she survive this?"

"Aye!" Jon yelled back. "The water is her cure. Hurry, friend, before we find ourselves in peril!"

No sooner had Dannan gotten knee-deep and set Muriel in the water than a whirlpool of black water swirled, heaving and lifting upward. Dannan splashed his way back toward them, ducking when a wall of a wave soaked his whole body, knocking him forward.

Jon raced to their sides, herding them all behind him. "'Tis Pricilla, you must run!" He yanked out his sword, the glint of steel under the almost full moon not terribly comforting when a gigantic half human, half octopus torpedoed from the depths of the ocean.

Pricilla shot from the water, bouncing upward, her tentacles swirling like the swing ride at the fair, whizzing, buzzing, cutting the water. Her silver hair, slicked back on her high forehead, shone under the buttery moon, her thick arms lifted high in the air as she waved her red-tipped fingers.

But her tentacles were quicker than Toni, who slipped on some seaweed and fell with a yelp of pain. Jon ran for her, his strong thighs pumping, and stretched out his arm. "Give me your hand, Toni! Reach for me!"

She tried to scramble upward as she reached for Jon's hand, but she couldn't get her footing; the sand was like ice, slick and evaporating beneath her at an alarming rate.

"Jon!" she screamed over the wind, just before something slimy and cold wrapped around her ankle and dragged her toward the water.

A bubble of laughter sounded, deep and malicious, filling her ears. "Look what I've found, pets!" Pricilla gloated, rolling her tentacle toward her body until Toni resembled a hot dog in a slimy bun.

Toni gasped for breath as the water pummeling her finally gave way to the image staring her down.

Okay, so yeah. This was probably as scary as it got, bar none. Dragons? Not so bad. Kinda pretty actually. Wings, colorful scales and so on. The teeth were a little off-putting, but whatever. The Truth Fairy? Hardly scary. Just misguided and in need of a gold intervention.

But this Pricilla? What nightmares were made of.

And now Toni planned to get right with Jesus, because there was likely no getting out of this. Fire-breathing and falsehood detector aside, she didn't have anything to fight off this fairytale villain.

Pricilla's bulging eyes peered right into Toni's soul, her thick ruby-red lips smacking. "Aren't you tasty?" she husked, her voice as deep as if she'd smoked a thousand cigarettes.

"Unhand her, Pricilla, or feel the wrath of my sword!" Jon yelled from below.

Toni almost rolled her eyes, but that was an effort because they were bulging. Jon was big on the sword wrath, but so far, it was kind of a dud threat.

"Tsk-tsk, my little prince," she cooed down at Jon. "You know better than to tussle with meee!" she screamed.

Toni didn't have time to reflect on Pricilla's words, instead, she was too busy praying her organs would stay on the inside as the sea witch squeezed her so tight, she almost retched.

"Toni! Listen carefully. Close your eyes—keep them shut tight!"

Not a problem, she thought. Who wanted this beast to haunt their dreams for all eternity? She did as Jon bade, scrunching her eyes shut as Pricilla's tentacles sucked at her flesh, pulling, squeezing until she was almost out of breath. But then she remembered why she had to keep her eyes closed—Pricilla's squid ink would blind her.

That would really suck if she couldn't see Jon anymore. He was so great to look at. So she closed her eyes tighter.

But then her feet began to tingle and twitch in that now-familiar way, and it was like coming home. Strength coursed through her body in tremors, waiting, pulsing.

Nina and Marty splashed below and screamed orders to one another to grab a tentacle, while Wanda and Dannan did the same.

But Toni almost didn't notice for the zing of pressure in her feet, and again, her brain spoke to her. *So look, here's the thing. Your feet aren't going to be a lot of help when you can't move, yanno? Just keep your eyes closed and roll with this to the end. No pun intended.*

But her body had different ideas. *Go limp, don't stiffen up. That's it. Relax. Keep your eyes closed and chill. The second she eases up on her grip because your pals are down there yanking her crank, use it to your advantage and bend at the waist then head-butt a bitch.*

But I can't even do a whole sit up! I'm out of shape. My soft, white underbelly really is soft! her brain revolted.

Find your core, Sunshine, and trust I know what I'm saying, her body insisted.

So she focused, and the moment Pricilla reacted to the girls grabbing her tentacles by easing her grip, was the moment she bolted upward, her body flying full-steam ahead, her target aligned.

Toni thwacked Pricilla right between her bulging eyes, the impact unbelievably making her fall backward. She crashed into the ocean like a rock, the sting of it making her cry out in agony. Icy waves pummeled her as Pricilla howled her rage and Toni fought her way to the surface, her feet mysteriously light under the water.

And then hands, several pairs, were lifting her, pushing her, driving her upward, shooting her out of the water, where she landed on Pricilla's head and latched onto her thatch of silver hair. She gasped for air, spitting the freezing water from her face and gripping tight.

From below above, she saw Nina, Marty, Wanda and Dannan, their hands wrapping around Pricilla's inky tentacles, but her mission made her forget everything around her.

Kill the bitch for almost freezing her tits right off—because heavy dress, plus water that was at best twenty below, equaled frostbite.

Pricilla began to roar her fury, shaking her head with wild abandon, spinning in circles like some mad whirling dervish, growing in size while the girls hung on to her.

Toni held on tight, too, keeping her eyes clenched shut, opening her mouth wide and spraying fire at Pricilla's silver head.

Her screams were raw, furious, but Toni's body wouldn't allow her to let go.

And as Pricilla grew to monstrous proportions, her head filling the night sky, Toni clung to her flesh, her mind racing to find a solution.

Then the slice of a sword in the wind, the sharp steel against flesh rang out. She finally looked down to find Jon using all that wrath he kept talking about as he took a whack at one of the sea witch's tentacles and severed it cleanly. It flew upward in the air, landing in the water with a muted thwack.

But black ink spewed from Pricilla's wound, forcing Jon to turn his face and lose his footing. He fell, swallowed up by the freezing water, and that's when panic really began to set in for Toni.

"Get Jon!" she screamed to Marty and Wanda, who clung to a tentacle in their effort to drag Pricilla from the water.

Jon appeared unconscious, his body buoying upward only to sink again. Fear like the ice-cold water raced through Toni's veins when she could no longer see his head.

But from the depths below her, through the snow mixed with rain and the roar of the ocean, Muriel's red head popped upward, her arm rising high when she hurled a shiny item upward to Toni. "I'll get Jon! You chop the bitch's head off!" she bellowed.

The moment she realized Jon was safe with Muriel, Toni's feet sprang into action without aid of her brain as she strained for the sword, managing to catch it just as it arced over her head.

The metal was heavy in her hands when she wrapped her fingers around the base and attempted to lift it as she dragged herself upward until she was on the top of Pricilla's enormous head where she managed to sink her heels into the sea witch's thick hair.

Toni grunted as the wind pushed her back to the edge of Pricilla's skull and she wobbled.

She couldn't even lift the damn sword, how was she going to cut this woman's head off from behind, no less? And by the way, ewwww on the head chopping, but she couldn't hack her head off from this vantage point. She needed more leverage. If she could just get to her shoulder...

Instead, an icy wave crashed into her, pushing her off Pricilla's skull and back into the water.

It was then the shoes began to heat her feet, and luckily, she landed on one of Pricilla's tentacles like she'd just starred in *The Matrix* and performed her own stunts.

Wrapping her legs around the thick length, she dragged the sword with her, inching her way upward, fighting the pounding waves crashing all around her.

"Get the fuck down, Toni!" Nina hollered just before a wave toppled her, pulling her under the water.

"Lass, no!" Dannan roared above the crash of the surf, but her feet weren't having it.

She fought her way along the tentacle as Marty attempted to shift into her werewolf form with a snarl, her eyes glowing in the turbulent black night.

Toni refused to give in to the sheer terror of seeing hair sprout on Marty's face and long claws grow from her fingertips—this was a woman who'd looked out for her and just because she was a hundred times scarier than anything she'd seen on TV, was no reason to chicken out now.

As Marty launched herself at Pricilla's side as though her feet had springs, her teeth bared, Pricilla caught her midair, snatching her up and rolling her tentacle around the werewolf.

And still, Toni climbed upward along a swerving, rocking Pricilla, ignoring the frantic screams from everyone below, gritting her teeth as she inched forward, the sword heavy and slowing down her progress.

You have a job to do. Cut the bitch's head off, her body said. *Do it!*

You know, I'm washing my hands of you. We're done. If you want to commit fairytale-a-cide, you go, girl. I'll wait, her brain said.

"Toni! Wait for me, milady!"

Jon?

She turned and looked back to find Jon, hot on her tail, using his strong legs as he, too, worked his way up Pricilla's body hand over hand, fighting the torrential downpour and the hard sleet that had begun to form. Relief swelled in her chest as he came closer, her heart pumping with joy.

When he caught up with her, he planted a hand on her butt and pushed her upward, sliding her along until she reached the large swell of Pricilla's hip.

That was when all hell broke loose. Pricilla flailed, her whole form shivering so violently, they were thrown into the air. Jon managed to grab her around the waist just as the witch launched them forward like tennis balls being shot from a machine. Toni clung to the sword with all her might against the brutal force of the wind.

They landed atop a rock, overlooking the ocean, the rough surface scraping against her skin as they skidded to a halt.

Jon was the first to rise, and in that moment, soaking wet, his wide chest heaving, his hair plastered to his face, Toni's heart did something so unexpected, she almost doubled over.

It pounded, throbbed, crashed at the mere thought of losing Jon.

"Give him back or I'll make ye my meal!" Dannan screeched from below, forcing Toni to her feet as she dragged the sword with her and looked down at the shoreline.

Pricilla had Carl.

No. No. No! Her pulse slammed in her ears, fear coursed icy-hot through her veins, her limbs shook, but the hell she was going to let this lunatic hurt Carl.

And poor Carl, helpless, his eyes wide, his reindeer form frozen in terror, pissed her off. *Fuck* panic and fear.

Dragging the sword to her side, her arm on fire from the ache, she gasped for breath and yelled into the wind, "Come and get me, you stupid bitch!"

Pricilla's head swerved, her eyes locking on Toni and Jon, her intent obvious.

Killing them.

As she raced across the water, her face demonic, her tentacles smashing everything in their wake, Jon rushed up behind Toni, placing his hand on hers. "Stay close!" he whispered, his lips cold at the shell of her ear.

Pricilla howled her rage, torpedoing toward them at a speed Toni knew would knock them to the moon if she made impact.

Jon's hand tightened on her waist momentarily, and just as the screams to run from below them rose, so did his sword.

He wrapped his arms around her shoulders and helped her to lift it high, twisting them at the waist like baseball players waiting to hit a homerun, and as Pricilla steamrolled forward, they swung the sword—*together*.

The point of impact was precise as they let out a warrior cry in unison. With a mighty thwack, the blade sliced through Pricilla's neck like butter.

The sea witch's head toppled off her body, her mouth open in a macabre, silent scream as it splashed to the water, bouncing on the waves, her silver hair floating in the froth.

Her bulky body crumpled seconds afterward like a deflated balloon as Jon and Toni fell to their knees, chests heaving.

But as Pricilla's tentacles flailed out of control, their instinct to survive strong, one stray rose up from the shadowy depths just as Jon was helping Toni to her feet.

The slimy limb drove into the side of her head, knocking her from the top of the tall rock to the beach below.

The last thing she remembered was seeing Jon's face as he yelled her name, and she fell to the sandy shore.

Chapter 11

She woke to a warm fire at her feet, restrictive shoes still firmly in place, a headache the size of Yankee Stadium complete with cheers from the roaring crowd in her head.

Toni fought to sit up, but the heavy weight of furry blankets stopped her—or she was just too weak to move, she couldn't decide.

"Lay still, milady. Let me tend to you," Jon said, his voice warm as he slipped his hand under her head and offered her a tin cup of liquid.

She took a grateful sip, letting the rich, savory broth warm her belly. "What happened?" she asked on a groan, her right arm protesting when she tried to sit up on her elbow.

"You slayed a sea bitch like a boss, so sayeth Nina." Jon brushed her hair from her face, his eyes tender, his smile affectionate. "You also scared the soul from my very body when you fell to the shore. *Never* do that again. I beg of you."

Toni chuckled, warmth spreading throughout her limbs as his words. At Jon's insistence, she leaned back against pillows.

Wait. *Pillows?*

She popped upright then groaned. "Where are we?" she asked as she looked around the room. Softly lit with a roaring fire, it was a crude bedroom, but she was in a bed, a soft bed with warm blankets, and a window where snow fell in a curtain of white. A small Christmas tree sat in the corner, strands of fragile tinsel draped across its thin branches.

Her dress hung by the fire, the remains of it sewn with patches of various materials to mend the holes.

"We are the guests of a very kind fisherman named Aegon and his wife Flauta. They saw you kill Pricilla from the cliffs and wanted to thank you by harboring us for the night. She has ruined a great many fishing expeditions for him with her tax on the ocean's depths."

She forgot about Pricilla for a moment and grabbed his hand, her heart racing. "Carl? The others? Is everyone all right?"

He pressed her to the pillows with an easy smile as he sat on the edge of the bed. "Everyone is fine, milady. This I promise. They're all resting quite comfortably. Fed, warm clothes, warm beds. All is well this night."

Closing her eyes, she leaned forward against him in relief, realizing she was naked beneath the blankets, but her limbs were too sore and tired to care about her modesty. "Muriel? Is she okay, too? She saved you from drowning."

"Aye. She's well, and quite happy in her native waters. No more talk. Now you must rest." He pressed a soft kiss to her forehead and rose to leave, but she gripped his hand and pulled him back down.

She needed to know where they were in relation to their destination. How many more days she had before she needed to figure out her life and what waited for her at the castle.

"The castle, are we close?"

"If all goes well, we arrive at nightfall tomorrow. Just one day before the Christmas Eve ball. Somehow, when we tangled with Pricilla it brought us closer to our destination."

And then she'd find out what this gift of happiness was about. What this journey meant. Whether she could stay here in Shamalot because there was nothing to return to back in Jersey. How she would survive here in a land that, while beautiful and far away from Stas, was also riddled with its own dangers, like a price on her head for something she knew nothing about.

"I'm afraid," she admitted on a whisper.

Jon scooted onto the bed beside her. "There is nothing to fear here. We're safe for the night, Toni."

She snuggled down against him, burrowing in his warmth, cherishing this moment. "No. I mean finding out what waits for me at the castle scares me."

"The castle is a wondrous place, Toni. Beautiful and serene. Whatever waits there for you, I know it will bring you only great joy."

She closed her eyes to steady the panic building. "You've been?"

Jon nodded his head. "A time or two. It's fit for someone as beautiful as you."

Her cheeks flushed as she focused on the buttons of his vest. "What if my happiness is finding my brother after all this time?"

He tilted her chin upward and looked into her eyes. "That would be a gift. A true gift."

"I'd...I'd have to go back to Jersey," she said, though the idea pained her, hurt her deep in her marrow. The thought of leaving Jon brought tears to her eyes even as the thought of her brother, alive and well, brought joy. As silly as it sounded after knowing him for such a short time, she wanted to get to know Jon more deeply.

"And I would not begrudge you the chance. Family is important. I see these women, who behave like family. These women who protect and honor their friendships or fall on the sword...I admire them. They are strong, smart warriors not only in the physical sense, but of the heart. They speak of their husbands and children and friends with pride I can almost taste on the tip of my tongue. They make me reconsider my anger with my own family."

Toni looked up at him, curious. "Why are you angry with them?"

His eyes drifted away from hers and to the window where he gazed at the snow. "They wish for me to do something I do not wish to do. A family obligation, shall we say. Yet, I long for them much the way you long for your brother."

"What do they want you to do? Marry some hot maiden in exchange for a barrel of fish and a herd of bison?"

He barked a laugh, stroking her arm. "Again with the funny words. What are bison?"

She splayed her aching arms outward. "Big, big cows."

"Ah, I assure you. No bison are involved."

Obviously, he didn't want to talk about whatever the obligation was, and if this was potentially their last night together, she wouldn't press. "What about this Queen Angria? Does she get some prison time for sending in every nut she could get her hands on to capture me?"

"The king will see to her punishment, of that I promise. The king is a fair, kind man at heart. He's a brilliant ruler for the most part," Jon said with an admiration she hadn't expected.

Somehow, she'd expected the king would be a douchenozzle like all the other fairytale kings she'd read about. Angry, greedy, hand happy with beheadings and doling out high taxes so he could dine on fine crops his villagers slaved day and night raising.

"That's good to know. I can't wait until he takes these shoes off. Have we figured out where these things came from and why the king has them?"

Jon shook his head. "I still know not. I admit 'tis an odd item for the king to have. Though, I don't doubt they're part of the reason you can now breathe fire and parse truths from lies."

"How crazy. All of this has been just crazy," she murmured.

"It has been an adventure, to say the least."

"Will you be happy to go back to your quiet life?" She was fishing. She knew she was fishing rather than straight-up ask him how he felt about her, and she didn't know why.

It wasn't in her nature to skirt big issues and she wondered if it wasn't because this was so important to her, she was too afraid to dig.

"I like your noise," he offered without commitment. "I like you. I like your friends. I would wish our worlds were more easily traveled to and from."

She smiled up at him, her heart fluttering wildly in her chest. "Really? And what would you do if you could travel back and forth?"

He appeared to give that some thought before he said, "I'd date you. I'd talk on this phone with you. I'd play this game Nina speaks of on the computer called *Minecraft*. I'd watch TV with you. I'd take you away from your horrible boss Bree and take care of you so you never had to fold another thong again," he whispered against her ear.

Tears welled in her eyes. He'd date her. She realized now, she wanted that more than she even wanted a cup of coffee and a pastrami and swiss on rye with stone-ground mustard. He'd really been listening to their road-trip chatter, absorbing their lingo, and that touched her heart.

Cupping his jaw, she ran her thumb over the stubble on his chin and whispered, "You would?"

Jon brushed his lips over her fingertips. "I would," he answered, just before he pressed his lips to hers, slipping his tongue into her mouth with that familiar rasp of silk.

She sighed, pushing her arms upward until she wrapped them around his neck, arching against him as he pulled her tight to him, his hands splaying across her spine.

He devoured her lips, licking, teasing, tasting, running his hands over her arms, the contact of his calloused palms on her hot flesh making her tingle.

Toni pulled him to her, gripping each side of his shirt, her nipples delighting in the delicious friction against the fabric and his hard chest beneath.

Jon rolled her to her back, lying on top of her, molding his thickly muscled frame to hers, moaning into her mouth. His fingers skimmed the underside of her breast then pulled away, skating along her flesh, moving the blanket farther down until she was almost naked.

Then he stopped just as suddenly, tearing his lips from hers and staring down at her, his eyes wide with concern.

"What's wrong?" she huffed, trying to catch her breath.

"Milady, we must stop. We must stop now." He began to move off her, but Toni grabbed him and pulled him back down on top of her.

"Explanation?"

"Your virtue."

She blew a bit of air from her lips. "Oh, that? Long gone."

"You have bedded men?" he asked, his sapphire eyes incredulous.

"Well, not by the dozens. Only three."

But Jon didn't look relieved. In fact, he looked horrified. "*Three?*"

"You say that like I said a million. Yes, three. For my age, I'd say that's pretty close to virtuous in this day and age, buddy."

"And what is your age?"

"I'm thirty-two. Too old for you?"

"No," he blustered, his skin flushing. "I'm in my thirty-fifth year."

"Then what's the hang-up here?"

"Where you come from, this is allowed?"

"Allowed? Well, yes. As long as you're over the age of eighteen. Though, that's not always the case. Most of us lose our virginity in high school. Not all, but a good percentage. It's when our hormones are at their freakiest."

"What is a high school and a hormone?"

"One of the most lethal combinations in the history of man."

"In our land, consummation is not allowed until you are wed."

Now her eyes went wide. "Aw, c'mon. That's not true. Is it? You don't really think there's not some woot-woot happening in Shamalot, do you? Do you really believe everyone in the land waits for marriage? Have you ever watched *Game of Thrones*? God, someone's always doing someone. Sometimes they do their own…" She paused to rethink her words. "Forget I asked that. I still don't get the problem."

"I will not be a party to endangering your stellar reputation. Or rather, your almost stellar reputation."

"Okay, I'm going to let that crack slide because we come from totally different eras, but this isn't about my reputation. I have no reputation in Shamalot other than that poor girl with a death knell on her head. I'm likely all the rage at the henchmen's dinner. So I'll say it again. That's not what this is about. What *is* this about?"

"I need a promise first."

"Speak."

He pursed his luscious lips. "First the promise."

"Okay, I promise."

"Promise you will not fall into fits of laughter, and remember, our worlds are infinitely different."

She nodded solemnly. "I promise—infinitely."

"My virtue remains intact."

She tried to keep a straight face. No way. "So you're a virgin."

"Indeed."

Toni grabbed a pillow and held it over her face to keep from screaming her frustration.

Jon pulled it away and peered down at her. "Milady?"

She sighed. "This is a predicament, for sure. You're taught to save yourself for marriage and I'm all enticing you to break your code of man-honor. Maybe you could have mentioned this much earlier." Like before they were grinding each other into the bed.

"Maybe you might have told me your experience with bedsport is vast," he offered in a comically haughty tone.

She poked a finger in his chest with a reproachful glance. "It is *not* vast. Where I come from, it's by and large sort of pathetic, and I'll thank you to stop mentioning it like I've pillaged and plundered every man from here to Jersey. I mean, who would ever in a frillion years think *you* were a virgin?"

He rose up on his hands above her, his brow furrowed, his expression adorable. "You say this why?"

"Because look at you, all muscles and ripples and angels singing over your head while shafts of light glow all around you—"

"Angels, milady?"

"Never mind. Anyway, *hello*. I can't believe someone as unbelievably gorgeous as you hasn't at least been tempted. I would have thought you'd use your amazing looks as a manipulation tactic to twist some pantaloons, which I realize is incredibly sexist, but where I come from, it happens all the time. It's wrong, but it happens. Sex sells and all."

"I know not the gibberish you speak of manipulations, but I follow a strict code of honor, milady. I made a vow to myself and my realm to wait for marriage. It is just what we do here in Shamalot. Thus, I do not twist pantaloons."

"Haven't you ever been tempted?"

"Including now?"

She hid a pleased smile. "Yes."

"Then yes, but I always consider the maiden and her good name. Hence, I would never sacrifice her reputation for a momentary dabble in the temptations of the flesh."

God, he was so chivalrous and decent. So what did a girl say to that? No way was she compromising his values for her own hormonal satisfaction.

Pressing a quick kiss to his lips, she said, "You're a good and decent man, Jon Doe. You're kind and smart and you care. It's one of the many reasons I like you so much," she said as she tried to slip out from beneath him.

"But wait," he responded, tucking her back under him and brushing his lips against her jaw.

"For?"

"Does anyone have to *know* I've sacrificed your good name for the temptation of your delicious flesh?" he teased, his shaft rigid, pressing against her thigh.

But Toni didn't want to take something from him he'd saved for marriage. He was thirty-five and he'd waited this long—she wasn't going to be a party to that, as much as she wanted to be intimate with him. To take that back with her to Jersey so she'd be able to revisit this moment.

Toni's throat clogged, but she was determined not to let him see her regret.

"See what this is? This is the hormone thing I was talking about. You're all hot and heavy in the moment, but when the hormones fade, you might regret giving something away you've saved for *thirty-five* years, Jon. No one has to know, that's true. *You'd* know, though. You've waited a long time for the right woman to come along. I'm not going to be the one to compromise—"

He pressed his lips to hers again, whispering against them, "'Tis true I've waited for the right woman to come along...and now she *has*."

Her heart thrashed against her ribs and her toes curled. She knew in her gut this was right. She didn't know why she knew, which was as cliché as it got. She didn't know how. She just felt it in her bones—in her heart—in her mind.

Rather than answer him, she reached up and cupped his jaw, letting her fingers roam over his chin, skimming her thumb over his lower lip, pulling him to her to place her mouth over his with a sigh.

And Jon responded in kind, driving his tongue between her lips, caressing hers with precise strokes, pushing the blankets away from her until she was naked, the firelight dancing over her skin.

He swallowed hard, his Adam's apple visible when he sat up and unbuttoned his vest, pulling it and his shirt over his head.

His chest was just as she'd imagined, wide, thick, rippling with muscle, his nipples dusky and erect. Skin dusted in bronze stretched over his arms, strong and long.

Jon looked down at her, his sapphire eyes following the line of her neck, her collarbones, until he reached her breasts. His eyes grew dark, stormy, his body stiffening with tension.

"Aye, milady. You are everything I imagined. *More*," he whispered into the room, his voice husky and deep.

Her cheeks flushed hot as her hands found his forearms, running her fingers over the muscled flesh, relishing his strength.

He lifted tentative hands, hovering over her breasts until she gripped his wrists and brought them to her chest.

Jon inhaled a sharp breath, running his fingers over her hardened nipples until she squirmed beneath him. Toni's eyes closed as he explored, brushing kisses over her shoulder, down along her sides and back up again, until his lips were on the underside of her breast.

He flicked his tongue out, drawing it up over the full flesh until he reached the tight bud. When he placed his lips over it, enveloping it with his hot mouth, Toni bucked beneath him, gripping his hair in her hands as her eyes rolled to the back of her head.

Jon let his body fall flush to hers, sliding to rest at her side as he stroked her nipples, nipping, pulling, tugging, as the heat in her stomach grew and the ache between her thighs began to swirl with need.

Her hands went to his breeches, unlacing the front of them, inching them downward as he traced circles of wet-hot heat over her straining nipples. He lifted his lower body, allowing her to push his pants off until they were both naked.

Rising up, he pressed his forehead to hers, their noses touching as he reached for her hands and held them still. His breath came in short bursts, their chests crashing together. "I fear I may burst, milady. I may not know the ways of the flesh as well as I'd like, but I do know 'twould not be pleasurable for you if my needs came first. We must slow our pace. *You* must be the priority," he said, almost as though it were an order.

An incredibly intoxicating, sensual order.

Arching into him, she ran her tongue over his lower lip and nipped it. "We should *both* be the priority," she whispered.

If this was going to be his first time, and if it would be their last, she wanted him to remember. She wanted him to understand how much she was coming to care for him—that she'd always consider this time with him a gift.

"Show me, milady. Show me what you wish. I have these thoughts...running amok through my brain like a herd of wild horses, but I want for you to treasure this memory. So tell me, and I shall do your bidding."

His tender words were a stark contrast to the powerful body lying so close to hers—so tender, she wanted to curl up next to him and stay in this moment forever, so tomorrow didn't have to come and she wouldn't have to make a choice she might regret.

Rather than give him direction, Toni decided whatever Jon wanted to do would end up pleasurable, so she pulled him close, placing a hand on his chest where his heart beat, and whispered back, "Do what your instincts tell you to do, Jon—do what your heart tells you."

Jon clearly needed no more words as he hauled her close—so close, their thighs touched and her breasts crushed to his chest. He kissed her with abandon, without holding anything back, until she almost couldn't breathe from it and the heat he stirred in her nearly boiled over.

Toni's hands went to his back, roaming over the wide expanse, her body arching into him to get as close as she could, to feel every square inch of his naked flesh.

And then he was pulling his lips from hers and slipping down along her body until his mouth was at the place where thigh and hip met. He brushed a kiss over her skin, making her buck and sending ripples of pleasure along her heated flesh.

Jon parted her thighs with a gentle hand, slipping between them and resting his palm at the apex. He shuddered a breath, the air fanning across her skin just before he slipped a finger into her folds and spread her wide.

When he placed his mouth over her core, she jolted with a groan, gritting her teeth to keep from screaming, the feeling so intense. His tongue slithered over her clit, tentatively then with bolder strokes, licking, tasting, exploring her until she squeezed her thighs together, unable to stop the roar of orgasm. Toni bucked beneath his mouth, pressing the pillow to her face to keep from screaming her pleasure.

White-hot flashes of light synced with the spike of her climax, spreading upward, climbing until she let go, falling into the abyss of her release.

Her chest was tight, her mouth dry, but she managed to drag him upward, pulling at his wide shoulders until his lips were back at hers.

Jon brushed the lone tear that fell from her eye, murmuring against her mouth. "This coffee you speak of, 'tis nothing I imagine compared to the taste of you."

She had to cling to him to keep the dizzy swell of his words from overwhelming her. No one had ever spoken to her like this. No one had ever stirred this kind of a response from her, and she wanted everything— all at once. Now.

Reaching between them, Toni smoothed her palms over his chest, down along the lean indentation of his hips. She enveloped his cock, thick, strong, hot in her hands, and circled it, stroking him, letting him thrust against her.

Slipping down along his hard frame, she savored each inch of his silken skin, brushed kisses at every available turn until her lips found his shaft. Toni ran her tongue along the length of it, smiled against him when Jon hissed and his hands went to her hair, clenching fistfuls between his fingers.

His knees raised upward, his muscles clenching as she kept him deep in her mouth, caressing his calves, swirling her tongue over his cock until his hips bucked.

Jon's fingers dug into the caps of her shoulders now, pulling her upward, rolling her to her back and crushing her with his heavy weight.

He was delicious as she absorbed his hot flesh and sinew, letting his body sink into hers, running her hands along his sleek lines, parting her thighs, welcoming him.

Poised at her entrance, Jon rose up on his knees, wrapping her thighs around his waist, looking down at her, his eyes flaming with desire as he took his first thrust into her body.

His head fell back on his neck then, the strain of veins and corded muscle pulsing along his throat as he adjusted to being inside her.

Toni fought not to squirm beneath him, fought to lie still and savor watching his first time, luxuriate in the emotion. She clenched him tight as he stretched her, deepening his thrusts until he was embedded inside her.

He sighed a long groan, falling forward onto her, slipping his hands beneath her back and pressing his mouth to hers.

She saw stars behind her eyelids as each stroke into her grew more confident, harder, more satisfying. Curling into him, she matched his thrusts, lifting her hips, reaching toward release.

Wave after wave of pleasure swept through her, pooling in her belly, tingling in her toes, stroking her core until she thought she might explode.

Jon began to rock against her, lifting her leg higher, pushing into her wet depths, his body greedy, his lips on hers, and suddenly it was more than Toni could bear.

A swift wave of bliss rolled over her, beginning at her core and rising upward. It was slow, lazy, fast, sweet and sharp all at once. She clung to him then, nipped his earlobe as she strained against him, feeling every definition in his abs, loving his pubic bone scraping against her clit as they came.

Jon grunted, feral and low in her ear, expelling a long breath as he whispered her name. She tightened her grasp around his neck, rode the last remnants of their orgasm until their writhing slowed and their bodies settled.

And then Toni closed her eyes, smelled his hair draped across her cheek, savored the feel of his flesh against hers, kept him as close to her as possible for as long as possible.

Lived in the moment.

For as long as the moment would allow.

* * *

As Toni slept in his arms, her beautiful face serene, Jon warred with his emotions.

This—*this* had been worth the thirty-five-year wait. Not just the beauty of their lovemaking, but lovemaking with the woman he knew was meant to be his for all time.

Yet, he had things he must tell her. Secrets he must share.

What if the king granted her happiness and sent her back to her homeland to find her brother? He would never ask her to choose between them. He would never require she give up the only chance she had to comfort her heart—to know her brother was safe.

Yet, his gut tightened. How could *he* leave behind his own family and obligations?

Still, he knew he would. He would learn to adjust to this place called Jersey, with phones and movies and a place called McDonald's where they crisped potatoes and made hams in buns.

But he must tell her one thing.

The one thing that could make her change her mind about how decent and good he pretended he was.

Forever.

Chapter 12

Just so you know, we have trouble. I don't just mean the kind of trouble that involves the queen's daughter Resplendant's heart, either. The sweet and fair Resplendant's been officially dumped by the prince upon his father's orders. There's been crying. So much crying, and wailing, and head-bent, draggin-ass moping, a common storyteller like myself could almost need an antidepressant to help her get through the day.

Also, for future reference to all those who wish to visit a castle because it's cool? Castle walls make for one helluva echo.

Alas, here in Shamalot, we don't have *Ben and Jerry's* and old T-shirts in the realm for our poor Resplendant's funk. *You* try soothing a broken heart with a new crinoline and some thistleberries with roasted boar. It's just not the same as a hearty scoop of *Chunky Monkey* and a vodka gimlet, you know?

Needless to say, nothing is easing our gentle Resplendant's pain-swollen heart, for she loves Prince Iver Daring with all her being. She is his one true love, no matter what the doddering old Roz says.

Since King Dick, on the advice of the Great and Wonderful Roz, ordered the end to his son's relationship with Resplendant. Prince Iver, too, has been moping about the castle, wandering from room to room, sword dragging pathetically at half-mast by his side, refusing to speak, let alone hear his father's reasoning.

But King Dick is certain he's made the right move for his firstborn and he won't hear another protest.

As you can imagine, Queen Angria's pretty bent out of shape at this point. Not only has her daughter been ditched, but she's been foiled over and over by a mere snippet of an icky human girl (her words, not this storyteller's. I personally like the kid's chutzpah), and she wants blood.

Spilled.

Everywhere.

She also wants to know WTF is up with this guttersnipe and her amazing warrior-like skills. Where did she learn to do battle with such adeptness? Who is her sensei?

Why isn't he working as one of the queen's masters in weaponry?

And where did she get those fabulous shoes? Oh, the sparkle—it makes her giddy.

The queen's beside herself now that our bedraggled band of realm-hoppers is almost to the castle. But she's decided, rather than bring the battle to them, why not let them bring the battle to her? Why not wait until the much-touted Christmas Eve ball and *really* turn it into a party chock-full of blood and gore?

Why not let them all believe they've made it to safe harbor, and then take everyone out in one deliciously fell swoop? King Dick and his precious son Prince Iver Daring for dumping her beautiful Resplendant, this misfit pack of wanderers who talk too much and have managed to escape her wrath, and Toni of the fiery hair and sparkly shoes?

None of the particulars mattered anymore. All that mattered was everyone had to die on a night that would go down in infamy as the night King Dick would always remember crossing Queen Angria was unacceptable.

In fact, why not make it a double coup—like an all-out massacre—and steal the castle *and* the kingdom while she's at it?

The queen's decided this could be LOL hilarious—a way to make her mark and force the inhabitants of Shamalot to bow down and worship the very ground she walks upon.

And she likes that. She likes that a lot.

Then there's our rugged, chivalrous Jon Doe, falling head over heels for a woman he might have to part with. Torn between two worlds—the one to which his fair maiden must return to possibly reunite with her beloved brother, and the one where he has many obligations.

Because our Jon has a secret. One I'm quite confident you've figured out by now.

However, it's the journey, not necessarily the destination, yes? Plus, for Nina—this entire tale in a yellow dress, bluebirds singing above her head—retribution *can* be good for the soul. Just ask this storyteller.

Anyway, there's a battle looming—filled with potential death and despair, and as we rejoin our band of misfits, everyone appears to be blissfully unaware…

* * *

Toni was the first to hit the top of the cliff overlooking the castle, her breath caught in her throat as she stared at the beauty sprawling before her. Snow-capped mountains surrounded the gray castle, their majesty rising into the low clouds above.

Stained glass windows in the shape of elongated ovals, glowing with candles, spanned the high towers, preparing for the coming night. Neatly trimmed, tall hedges nestled along the endless miles of the castle, almost glittering in the freshly fallen snow. People milled about the small knoll in front of the steps dressed warmly, selling goods and fresh market fare.

Carriages bustled in and out of the square in preparation for the coming ball, weaving in and out of trees glistening with some kind of green fruit that appeared to have been dipped in sugar like the leaves in the Garden of Wings.

Water swelled below them in ripples of ebony and frothy white, crashing against the boulders near the shore. The salty spray made her heart beat faster. They were here. They were finally here.

She grabbed Jon's hand as he came up behind her and tucked her to his chest.

"It's magnificent, milady, don't you agree?" he said at her ear, making her shiver.

She sighed against him, stealing yet another moment where she could be close to him. "I've never seen anything quite as beautiful."

"I have," he admitted in husky tones. "You, last night, with the fire gracing your perfect form and the serenity upon your face as you slept beside me."

"It had to be the pillows. It feels like a hundred years since I slept on a pillow," she teased, closing her eyes and smiling.

"Naturally, it had nothing to do with my quick aptitude at beginner's bedsport."

"Bedsport? I forgot all about that," she joked, nudging his ribs with her elbow.

He turned her in his arms with a chuckle. "Tell me something, milady."

Toni rolled her eyes at him. "Are you going to make me rate your bedsport performance on a scale of one to ten?"

"Nay," he muttered, his eyes serious. "I'd like to ask you a graver question."

"Rating the bedsport isn't grave?"

"Toni…" he warned, letting her know he was done indulging her.

"Okay, fine. Ask away."

"If it 'twere possible, would you live with a man such as myself—one without riches, in a small cottage in a clearing without phones or intor-nets or coffee spouts, and help me raise reindeer? Could that make someone like you, from a vastly different world, happy?"

Resting her cheek on his chest, she smiled against the hard surface. "Coffeepots. Not spouts. And yes…I think I could."

"This is good to know."

"Hey, are we doing the regrets thing? I thought we made a pact?"

"Nay, milady. I simply ask in order to stroke my vast ego," he said on a rumble of laughter.

She laughed as her cheeks flushed despite the bitter cold. Lifting her head, she gave him a soft kiss, fighting the butterflies in her belly. "No regrets, right?"

"Not a one," he said against her lips.

They'd decided to see what they could see rather than focus on when or if this would all end. Nothing was set in stone at this point. The king and this happiness she was supposed to find hadn't been handed down yet.

She gnawed on her knuckle, thinking.

"What troubles you, Toni?"

"Just a feeling, I suppose. Here we are, finally at the castle, and this Queen Angria still hasn't shown up. Why is that? You'd think after a couple of unsuccessful attempts to kidnap me, we'd have run into her by now."

"Nay. The queen does not dirty her hands with such matters. She leaves that to her henchmen."

Something just wasn't sitting right with her. "Okay, so did she just give up? Call it a day? Realize there's nothing I have that she wants?"

"This I do not know. Not even with all the asking I've done around the forest. However, you are here now and safe, and no one will harm you in the king's care. This I know."

"You keep saying that like he's an old friend. Do you guys do lunch on occasion? Hit Happy Hour at the *Stool and Gruel* once a week?"

Jon smiled as he looked out over the ocean's vastness. "I only know the kind of ruler he's been in my thirty-five years. Fair, kind, if not a bit eccentric. He would never allow a faithful subject to be harmed. There has been peace for many years between him and Angria. I imagine once he finds she's sent men for your capture, he will be quite displeased. Please trust this."

She took a deep breath and tried not to allow her jitters about her fate to take over. "Okay. I trust you."

"Now, I must go prepare for our crossing, milady. Sit tight," he said, dropping another breath-stealing kiss on her lips before taking his leave.

Nina came up behind her, the bluebirds now contentedly sitting on her shoulder, still whistling their happy tune. "You ready, kiddo?" she asked, placing a hand on Toni's shoulder.

She wanted to say yes. She wanted to be brave in front of Nina because that's what you did with the biggest badass in the land. So she nodded. "I think so."

"Bullshit."

"Can I ask you a question?"

"Yep."

"If I go back to Jersey, if that's where this happiness I'm supposed to be granted is, can we text each other sometimes, maybe? Call or something?"

"Are you gonna wanna do lunch? Shop or some bullshit? Get our hair done?"

"I'd rather have my throat punched." She paused a moment, fighting the swell of loneliness she'd staved off every day and night for three years.

She'd always thought of herself as independent, capable of handling anything. But this loneliness, the empty nights with nothing to look forward to but a cheap TV dinner, being without her brother, had seeped into her bones.

As though a fog had lifted, being with these people had reminded her that she'd been doing nothing more than surviving. Yet, she wanted more, and if Jersey was where her happiness was, she wanted to have a life again. She wanted friends and maybe a hobby—something to fill the void she was so afraid of slipping back into if she had to go back.

Clearing her throat, she asked, "So maybe we could see a movie—your choice, of course. No rom-coms. Or just have a conversation sometime? I'd like to keep in touch with Carl, too…"

Nina nudged her shoulder. "I'm kidding, Princess Sparkly. Of course we'll text and hang out and do all the fun shit we paranormals do. Christmas and Easter and effin' Groundhog Day included. There's always something to celebrate with this lot. Because that's what we do. I'm not talking about the vague, empty promises people make when they say those words, either. We really do this shit. Besides, Carl would miss the crap outta ya if you didn't keep in touch, kiddo. Since Quinn became Aphrodite, she's been crazy busy making matches and hasn't had a lot of time to read to him. He loves your stories—even if you can't remember *Sleeping Beauty* didn't have seven dwarves and a fucking library the size of NASA."

She fought the lump in her throat, keeping her eyes down so Nina wouldn't see her cry, and whispered, "Thank you."

"You do know you'll never be alone now, right? We'll always be there, Princess. Sometimes you won't even have to call. We'll just show the hell up with some crappy casserole Marty baked that I can't eat, or extra fresh loaves of bread hot out of the oven from Arch, who doesn't know what to do with them, and who you haven't met but will make you what I hear are the best chicken wings on the planet. Like I'd fucking know, right? You still need to meet Darnell, because who the fuck wants a day to go by without a bear hug from our favorite escaped demon? We'll Skype you, and text you, and in general torture the living shit out of you every damn time you think you might be safe from us bunch o' nutbags. Most of all, we'll protect you—"

Toni lunged at Nina, stopping her words, words she so needed to hear. Wrapping her arms around the vampire's waist, Toni buried her face in her shoulder.

Nina thumped her on the back with an awkward pat, letting her chin rest on the top of Toni's head for the briefest of moments. "No one will hurt you ever again. Count on that crap."

"Group hug!" Marty called out, wrapping her arms around them, with Wanda right behind her.

Dannan joined in, too, sheltering them with his big body as he pulled them all close and purred a grumble.

"Princess thought if this King Dick says she has to go back to Jersey, she'd be rid of us. Now get the fuck off me and tell her we're framily. You know, the friends-and-family shit, and then tell her ditching us just won't fly."

"How could you ever think something like that, Toni?" Wanda asked, tugging a length of Toni's hair. "Who else understands you and what you've been through better than us?"

"I said that shit," Nina groused, rubbing her knuckles on the top of Toni's head.

Marty brushed Toni's tears away from her cold cheeks and dropped a kiss on her forehead. "Aw, is Nina being reassuring again? God, just when you thought it was safe to go back in the water, huh?"

Nina flipped her the middle finger. "Fuck you, Marty."

Marty swatted her with the furry muff Flauta had given her to keep her hands warm for the last leg of their journey. "That's so mean! Take it back."

"Okay, unfuck you, Marty."

Toni laughed, wiping away her tears and squaring her shoulders. "Okay, enough of the girlie crap, let's get this show on the road. We have a ball to attend and we need to get you guys back home so you don't miss Christmas with your families."

"About the castle," Jon interrupted them, clearing his throat.

"What about it, Flawless?" Nina asked, her eyes wary.

Jon gave them a sheepish glance. "We have a small problem."

Alarm skittered up Toni's spine. "Which is?"

He sighed, his wide chest puffing outward. "The mote below us and no boat to take us to the land's edge. They must have taken all the boats inland after bringing the guests from the surrounding mainland for the ball tomorrow."

"Is there no way to send a signal, lad?" Dannan wondered.

"Who would be in the towers now, my friend? The drawbridge is up. Everyone is preparing for the ball. No enemies dare interfere. You know the king and his parties. Even some of our least supportive wouldn't dare miss it."

Toni's feet began to tingle as she looked out over the cliff. "So you just need someone to put the drawbridge down?"

"Well, yes. And I also need someone to magically produce one of your planes to transport me back and forth from my world to yours. It is not so simple, milady," he said with sarcasm.

She fought a girlish smile at the thought and asked, "Is it hard to put the drawbridge down?"

Jon looked at her as though she'd sprouted two heads. "No. It's quite simple, though it takes some strength. But what does this have to do with *getting* to the drawbridge, Toni? It is there," he pointed to the distance, "and we are here with no transportation." He then pointed to his feet as though she'd missed the class on logistics.

"Yeah, yeah. I get that."

"'The water is too cold to swim the mote to get to the drawbridge for us humans. We would freeze to death, and though the ladies are the logical choice. I cannot risk their health with their powers depleting. I will not chance this."

Toni nodded. "I get that, too, I was just asking a question." *But why are you asking the question?* her brain wondered.

Nina scowled, placing her hands on her hips. "Damn Brenda the Flaky Witch. If she'd left GD well enough alone, I could fly the hell over there—"

Toni backed up and got a running start at the edge of the cliff, jumping off the rocky surface with a piercing yelp of surprise.

As she shot toward the murky-cold water, she felt no fear. None. Not an ounce. It was as though she'd been doing this all her life.

As she screamed toward the water, her dress billowing upward like some reverse parachute, she clenched her eyes shut and hit the water like a cliff diver who'd just executed the most beautiful swan dive ever. With grace and speed, the impact almost nothing.

Her legs shifted, she heard the crunch of bone in her head, felt her lower body streamline, felt her feet all but disappear. She tumbled under the water, forcing her eyes open to encounter her lower body.

She had a tail. Shut the front door!

Or more appropriately, a tail scaled in the most beautiful purple and silver. Her fin swished in the water, swirling around and chasing away smaller fish.

What the hell?

And then it struck her. Somehow, after her battle with Pricilla, she'd inherited a tail. That was the only logical explanation for her new appendage.

Remember when I said I was done with you? That you were dead to me? Now you're more than dead to me. You've reached moronic levels here, dummy. You're going to freeze your ass off in this water and die. You came all this way just to damn well die right before you find out what the hell is going on? No can do," her brain complained.

But her body? It said, *Swim, bitch, swim, like the mermaid you've become! Work that fin, honey!*

Toni forced her way to the surface, gulping the air and looking over her shoulder where everyone waved frantically to her to come back to the bottom of the cliff. Yet, she knew she could do this.

She was going to let that drawbridge down so they could attend this ball and get on with it already. As she sliced through the water, riding each wave as she swept upward for air, the name Flipper came to mind. She felt a lot like what she guessed a dolphin must feel as he soared through the air, skipping over the ocean with abandon.

The water didn't feel cold at all—in fact, it gave her life, purpose, a freedom she'd never known. It felt as much her home as the land did.

Rising to the surface to pinpoint her location, she saw the shore, where small boats decorated with ropes of pine and red bows lolled at a dock.

Flapping her fin with furious strokes, she pushed the last few yards to the water's edge and prayed when she got to shore, she'd have feet again.

Shooting herself over the last leg, she rode a wave in, hitting the rocky shorefront with a grunt as the stones scraped her chest and face.

Toni dragged herself over the uneven surface and spat water from her mouth, using her forearm to wipe her long strands of hair from her face. Gazing around, she noted it was deserted. Clearly everyone really was off to prepare for the ball tomorrow night.

Looking down the length of her body, she was relieved to see she did indeed have feet again, the shoes still firmly attached. Gathering her soaking gown, she hopped up and made her way toward a long stone tunnel, dimly lit with fiery torches, that led to a small courtyard, festively decorated for the holiday.

So where would one hide a drawbridge opener anyway? As she crept along the wall and into the courtyard, dripping, her teeth chattering, she spied a huge wheel attached to pulleys and weights with thick chains.

With shaky hands, Toni went for it. Grabbing the handle of the wheel, she jumped upward and gave it a hard yank, knocking snow and leaves down onto her head.

She heard the creak of the chains, cringing at the thought someone might catch her, but she managed to get it moving with a slow groan.

As it lowered, Toni fought the butterflies in her stomach. For all Jon's reassurances about how she needn't fear the king, she feared.

Big time.

How would Jon—a commoner, if one went by fairytales—know anything about the king and whether he was a standup guy, anyway? Did the king mingle with the little people? Was his opinion based on general Shamlotian opinion?

Or maybe she was just being a totally pessimistic bag o' dicks based on her own experience with American politics. Maybe King Dick was a decent guy who ran Shamalot fairly, a guy who was an interactive king, so to speak, and she was just cranky because she was soaking wet and she'd battled half the inhabitants of Not So Sherwood Forest to get here to return a pair of shoes that had apparently helped her absorb her foes' powers.

And her lips were chapped. Really chapped.

But whatever this king had to give her, she had to believe Brenda wouldn't have sent her here if she knew he was going to chop her head off. That wasn't very happy.

Right?

"Toni!" a voice whisper-yelled.

Her eyes squinted at the tunnel as Jon rushed toward her, his eyes glinting in the torchlight. "Have you lost your senses, milady?"

"I have not. Did you see me? I was a regular Ariel out there."

"Muriel," he corrected.

She flapped a hand at him. "Whatever. I got the job done, right? What's the big to-do?"

He grabbed her hand and pressed it to his chest. "Doth thou feel that?"

Toni nodded on a shiver. "Thou doth. Did you run over the drawbridge?"

"That is the beat of terror. With no warning at all, you hurled yourself from the cliff's edge. A conversation prior to such an act would be kind on your part."

She couldn't stop the giggle that escaped her throat. "I'm sorry. It just—"

"Happened," he said on a weary sigh. "This expression I know all too well with you, my dove. Clearly, you garnered some of Pricilla's sea worthiness."

"Did you see?" she asked from trembling lips as salty water dripped from her hair. "I had a tail. A tail! It was amazing. Do I get to keep all this stuff if I go back to Jersey? I mean, Bree could really use a good fire under her ass, don't you think?"

Jon cupped her jaw as she heard the others footsteps coming from the tunnel. "Speaking of fire, you need to be near one as soon as possible." He took his pelt off and wrapped it around her shivering body, rubbing her arms.

As Marty and the others came out of the tunnel, Toni asked him, "Now what? Where do we go from here?"

Jon pulled her aside as everyone began to cluster around them, dragging the hood of his cloak over his head. "This is where I leave you momentarily, Toni. I must tend to Oliver at the stables and settle him for the night. But I shall come find you the moment I have done so."

Leave her? She was going to just knock on the king's door and say, "Howdy, neighbor! Resident realm-jumpers here. Your pal Brenda said to drop in anytime."

Toni gripped his arm in panic. "I can go with you and we'll see the king together."

"You must dry off, my beautiful fish. You do not wish to catch a cold and miss your debut with the king, do you?"

What was all this? "Well, runny nose aside, I kind of don't want to do it without you with me. I don't know anything about Shamalot's formalities and its dignitaries. What if I insult him by using the wrong word—phrase—sentence? Do I curtsy? Bow? I need you with me to help me do this right. What is it with all this 'Bye, Felicia'?"

"Who, pray tell, is Felicia?"

"Not the point. The point is, I'm a little nervous after everything we went through to get here."

"You have nothing to fear, milady. The king is a kind ruler. He'll welcome you and the return of his shoes with open arms. You are safe here at the castle. This I promise. Now, kiss me, wench, for I long to have your lips upon mine."

She raised her face to his, even as confused as she was by his words. They'd been all gung-ho, yay castle, and now he was just dropping her off like a baby in a basket at a church? Just leaving her without the secret password?

Jon kissed her hard, his arms wrapping around her possessively, making her forget everything but his mouth on hers. Pulling away, he pressed the tip of his nose to hers and whispered, "Go right to that door and knock. There will be a guard by the good name of Heinrick. Show him the shoes and tell him Brenda sent you."

Still, she clung to his large frame. "Are you *sure* you don't want me to go with you?"

"Methinks my novice attempts at the bedsport were better than you let on," he teased with a soft chuckle.

Toni rolled her eyes on another violent shiver. "Bedsport, schmedsport. All you men, even ones from different realms, need to have your egos stroked, don't you?"

Nina parted them by sticking her beautiful face between their heads. "Okay, lovebirds, it's time to get this shit done. I miss my kid and my man and a good Netflix binge of *Longmire*. Say your goodbyes and move along little doggies, before you catch some otherworldy plague we have to find the tears of a Dutch maiden to cure, huh?" She gave Jon an affectionate slap on the back for good measure.

Jon pulled away from Toni, his eyes warm. "Do as Nina says, milady. I'll see you soon." He pressed one last lingering kiss to her lips before he was swallowed up by the night, followed by Dannan's thundering footsteps.

As the girls pulled her toward the door Jon had directed them toward, Toni wasn't sure if she was being melodramatic, but his kiss had felt like a kinder version of the Old Yeller of goodbyes.

Sweet.

Gentle.

Final.

Chapter 13

"So are ye gonna open yer flytrap sometime soon, lad, or will ye have Toni believe yer tendin' Oliver till the morrow?"

Rubbing Oliver down, he gritted his teeth, kicking himself for being the coward he was. "She'll be well with the women, yes?"

Dannan wagged a long blue finger at him. "Oh no, lad. Ye are not soothing yerself with that justification. Ye should have gone with her. Not a one of the lasses knows royalty the way ye do. She's nervous as a stray cat in the square. Her comfort is compromised, and I do not like ye for it."

He dropped his hands to his side, consumed with guilt. The king was kind and fair, and he'd never harm her, but leaving Toni on her own in a strange setting was beneath him.

Jon tucked the hood of the cloak her wore closer, keeping his head down as some of the stable boys passed by. "There is so much at stake. This is not, as you well know, just about me, friend. There are others involved here who would potentially suffer. I'm trying to protect everyone, Dannan. I must have time to investigate the well-being of the others and make the appropriate move for all concerned. I would have never sent Toni into the castle had I feared for her safety. You know this."

Dannan nodded, leaning on the edge of the stable doors. "Aye, lad, and I know gettin' word to the castle was impossible with the weather takin' the turn it did, and ye cannot stop what will happen now that yer so deeply involved. But you must tell her if ye don't want to lose her. Ye can only take the honest path, and that path is telling Toni the truth. Let the chips fall where they may, but at least ye can say ye were honest in the end."

Where had this all gone so wrong? Why hadn't he just owned up to his truths earlier instead of putting off the inevitable?

Because he'd forgotten where this little adventure ended and his true life began. The edges had become blurred, lines crossed.

"Have ye heard the gossip from the castle about the prince?"

In aggravation, he threw down the blanket he'd planned to cover Oliver with. "We've been here nigh on a mere hour, ogre. What could I have possibly heard?"

"The king has sent Resplendant away, lad. Brokenhearted and blue are the words I'm hearin'. King Dick has broken the pact with the queen for their marriage and the merger between the two castles and lands. The king claims that bats-in-the-belfry Roz has seen the face of the prince's beloved in her mirror, and 'twas not Resplendant. They say the prince is brokenhearted, too."

Jon's stomach nosedived, his fists clenching. "Nay. This cannot be true. Why have we not heard this?"

Dannan rolled his big eyes as he attempted to stretch out a leg. "Because we've been deep in the forest, ye fool! If ye couldn't get word to the castle, how would ye expect we'd hear this information? This news makes for a very angry Angria, I suspect."

Jon clenched his jaw. When he got his hands on Angria, she was going to wish the merger with the king were the biggest problem in her life.

Yet now, everything made sense all at once—and one thing was for certain, he had to get to Toni immediately. He had to tell her.

Dannan placed a large hand on his shoulder and squeezed. "Ye must get on with it, boy. Ye must stop skulking about the grounds and find yer woman. If ye will not, I shall. I wish no harm to come to the lass. She's grown a fond place in my heart. Yer little adventure is over now. Ye must make this right for the honor of true love's kiss."

True love's kiss. He'd thought it all bunk, but not after last night and their lovemaking. After last night, he knew Toni was the woman for him.

Dannan guffawed. "I see that twinkle in yer eye, boy. Ye are in love."

That he was. He was certain of it. The fair Toni wasn't aware of her true heart right now, but she loved him, too. He knew it as sure as he knew he must fix this.

Damn, this had all fallen apart so quickly. He'd hoped to handle some of his affairs privately and attempt to make a smooth transition, but not with Toni and her head at stake.

"Will you tend to Oliver for me?"

"Aye, lad. Go. Hurry!"

Just as Jon turned to head for the castle doors, the castle guards, lined up, thwarted him, swords drawn and pointed at his chest. "Halt, Jon Doe!" one yelled "You are under arrest by order of Prince Iver Daring!"

As the pale, discontent Nina would say, *fuck*.

* * *

"One more bow in this GD beehive and someone dies. You got that?" Nina groused, flapping away the hands of the very patient handmaiden who'd reconstructed her hairdo, as the bluebirds settled back into the nest of her ebony hair.

If she only knew how utterly surreal she looked, the soft lemon color of her dress, rather than taking away from her paleness, accentuated it. But she was wearing down, and it was beginning to show, endlessly worrying Toni.

Marty sighed as another handmaiden fluffed her amazing gown of lavender silk and taffeta. The gorgeous detail of the bodice alone, with its swirls of flowers and leaves, would be the envy of every female ball attendee.

The puffy sleeves off her creamy shoulders bounced as she sighed. "Ignore her, girls. Please. And if she keeps complaining, give her a clove of garlic. That shuts her right up."

Wanda rose from the poofy white lounging chair she'd been quietly sitting on and shook a finger at Nina. "Don't be so ungrateful. They're just doing their jobs."

Nina whipped around, the skirts of her heavy gown whispering across the floor. "I'm gonna pluck those wings right the hell off your back, Wanda. I know this has been a whole princess party come true for the two of you, but me? Sheer effin' hell. I want out. I miss my kid, and my man, and my own GD castle."

Marty's blue eyes became watery, her lower lip quivering as she fought tears. "I have to admit, I miss Hollis and Keegan like crazy. I don't know if time passes the same here as it does back home, but if it does, I hope Keegan remembered to help our girl make cookies for Santa. She loves that more than I think she even loves opening presents."

Wanda was the first to reassure her, her eyes filling, too. "You know Archibald and Darnell are on top of things, Marty. All of the children will be taken care of, if that's the case. Arch isn't going to let them miss a thing. In fact, if it *is* Christmas Eve back home, know what they're doing right now? Sleigh-riding down that big hill behind Mara's old place. Keegan's dragging the little ones to the top of the hill while Greg waits at the bottom. Heath is making snowmen with Darnell, and Arch has them dressed like they're in Siberia, waiting for them to finish so he can tuck them under those awesome heated blankets with a huge carafe of hot chocolate, brimming with the mini-marshmallows they love so much. It's our Christmas Eve…tradition," she said, her voice cracking.

"You think Katie, Shaw, the twins and Teeny are there?" Nina asked, a smile reaching her eyes.

Wanda smiled brightly. Almost too brightly. "Of course they are. Teeny's trying to sneak off for a smoke while Grandma Lou, Clay, and Casey chase after her."

Marty nodded, her smile growing. "How much you wanna bet Quinn's trying to hook Arch up with Teeny again?"

Nina barked a sharp laugh, slapping her thigh. "You remember what Teeny said about him the first time Quinn tried that shit?" She hunched over and scrunched up her beautiful face, mimicking Teeny. "He came at me like he was gettin' ready to lay one on a damn fish. I don't want no stuffy old man. I want me a youngin' with abs o' titanium and a tight butt!"

All three of the women laughed. Their combined memories were what had kept them going on this trek to the castle. They were always talking about one incident or another they'd shared together as they'd trudged through the forest, while Toni had stayed in the background and eavesdropped on their happiness. Her heart clenched tight. They were all so close—so intertwined in each other's lives.

She rose from the magnificent four-poster bed with inlaid wood, sitting in the middle of the breathtaking room she'd been whisked away to last night, the rustle of her beautiful skirts hindering her stride. She crossed the room and squeezed Nina's arm, shooting Marty and Wanda an apologetic glance.

"I'm sorry, Nina—all of you. I know how much you've sacrificed to help me. But this will all be over tonight. You heard what the king's messenger said, right? He said he'd take court with us this evening at the ball. It won't be long now."

Nina squeezed her arm back. "Sorry, kiddo. I'm low on this damned elixir crap and it's just making me crabbier than usual. This fucking dress doesn't help. Who the hell thought this contraption up? If I had organs, I'd have fekkin' yarked them up by now, it's so damn tight."

"I'll treasure this always," Toni said with a grin.

"What?"

"Your apology."

"Shut it or I rip your ankles off."

Toni stroked Nina's cheek with the back of her hand, smiling sweetly. "You will not. Know why? Because you're my framily," she teased, straightening one of the bows down the front of Nina's lemon-colored gown.

Nina batted her hands away. "Fuck you and fuck your framily. Now when does this damn shindig begin? Because I want the fuck out."

Toni ran and grabbed the official scroll the king's messenger had sent, holding it up for Nina to see. "Nine sharp. It won't be long now."

Turning her back to the group, she bit the inside of her cheek to stem the tears and dropped the scroll on the beautiful dressing table, where her own personal handmaiden had twisted and turned and brushed her hair into the most fabulous up-do Toni had ever seen.

It swept upward in a riot of auburn curls swirling around her head then fell down the middle of her back in the tiniest of ringlets. She wore a gown of the softest dove-gray silk, the ruched bodice in deep purple with lavender beads dripping along the front, leading to her waist. The heavy crinoline beneath it gave it a bell shape, swaying to and fro and she moved.

Nina tucked a stray curl that just wouldn't behave behind her ear, adorned with an earring made of lemon-colored crystals. "So have we figured out where the fuck Flawless is? Because when we find him and all his GD perfection, I'm gonna personally kick his ass from here to Jersey for abandoning the kid like this. No-good son of a bitch. I knew he was too damn good to be true."

Yeah. Where *was* Flawless? After he'd left them at the castle doors last night, she'd tried to tamp down the fear she'd never see him again. All while they'd spoken to the king's advisors, while they'd been fed and drawn hot baths, and while they'd been settled in connecting rooms, she'd wondered where Jon had gone.

As she'd stared out the window of her room late last evening, she'd hoped to catch a glimpse of him in the courtyard below, but it was as silent as a church mouse.

When they'd inquired about him this morning, her personal guard—appointed to her by the king because she still had the damn shoes—as well as most of the castle's staff claimed they knew nothing of a Jon Doe. Never heard of him, in fact.

And that just made everything worse. It was as though he were some figment of their imaginations—as though that long trek they'd just shared had happened with the Invisible Man.

This morning, as she'd risen in her incredible bedroom in her equally incredible bed, her chest was tight, her throat sore from crying, her eyes swollen from a restless night. If Jon had meant goodbye last night, surely he could have had the decency to have been honest about it, rather than say all those pretty things only to desert her in the end.

Okay, so he'd said some things in the heat of the moment that maybe he didn't really mean. She was a big girl. She could have taken that. But this silence? This deafening no-show? It hurt.

Jerk.

Wanda fluttered behind Toni, wrapping her arms around her shoulders from behind as they looked out the stained glass window toward the bustling courtyard, where the staff of the castle was in high gear with Christmas Eve ball preparations.

She leaned back against Wanda and fought more tears. It was Christmas, for Pete's sake. These women belonged with their families and their Christmas trees and lights, and Carl deserved a visit with Santa Claus.

Christmas had come and gone for her these last three years since Cormac had been gone—it was just another day where most everything was closed and she'd have to choose between a Salisbury steak TV dinner or boxed mac and cheese.

But these women—these women who'd jumped on the get-Toni-to-the-castle bandwagon or bust—had traditions they'd miss if they didn't get home tonight.

Nina had told her all about the feast Archibald, Wanda's manservant, served for their OOPS extended family. At least fifty plates covered a formal table filled with turkeys and roasts and mounds of creamy mashed potatoes and all the trimmings. They toasted their lives together, they laughed, they danced, they had a secret Santa with Darnell playing the starring role.

She wanted them to have this night—or at least to salvage what was left of the season. She *needed* them to have it back, and looking for Jon would keep them from their appointment to go home.

"You three have to go meet the king. But I have to look for Jon and Dannan," she murmured.

Marty sighed a breathy sigh and smiled fondly. "Ah, love. You're in love."

Was this love? Did this gnawing ache in her belly, this panic she felt without him at her side, mean love? "Can I ask you all a question?"

"Always," Wanda whispered.

"You'll think it's stupid."

"Probably," Nina agreed with a grin. "But ask anyway. I need some shit to snark while we figure out what to do next, and you amuse me."

Toni looked down at her hands, fiddling with the front of her dress. "When you first met your husbands, did you see a glow around their heads and hear a harp strumming softly in the distance?"

"Oh, 'tis true love, milady!" one of the handmaidens said on a wistful sigh as she gathered brushes and bows, putting them back in her basket.

"I don't understand."

"When a maiden falls in love—*real* love—her true mate presents himself with music and beautiful lights shining down from the heavens. 'Tis how you know he's the one," she said on a wink.

"But it's so soon… We've only known each other a little while," she managed to murmur. Not a chance in hell would she hook up for life with a guy she'd only known a few weeks if she were back in Jersey.

The handmaiden smiled knowingly. "That is what the inside of your head tells you, but the inside of your chest, right here," she said, pointing to her heart, "it always knows best. For now, I must go tend to the others, but I wish you, your true love and everyone in your party the very best of the holiday season." She waved and skipped off to the door of the bedroom.

"A harp, huh?" Nina asked. "I saw stars for sure. I think I remember flashing lights, too."

Marty nodded, a soft smile spreading her lips. "Yeah. No music, but I knew. I just knew."

Wanda gave Toni a tight squeeze. "I need you to trust me about something, Toni, okay?"

"Okay," she said with great hesitance.

"I don't know what's going on. I don't know why no one seems to know who Jon is, but I promise you this—he's crazy about you, and I think you're crazy about him, too. I know you're warring with that notion because it appears he's deserted you and you want to hate him for making you care. But don't. Not yet. Your heart is sending you a message your head wants to overrule. But something's happened with him, *to* him. *Something*, and I intend to find out what that something is. Until then, promise me you won't let your crazy imagination get the best of you. Jon did *not* desert you. He just wouldn't do that."

How Wanda could be so sure baffled her. Maybe Toni was too thick in the mud to see clearly.

Her nod was slow, but she still wasn't totally convinced. "You know, you once said to me something wasn't right about him. Should I trust that, too?"

Wanda nodded, her hair never moving. "You absolutely should. Something *isn't* right. I think I also said I thought he was a good guy or something to that effect. I don't necessarily think what I said has to do with some kind of deceit that would hurt you. I refuse to believe he's willingly not by your side. So until we figure this out, promise me you won't jump to conclusions? Let's get the entire picture first. Until then, it's Christmas, for crap's sake, and I believe in miracles."

Toni shuddered a breath and prayed for one of those miracles. "We don't have a lot of time left. Once we see the king and he gives me whatever I'm supposed to get, and you all prove you've done your tasks as fairy godmothers, I'm assuming you can leave. At least that's what Brenda implied anyway. I'm not going to let you waste another second here in this realm if you're missing the holiday with your families. I just won't."

"Then we go find the fuck before we meet the king," Nina said. "Then I beat Flawless's ass for ditching us like so much landfill and make him squeal like a girl. And if I find that damn knock-off of Shrek, I'll beat his ass, too. Can't believe after all that all-for-one-and-one-for-all musketeer bullshit, he just left us like we didn't mean shit."

But Toni offered a sobering thought. "Have you seen the size of this castle? It could take a week to find the kitchen, and that's if you know where you're going. How will we find him in this maze in less than an hour? No way am I letting you guys miss this appointment with King Dick. If I'm not going back to Jersey, you three most certainly are. No matter what. Especially you, Nina. You can't hold out much longer like this without a good infusion of some blood."

Marty rushed to Toni's side and grabbed her hand, her blonde hair erect as ever. "No one's leaving anyone anywhere, honey. We're a team—Team Toni. Period. Now, I'm not a werewolf for nothing. I know Jon's scent, and if he's still here in the castle, or on the grounds, I'll find him. Nina's got the same superpower I do, as does Wanda. Our senses might be dulled because of whatever Brenda did and this crazy fairy godmother stint, but I'm pretty sure I could smell a man as fabulous as Jon even without my full werewolf senses. So I say we split into groups of two and we do this. You in?"

Nina nodded, her head's up-and-down bob sluggish. "Yeah, yeah. Wonder Twin powers activate. Let's roll before I collapse the fuck all over the floor."

Wanda nodded her perfectly coiffed head, her wings throbbing a muted whir. "We meet in the ballroom in forty minutes. No longer, understood? We all need to be accounted for before we take this a step further. We'll regroup then if we don't find him."

Toni looked to Carl, who, while considered odd by the castle members, was allowed to stay indoors and wander throughout their connecting rooms. "You with us, buddy?"

Carl stomped his hoof in favor of finding Jon.

"All right, girls," Wanda said, raising her arm high. "Let's really storm the castle!"

* * *

"Who dares to imprison us, Günter? Answer the question!" Jon raged, shaking the bars of the cell he and Dannan were stuffed inside, in the prison below the castle.

But the guard refused to turn and address them, keeping his back to the cell.

Dannan, the top of his head bent sideways with his cheek against the cell's ceiling, poked him with a big toe to his shoulder blades. "Lad, quiet! I cannot think when yer caterwaulin' like a woman!"

Jon sneered, gritting his teeth. "We must get to Toni before she sees the king and possibly leaves the realm forever. How else would you have me do that but make demands, ogre?"

If she left the realm without giving him the chance to tell her of his heart, to tell her the truth, he'd never forgive himself.

"Has it helped ye so far? Nay. Now pipe down and let yer old friend think."

"The women will never find us here in time, Dannan. We must find someone who will listen to the truths I speak. Unlike Günter, who has clearly been ordered to ignore my commands at all costs!" Jon spat.

"Ye should have thought of what the prince would do if he felt threatened. He is not as strong as ye, lad. We are imprisoned because his decisions are based on fear. And ye should have thought to tell yer lady love much sooner, ye fool!" Dannan grumbled.

Jon paced the floor, knowing his friend was right, knowing exactly why he was locked up in this cell. "Aye, but that is done now. I cannot change such. Now we must find our way out of here quickly." Before he lost the woman he wanted to spend the rest of his days with.

"'Tis good ye are my friend or I would have eaten yer foolish hide by now."

He grabbed onto the bars again and rattled them, his knuckles going white from the effort. "Damn you, man, you must listen to me!"

But Günter refused to turn, making him a loyal guard to the king, but hellfire and damnation, now wasn't the time to prove his worth.

"Lad?"

Jon whipped around, and if not for their circumstances, he'd roll on the filthy cell floor with laughter at the sight Dannan made, squished into a corner as though he were a rag doll a child had shoved into her tiny dollhouse. But right now, he was too angry.

"*What, man?*"

He grinned, wide and mischievous. "I think I have a plan."

Chapter 14

Toni latched on to Nina's arm and pulled her close, growing more worried by the second at the vampire's paler-than-pale skin. "Are you okay?"

"I'm fine. Get the fuck off me and stop doing the mother-hen shit. I get enough of that crap from Marty and Wanda. Just shut up and keep moving."

But Toni gasped, clamping her hand over her mouth.

Nina stopped dead in the middle of a long halfway that appeared to go on for a thousand miles with nothing in between the beginning and end. "Now what?"

She lifted a finger and pointed at Nina's face, her eyes going wide. "*You're lying.*"

Nina squinted at her. "Did you just call be a liar? Who the fuck do you think you are?"

Now Toni narrowed her eyes and shook her finger. "You're lying about feeling all right. The proof is in the pudding. The pudding being your nose!" She gave the end of Nina's nose, pushing farther from her face, a tweak, fighting hysterical laughter.

The vampire lifted her hand to her face and snarled. "Goddammit, Sparkly Pants, fix this!"

Toni gave her a look of innocence, throwing up her hands. "I don't know how to fix it, remember? Now stop bullshitting me and slow down. We need to get you somewhere you can rest with Carl and I'll go the rest of the way alone."

Nina grabbed Carl's harness, pulling him close. "Um, nope. You go nowhere alone, kiddo. We tag team or we call it quits. I'm the muscle, and I always have been."

"Well, here in the realm you're not so muscley, now are you? So stop being so damn difficult and let's find you a place to catch your breath."

"I don't breathe, twit."

Toni rolled her eyes and gave Nina a shove forward. "Then let's find you a place where you can *not* breathe, Crusty."

When they finally made it to the end of the hallway, they found themselves at a beautiful balcony, graced with sweeping pine boughs and red silk bows. Holly hung from the strands laden with pinecones and berries coated in glistening white sugar.

Standing on her tiptoes, Toni looked over the edge and inhaled at the sight below her. It was the ballroom. My God, it was amazing. Like every fairytale she'd ever seen come to life on a big screen.

"Oh, Nina, it's magnificent."

Tall pine trees decorated identically to the boughs on the balcony lined the entryway, where wide doors made of gleaming dark wood stood wide open. A long red carpet ran through the center of the ballroom, leading to the king's throne.

Gripping Nina's upper arm, she led her down the stairs to get a closer look. Guards stood just inside the smaller doorway in suits of armor. Tables with crystalline ice sculptures of Christmas trees dressed the tables. Torches and lanterns glowed from every available corner while a string quartet and a harpist played a soft melody.

The ballroom was alive with energy. Men in crushed red velvet coats, matching breeches and white stockings ran around the ballroom, readying the space. Fluted glasses with the castles infamous thistleberry wine sat upon sterling silver trays, balanced on the hands of their servers.

The white marble floor gleamed, the intricate pattern of Castle Beckett's crest square in the middle, drawing her eyes upward to the vaulted ceilings, where more swags of pine hung. The wide steps leading down into the ballroom were lined with bouquet after bouquet of red and white poinsettias in silver and gold urn vases, picks of pine sprays gracefully draping from them.

And it was amazing, fabulous, gorgeous. Yet, the beauty was dimmed without Jon to share it with her, dimmer still somehow by the reason she was here. If she wasn't in such a state of panic that she'd never see Jon again, she would love to soak it all in.

"Kiddo? We need to get ready to meet this King Dick. Look at the clock."

Toni's eyes flew to the grandfather clock, standing like some ominous entity just inside the ballroom doors. Five minutes until Wanda and Marty showed up and they had to prepare.

Her heart crashed against her ribs as a man with a trumpet took his place at the top of the steps. They were getting ready for announcements—which meant the king would be taking his place on the throne directly at the other end of the ballroom at any minute.

If she could just get to him before he became involved in the evening's activities, she might have a shot at finding Jon—or at least explaining her circumstance.

It had to happen as soon as possible so he could grant the women their wish to go home, at the very least. Forget about her and her happy-sappy whatever. Nina couldn't hold out much longer, and Toni would do everything in her power to make sure she saw the king ASAP.

She turned to Nina and pointed toward a potted pine tree dotted with silk bows in gold and silver just outside the ballroom doors. "Okay, you stay here and wait for Marty and Wanda. Sit on that fancy chair and don't move. I'm going to try to hit up the king before this shindig begins. Maybe he can help me find Jon."

Nina shook her head and gripped Toni's arm with the weakest grasp she'd displayed since they'd begun this whole thing. Glowering down at her, she said, "Not gonna happen. We stay together or we don't do it."

Marty and Wanda flew down the wide staircase, out of breath, their dresses floating behind them as they rushed up to them. Marty's eyes went wide when she saw her friend. "Nina! What the hell happened to your nose? Can't we leave you for five seconds?"

"Shut up, Blondie, or I'm gonna clip those wings!"

Toni ignored Nina's outburst and looked to them with hope. "Anything?"

Marty shook her head, her cheeks flushed and what looked like vanilla icing at the corner of her mouth. "No, but we heard the craziest story. Apparently that Angria who wants your head? She's got more trouble than just you, kiddo. The king called off an engagement between her daughter and the king's son, Prince Somethingorother. The cook claims that the queen's daughter was supposed to marry the prince since their births, but the king called it off because his psychic or whoever said the queen's daughter isn't his one true love. Or something like that. They say tonight is the night this psychic is supposed to reveal who the prince's true love is. Anyway, it's all the talk in the kitchens, where, I might add, they have the most fabulously moist cake I've ever stolen a swipe of frosting from."

Wanda licked her thumb and wiped Marty's mouth. "This has something to do with you, Toni. I know it does. I just can't figure out what."

Toni shook her head in confusion. "That can't be right. What do I have to do with King Dick's son? Nothing. That's what. Now, you three stay with Nina. I'm going to go find out if I can't get the king to see me so I can figure out how we might go about getting you three home, pronto." She turned to leave, but Wanda grabbed her by the arm.

"Um, no. You go nowhere alone. Are you forgetting this queen wants your head? Are you forgetting she's sent out every jackhole from here to eternity to try to stop you? I'm telling you—this little castle drama has to do with *you*. I feel it in my gut. So if we go, we go together. Marty, you stay with Nina and Carl."

Nina grabbed Toni's hand just as she was about to make her way inside the ballroom. "Listen to me, kiddo. Shit feels off. Wanda's right. I know my vampire senses are all fucked up here in Never-Never Land, but I just have this bad damn vibe I can't shake. You keep your eyes and ears open. Don't leave Wanda. Got that?"

Toni tugged one of her beautiful curls and smiled, trying to keep her hands from shaking. "Got it, Fairy Godmother."

She and Wanda clasped hands and began to fight their way into the ballroom, past the dozens and dozens of servants milling about, setting tables and fluffing flowers, while Toni tried to shake off the same bad vibe she was apparently sharing with Nina.

* * *

Just a little more," Jon urged Dannan as he reached his long fingers between the thick bars of the cell to try to retrieve the keys.

Dannan grunted as he strained to yank them from the unconscious Günter's waist.

"To the left, my friend. The left," Jon directed as he stood on top of the lone barrel in their cell, looking out into the prison's exterior.

The ogre's blue fingers swept across the dirt floor, stretching, reaching, all while he grunted.

"How did ye know about the guard's distaste for the sight of blood, ogre?"

"Ye trained with him often while I watched from the woods. When one of the lads was nicked by his opponent's sword, a mere scratch if ye were to ask me, the boy fell to the ground as if he'd been gutted like a fish when he looked upon a single drop of blood."

Jon looked down at the deep gash in his arm from Dannan's teeth, where he'd bitten him in order to draw enough blood to frighten Günter into passing out. "You bit me, Madman."

"I did. 'Twas delicious. Should I ever go back to the ways of the old order of picking humans' bones clean, I'm comin' for ye, lad," he said on another grunt as he finally got ahold of the keys. He swung them around his finger with a grin then tossed them to Jon.

Jon reached between the cell bars and unlocked it, letting it swing wide as Dannan spilled out of the cramped space with a loud moan, crashing to the hard dirt floor.

Jon dragged Günter to the far wall of the dank cellar and sat him in a corner, straightening his jacket for him before giving the guard a pat on the shoulder and muttering, "Sorry, friend. I'll make it up to you. Merry Christmas to you and yours!"

Dannan clapped him on the shoulder. "Leave him. He will recover. We must go, lad—the hour has just struck nine!"

As they made their way through the maze of the prison beneath the castle, ducking one lone guard and taking back his sword from the artillery room, Jon could only think of one thing—he would either always remember this moment because he'd won the heart of the woman he would love eternally.

Or she was going to, as Nina said, kick his ass to the curb and return to her land of Jersey without ever looking back.

* * *

Toni began to make her way through the crowd, her eye of the tiger on the king's throne, still empty. The crush of people entering the ballroom thickened, swirls of colorful dresses and men in formal jackets crowded her path as they all waited to see the king's entrance.

Wanda clung to her hand. "Slow down," she warned, just before Toni heard the soft sound of a piccolo.

She cocked her head and listened again, closing her eyes and inhaling the musical magic.

She knew it was a piccolo because in eighth-grade music, she'd been assigned one and she'd sucked monstrous balls at it. However, whoever was playing it would have garnered an A from crabby old Mr. Bartowski.

Her hand was somehow separated from Wanda's as she crowd swelled, swallowing her up and Toni followed the sound, unable to stop herself.

Maybe it was Jon? Harps were usually the instrument of choice for her True Love Top Forty, but she couldn't take a chance it wasn't him somewhere in this vast room. Maybe one's true-love tune changed when they were in someplace as grand as a castle?

So she followed the sweet strains out of the ballroom, down a long hall, powerless, mesmerized by the sound, her heart pounding in the hopes she'd find Jon and they'd fix this misunderstanding.

She was convinced that was what it had to be. But wait. Maybe he didn't hear music or see halos glowing over *her* head. Maybe he was her true love and she wasn't his?

Yet, suddenly, it didn't matter. The beautiful tune lulled her, pulled her toward it until she was in a room with a man standing in the shadows cast by long curtains hanging from the floor to ceiling windows, the silhouette of his piccolo evident in the dim lighting.

"Jon?" she asked, knowing it was ridiculous. This wasn't Jon. He was too portly, his jaw too slack.

He spun fully around, letting the piccolo in his hand fall to his side. He puffed out his chest and smiled at her, drawing her to him without saying a word.

Her feet began to tingle, making her question who this man actually was, but his smile was so serene, his face warm and inviting, that she couldn't help but move closer.

He bowed regally, his silver-white hair gleaming, his sweet blue eyes twinkling when he raised his head. "Welcome, milady. I am Sir Kenneth in the Key of G. And you are?"

She did a clumsy curtsy, reaching for the back of a chair to steady herself as she wobbled. She really needed to work on her curtsy. "Toni

Vitali," she murmured, hearing the words escape her lips, but they sounded foggy and muted.

"'Tis a pleasure. I hope you'll enjoy my happy tune," he said before placing the piccolo to his mouth and playing another melody.

As he played, he wound his way out of the room, his feet light, his white stockings almost a beckoning beacon.

Toni couldn't look away. The tingle in her own feet roared, yet it only felt like a distant nudge, one she successfully ignored as she followed Sir Kenneth, needing him to continue playing—to continue feeding her this amazing gift as it floated around her.

Her eyes glazed over as his back became blurry, tilting and swerving along another long hallway. Yet, she continued in his wake, compelled to reach him, but he only seemed to get farther away.

No! He couldn't get away. This music gave her life. She *needed* it!

The music began to whirl around her, as though it had become a wave and she was driftwood lost at sea, bobbing, weaving. The melody took her to a place she was almost sure she didn't want to go, but couldn't seem to stop herself from propelling forward toward.

And then the melodic, mournful tune stopped completely, and so did her feet.

When the haze cleared and her eyes focused, she had one thought as she scanned the room.

The fucking Pied Piper. Goddamn it! She might not have her fairytales entirely straight, but she knew this one. He'd led her like some lost lamb straight to the lion's den.

A maniacal cackle grew until it bounced off the room's walls, and then a husky, sultry voice said, "I've got you now, my pretty. I've been waiting for you!"

* * *

"Wanda!" Jon managed to grab her arm as he pushed his way through the throng of incoming guests, keeping his face tucked into the hood of his cloak.

She whirled around, her bell-shaped dress swaying, her wings fluttering. "Jon! Oh, thank God. Where have you been and why are your clothes dirty and torn?"

"'Tis a long story—one I shall share with you all as soon as I can. Where's Toni?" he asked, his eyes scanning the vast room frantically for his beloved.

Wanda gripped his arm, her eyes filled with a worry he didn't like. "I've lost her! She was going to try to see the king before our appointment to ask after you, but I lost her in the crowd. I don't know where she is and I'm panicked!"

Marty flanked him as she rushed up and gave him a hurried hug. "Where the hell have you been, Prince Charming? You had us all worried, not to mention Toni's beside herself. Speaking of, where is our fair maiden? It's almost time to greet the king."

Nina knocked him with a weak fist between the shoulder blades. "Dude! Why you gotta create so much drama? Jesus. Is it that hard for all of us to get this shit together? Lemme be clear—we need to stick the fuck together, Flawless!"

Jon gave them a quick bow. "My deepest apologies, maidens. We were thwarted by the king's guards, and I promise to tell you all about it, but for now, we must find Toni."

But horns began to blare a familiar blast of announcement, sounding out the king and queen's arrival.

As the crowd parted, hushing in reverence, King Dick and Queen Jane appeared at the top of the long staircase and, arm and arm, they made their way down.

Wanda gripped his arm, leaving him no choice but to stay right where he was as the royal couple proceeded down the stairs and moved toward the throne.

He let his eyes fall to the floor, waiting until the couple passed before he tried to move silently away from the crowd. But Marty clung to his other arm, her grip literally like steel. If her powers were weakened here in the realm, then he was but a mewling kitten compared to them.

"Stay put, buddy. I'm not getting my head chopped off because you committed some royal faux pas. Plus, hello. A real live king and queen!"

He would laugh if things weren't so dire—because on cue, Prince Iver Daring appeared at the top of the stairs, ready to make his descent to his chair beside the king and queen.

As he did, moving slowly down the procession aisle, his coat gleaming under the light of the torches, his hair pulled back from his face in an ebony ponytail, it wasn't until he was just a hair past them when all three women gasped.

And that was when Nina grabbed him by his shirtfront, lifting him high in the air, her face a mask of anger as she yelped, "Who the fuck are you, Jon Doe?"

Chapter 15

Long fingernails scraped beneath her chin, their tips digging into Toni's flesh as she tried not to wince. She lifted her chin, looking up and asked, "Queen Angria, I presume?"

The queen stepped backward a few feet and tossed her crowned, inky-black head on her shoulders, laughing again, that same bone-rattling masterpiece of a cackle she'd screeched just before she'd waved her spidery fingers in the air and glued Toni to the chair she was now unable to move from.

The queen's razor-thin black eyebrow rose haughtily, the high collar of her silk gown just grazing her pointed chin. "My name precedes me, eh?" she asked, her voice husky, her words precise.

She swept back across the room, the tail of her black and deep-purple dress following in her wake, to stand before Toni, searing her with her gaze.

Toni lifted her chin, her eyes narrowing as she tried to peek over the enormous skirt of her dress. Yet, she wasn't afraid. Why wasn't she afraid?

"Well, your henchmen do, anyway. You sure don't kid around when you want something, do you? Dragons and Starbucks and truth fairies and smelly guys with glowing eyes. Heh. That rhymes. Anyway, it was a lot. Just so you know, you have the market cornered on creepy employees. Anyway, let's cut to the chase. What do you want from me? I never got to the part where I had a conversation with any of your bad guys so we could discuss your terms. It was all rawr, and hiss, and poof, you're now the Truth Fairy."

"Your head, of course," she drawled long and low, as she ran a fingertip over the surface of a shined-to-perfection tabletop next to the chair Toni was pinned to, dragging her hand as though she were deep in thought.

"Because?"

"Because I was told just this day by a spy here in the castle that you, my interfering guttersnipe, are the face of the prince's one true love!"

Toni squinted in confusion, blowing the material of her bell-shaped skirt out of her face as it rose again. So this wasn't about the shoes? And hold the damn phone. The prince didn't even know her, and she sure as hell didn't know him. This was ridiculous. Again, more piss-poor miscommunication.

"You Shamalotians need phones so this won't keep happening."

"A what?"

Toni rolled her eyes in otherworld frustration. "It's this thing you talk into. You dial it, it rings, someone picks it up on the other end and you communicate without all this back-and-forth nonsense. I think everything would go much more smoothly if you could just give each other a call. For instance, you could have just called me and told me what all this was about."

"'Twould not matter if I called you on this phone or sent a message by horny toad. The answer would still be the same. *You* are the prince's true love!" she screamed in outrage.

"Horny toads carry messages? Is that like Shamalot's version of carrier pigeons?"

"Shut up with your endless prattle before I behead you here and now and watch your blood spill at my feet!"

"Whoa, Nellie. Easy there. Now, just say that one more time. Because I think I missed the impact of the statement. I'm the prince's *what?*" she asked, still absorbing this new information.

"The prince's one true love, moron!" she bellowed with agitation, gripping the sides of her lush gown in white-knuckled fists. "The Great and Wonderful Roz saw your face in her mirror, and that soft-in-the-middle King Dick took her advice. I have it on good word it was *you* the prince will spend the rest of his days with. The king sent my Resplendant away as though we'd never bartered at their births to merge our lands via marriage!"

The Great and Wonderful Roz? Priceless. Really. This predicament was priceless. And she'd laugh, because one of the only things on her body she could move was her lips anyway, but she had a sneaking suspicion she was going to die if she went too far.

Instead, she attempted to sympathize with the queen. "And who's the Great and Wonderful Roz? Is she the authority on true love? Did she perfect the art of matchmaking and I missed it?"

"She's the king's advisor, his oracle, and whatever that crony says, he does. Without thought!"

Toni popped her lips. "Ahh. Got it. I understand your frustration. So does the prince love your daughter Splendid?"

The queen's eyes lit up, almost rolling to the back of her head. *Resplendant!* And it doesn't matter who the prince loves, you simpleton! It only matters that on the advice of some doddering, centuries-old woman, the king has canceled our contract because he wants his son to be," she made air quotes, "*happy*," she said on an eye roll as she began to pace the length of the room in quick, fiery steps.

"Okay, so here's a thought, and it's one I've considered often when it comes to you villains in a fairytale. Why not just communicate? I mean, say you invite King Dick over for a cocktail. Something holiday-like. Egg nog, a candy cane martini, maybe. Then you sit, you chat, maybe you make some weenies in a blanket, because food really is the universal language, right? Then you do something totally crazy, like say, 'Hey, KD, you made a deal with me. I don't like that you broke your promise. It makes my feelings all hurty.' Then he responds by saying, 'I'm sorry, Angria. I wasn't being very sensitive to your feelings, was I?' There'll be a lot of ye's and 'tis's and whatever, but you get the general picture, right? Why does everything have to be all-out war? It's Christmas, for the love of Cheetos. Peace. Love. Harmony."

The queen raced across the floor toward her, her heels clacking against the hard marble in her mad dash. She bashed down Toni's skirt with a fist, effectively crushing her crinoline.

"Are you mad? He humiliated my daughter! He refuses to budge. That mealy-mouthed mule sent me a message via my liege, and told me my beautiful Resplendant is not the proper wife for Price Iver, and he won't have any son of his unhappy for eternity. He will not move an inch! Thus, you must be beheaded before his very eyes!"

"Is the prince's name really Iver?" Toni asked on a giggle-snort. "Who wants to marry a guy named Iver, anyway? Do you really want to look across your Thanksgiving table, which I'm sure is fabulous, and call your son-in-law *Iver?*"

"*Shut up!*" she screeched in Toni's face, shaking the crystal chandelier in the center of the ceiling. "You will pay for this! Everyone will pay. All of Shamalot will see its bitter end when I'm done!"

Toni refused to cower, but wow, this woman was scary with all her white teeth, shiny red lips, and glittering angry eyes. "But wait! What if I told you I love someone else? What if I told you I don't even know who Prince Iver is? What if I told you I don't even come from this time, and I can leave and go back home and then you can force the king to allow your daughter to marry the prince?"

That stopped her dead in her tracks. "*What?*"

Toni licked her lips while she tried to move, but she was cemented to the damn chair. "It's true! I'll hit the road, sayonara, later gator. The king can't make Prince Whatever marry me if I'm outtie, right? We just remove the problem and poof, instant marriage and land and whatever else it is you want."

The queen straightened; her spine so stiff Toni thought it might crack. "What maiden in her right senses wouldn't want the riches of the king?"

Now Toni rolled her eyes hard with a grating sigh. "*This* maiden, lady. I'm good with TV dinners and a drippy showerhead forever if it means I get to live. I've been beaten down, spit at, yelled at, punched, dumped in the ocean, knocked out, wore these damn uncomfortable shoes for miles and miles in more snow than I think Siberia's ever seen. I'm happy to hit the road if it means—"

She snatched up Toni's right foot, effectively silencing her. Swirling a finger along her calf, Angria eyeballed the sparkly purple shoe, still as perfect as when she'd first been forced to wear them.

Her eyes went from wonder to a narrowed pair of slits in her head. "These shoes? Where did you get them?"

Toni fought to keep her face impassive. She really didn't know about the shoes? Who was she kidding? They didn't even really know anything concrete about the shoes either, other than they'd guessed the shoes allowed her to absorb her foes powers.

But they didn't know that for sure. Still, she felt a little smug the queen was blissfully unaware, and she needed to keep it that way for just a little longer.

"I said, where did you get the shoes?" Angria demanded.

"Um, Brenda, the Good Witch of the South. She y'alled 'em right onto my feet."

"And what do they do?" she drawled, her interest clearly aroused as she squeezed Toni's foot.

Now Toni smiled, her grin wide and accommodating as she pointed her toe to show off the shoe. She just might stand a chance at getting out of here and warning the king he was about to see his kingdom crumble because he'd made a stupid decision.

"Wanna see?" she asked, all sweetness and light.

The queen lifted her sharp chin and dropped Toni's foot, sucking in her cheeks. "*Show me.*"

Hell yeah. "You bet," she said affably.

Toni cleared her throat and rolled her head on her neck to work out the kinks. Opening her mouth wide, she inhaled and exhaled with slow precision—before the burn of a stream of fire rose upward and exploded from her throat in billowing fashion.

She aimed the flames directly at the queen, spraying her thoroughly. Queen Angria fell to the floor with a howl, her black and purple dress splaying out behind her.

"*I'll kill youuuuuu!*" she bellowed, shaking the entire room as she threw her hands over her face to shield herself.

As if she hadn't heard *that* before.

But lucky for Toni, as Angria fought the flames, she also released the spell gluing her to the chair, giving her a chance to make her escape.

Lunging from the chair, she bolted toward the door, hoping against hope she could find her way back to the ballroom to warn the king that Angria was here and on the warpath.

* * *

The entire ballroom stopped all motion as Nina lifted Jon high in the air and demanded an answer, her arm trembling. "I said, *who. The. Fuck. Are. You?*"

Marty and Wanda grabbed at Nina's arms. "Put him down, Nina!" they yelled in unison.

But Nina wasn't letting go, and his warrior's heart, despite the dire circumstance, smiled. First, it meant she still had a bit of her strength. Second, she was fiercely loyal, unafraid to protect her own, and Toni had become one of hers by circumstance. If Toni chose to return to her homeland, she would be well cared for.

Gripping her wrists, Jon looked down at her from the shelter of his hooded jacket, keeping his voice calm, his eyes steady. "Please put me down, Pale One, so you do not tax yourself, and I shall explain."

Nina gave him a good hard shake before she let go of him, dropping him on the floor in a heap as she said with a sneer, "You damn well better, you piece o' royal shit. Why do you look exactly—and I don't just mean a little, I mean *exactly*—like the damn guy in the fancy pants and stupid knee-highs?"

"My stockings are not stupid! Arrest her for—for—I don't know for what!" the prince shouted in a bluster of red cheeks and spittle flying from his mouth. "Just arrest her for insulting me!"

The king turned with a sharp pivot of his foot just as the prince issued the order, stopping the procession toward his throne. The crowd all turned to stare in Jon's vicinity, their eyes wide.

This was the very reason Jon had been avoiding this Christmas Eve. He'd hoped to do this quietly, privately. Alas, nothing was going quite the way he'd planned.

Wanda jammed a finger under his nose, her ivory wings feverishly flapping her ire. "I knew it! I knew there was something just a little off about you, Hot Pants. Not something bad, but something off, and I'm never wrong," she yelled, yanking him to his feet. "What gives, Flawless?"

Marty crossed her arms over her chest and nodded her head vehemently. "'Rucy, you got some splainin' to do."

"Who are you? Remove your cloak's hood and reveal yourself!" the king shouted, barging through the crowd to stand before Jon as the queen and the prince followed behind, their eyes peering over his shoulder.

Jon instantly bowed, sweeping his arm across his midsection. "My apologies for disturbing your festivities, Sire."

"Rise!" the king thundered as his guards surrounded him on the chance Jon was a threat.

Jon did as he was bade, standing to face the king, his jaw clenched, his determination in place for what was about to come. He pushed the hood from his head.

And then the king gasped, as did the queen.

Aka, Mom and Dad.

His mother clutched the glittering jewelry at her long neck with a gloved hand, her eyes wide, her ageless face full of horror. *"Who are you?"* she hissed.

Well, if he was ever going to, as Marty said, shoot his wad, it would be now. "I am Prince Iver Daring, firstborn of King Dick and Queen Jane of the beloved Shamalot."

Chapter 16

You could have heard a pin drop, but only for seconds before the crowd burst into a ripple of gasps.

Toni's mouth fell open as she hung over the balcony, watching Jon's confession unfold. And as it did, everything made sense. His chivalry, his immaculate manners, the slip Muriel had made with his name, how sad he'd been about missing his family, those obligations he'd talked about.

All of it.

She was going to kill him. Gut him with his stupid sword of wrath. Because what Queen Angria had said was true—she really *was* the love of the real prince's life, and *her* life had been in imminent danger because he was off playing Robin Hood, Prince of Stealing Other People's Identities.

"You lie!" the fake prince yelled, pointing to his ruffled chest. "*I* am Prince Iver Daring!"

Jon shook his head, his expression full of sorrow as he clapped the fake prince on the shoulder. "Nay, Jon. There is no reason to play the part any longer. You had us locked in a cell to keep us from the inevitable happening. I know it was your fear that made you respond as such. You somehow found out about our arrival, and you did not want to risk being exposed. Was that not the way?"

The prince waffled, his face, so identical to Jon's going red, but he remained silent.

"'Tis as I thought. But now we must tell the truth, Jon Doe. Would you lose Resplendant, the love of your life for all time by pretending you are something you are not? Do riches mean more to your heart than true love? Do you wish to be wed to someone you do not love? Isn't that how this whole adventure started? Because I did not wish to be wed to someone I did not love."

The prince waffled, his eyes straying to the king and queen in guilt, but he didn't appear to be backing down. He was staying in character to the bitter end. "He lies, I say! Guards, arrest him!"

The slice of steel in the air as the guards drew their swords made Toni scream, "No!"

An old woman from the far corner of the room, wearing a magnificent coat in red crushed velvet lined with white fur and a hood shadowing her face, pointed upward, her wrinkled finger aimed at Toni. "It's her! Price Iver's one true love!"

The crowd gasped again, followed by murmurs and whispers behind their gloved hands.

She watched as Jon's eyes flew upward to meet hers, his face a mixture of relief and guilt and more relief.

But she wasn't having any of it. He'd lied to her. Boy, had he lied, big time.

She narrowed her gaze in his direction and jabbed a finger in the air. "Oh, Jon Doe or whoever you are, are you in for a rash of shit from me! All this time you had me believing you were some simple reindeer farmer and you're a *prince*? What was it you asked me just yesterday? If I could stay here with you, would living with a poor farmer make me happy? Yep! That's what you asked me, Reindeer Whisperer. Was it some kind of test to see if you could get someone to fall in love with you if you were poor? You *lied to me*, buddy, and you owe me an explanation!" she called from the balcony as she raced toward the first few steps of the staircase, only to have the guards stop her.

Nina pushed her way from the edge of the throng of people and ran up the steps. "You hurt one little hair on her red head, I eat you!" She leered in the face of a guard, who shrank back from the flash of her fangs.

Jon moved from the crowd, but the guards grabbed his arms, too. "You know 'tis not true, Toni. I have been gone from the castle for nigh on a year now. This plan was set in motion long before I knew you. Just ask *him*," he said sarcastically, thumbing his hand at the prince—who wasn't really the prince.

Oy.

"Silence!" the king roared upward, shaking his gold scepter, his jewel-encrusted crown rocking on his dark head as guards grabbed Toni's arms, thwarting her descent. "You will all be silent until I command that you speak!"

Jon stopped straining against the guards, as did Toni, but the second she got the chance to give him a good tongue lashing, he'd better take cover.

"Now, I would ask that you offer me an explanation," King Dick said, peering at Jon. "Who are you and how dare you use this sacred night for such deceit?"

Yeah. How dare ye!

Jon looked to the king, remorse in his sapphire eyes, but he lifted his jaw high with clear pride. "I did not plan it this way, Father. I ask that you hear my story before you judge, and then you may do with me as you see fit. But in the process, I ask that you spare the real Jon Doe your wrath. He is not guilty of this caper. 'Twas I who convinced him. "

The king crossed his arms over his gold-and-white jacket, his lips, so like Jon's, thinning. He rolled his hand. "Carry on," he ordered curtly.

Jon shrugged the guards off to stand before his parents. "I did not wish to marry Resplendant, Father. We are all wrong for each other. Still, I knew the merger you made with her mother was important to you. So one day, whilst in the woods pondering thus, I met Jon Doe. Neither of us could believe how uncanny 'twas that we looked so much alike. As we talked, I came to discover he and Resplendant were deeply in love. Yet, Queen Angria would not hear of a peasant marrying her royal daughter. They hid their love, and I saw the pain in his eyes. The timing was, as one would say, exceptional and uncanny. So we struck a deal to switch places…"

"And?" asked the queen, beautifully regal and blonde.

"And I knew this was what I must do. I would rather be a poor farmer than marry a woman I do not love. Surely you understand that, Mother? My heart does not twist in my chest when I see Resplendant's face, beautiful as she is. My wish to share a moment of wonder or a happy tale is not one I wish to share with her. 'Twas that not what you claimed was true love? Did you not feel that way about Father? 'Tis unfair to allow Resplendant to marry a man who will never love her the way she so deserves. Do you not remember the story you told me of true love's kiss?"

Queen Jane gave him a guarded glance as she circled him. "All this time…" she murmured, and then her eyes, the exact color of Jon's, opened wide. "I could not place my finger on it, for you are identical." She turned to the fake prince then. "Yet, my heart did not know yours. This—*this* explains it all."

Jon gripped his mother's hands and pulled them to his lips. "Do you understand what I speak, Mother? I did not wish for this life you and Father settled upon with the queen before I was even born. And I did not wish to deceive you, but I was left no choice, and Jon would have been a fair ruler. I would have seen to it myself. Yet, I am no good as future ruler of Shamalot if I am unhappy in the most important relationship of my life. Father preaches of balance between ruling the kingdom and his life with you. And finally," he paused, his eyes finding Toni's across the room. "Though I have missed you both, I cannot—will not marry Resplendant when I love another."

Toni's heart melted just a little. Not a lot, because he was still a lying jerk, and he'd kept it from her even when they'd finally gotten to the castle and then made her worry herself sick when she couldn't find him. But if anyone understood not wanting a life thrust upon you by someone else's hand, it was her.

He moved through the crowd, taking the steps two at a time until he reached her, and the guards backed away. "I do not know what will happen this night when you return the shoes. I do not know if Jersey is where your true happiness lies. I only know *my* true happiness lies with you. Always *you*."

In that moment, that beautiful, perfect, harps-playing-in-the-background moment, Toni knew, too. She knew, no matter what it took, she wanted to be with this man forever.

For always.

She lunged for him, throwing her arms around his neck, latching on to his lips as he wrapped his arms around her and held her tight, kissing her soundly.

The people of Shamalot cheered as Nina slapped Jon on the back, and Marty, Wanda, Dannan, and Carl rushed up the stairs to hug them.

"My shoes!" the king cried from the foot of the staircase, racing toward them, losing his crown along the way.

Toni slid from Jon's embrace, dropping to the step. "Yes. Your shoes. Brenda the Good Witch of the South sends her love." She curtsied, rather awkwardly, but the good intention was there.

The king assessed her with critical eyes, strutting along the step in all his gold-and-white embroidered finery, the ruffles on his shirtfront billowing. He stopped to stare down at her, his face a more mature version of his son's.

"Who is this woman who has been called your one true love, son?" King Dick asked, one eyebrow raised.

Jon smiled, his arm firmly about Toni's waist as he introduced her to his father. "This is Lady Anonia Vitali, Father. From the land of Jersey."

A rumble of thunder interrupted their introductions, shaking the urns filled with flowers.

Oh shit.

In all the excitement of finding out who Jon really was, she'd totally forgotten about Angria.

"Save the introductions for later—we have trouble!" she yelled, just as a screeching fireball sailed across the ballroom.

King Dick looked surprised, but he immediately grabbed a sword from one of his guards. "Who dares bring chaos to this night?" he asked his son as the stairs began to buckle and moan.

Toni grabbed the king's hand and began to drag him from the staircase as they started to crumble in angry shifts, cracking, collapsing, sputtering.

"Angria is here and boy, is she pissed at you!" she yelled to him.

They raced down the steps, Toni pulling the king as Jon called her name and threw the knife he kept in his boot to her before running for his mother and the fake prince, bundling them off with the guards in order to protect them.

"Where-oh-where are you, true love of Prince Iver?" a voice bellowed, echoing throughout the room. "Show me your face, so that I might remove it from your head for hurting my precious baby girl!"

As people began to scream and scatter in hordes, Toni pinpointed the source of all her trouble since she'd come to Shamalot.

Angria rose from the far shadowy corner, a dark, beautiful figure with crimson lips, dressed in deep purple and black, her arms outstretched, her hands clenched in tight fists. She changed, grew in size just like Pricilla had, twisting her body until she was a massive version of herself.

She swept her arm in a graceful arc, bringing with it a wave of fire. Setting the curtains ablaze, zigzagging across the room, illuminating the walls with its hot ire.

Marty screeched in anger as flying embers zapped her wings and caught fire while she ran toward Angria, attempting to shift into her werewolf form.

She half-morphed, the thrust of her skull and muzzle thwarting as though stuck; yet her hindquarters appeared, strong and lean as they ate up the floor. Marty howled, a long, frustrated, feral sound ripping from her throat.

God, they were getting weaker by the second.

"Marty! Stop! Drop! Roll!!" Wanda cried, grabbing glasses of thistleberry wine and launching the contents at Marty's wings, shoving her to the ground and rolling her until the fire was out.

King Dick flashed his sword, the steel glinting under the torches as he went on attack, rushing Queen Angria, slicing the air, his movements quick. But they weren't quick enough. The queen scooped him up in her hand, curling him into her palm and throwing him against the wall.

"Father!" Jon yelled, dodging a piece of the ceiling.

Carl, smack in the center of the room, leaned back on his reindeer haunches and shot forward, aiming straight for the queen's legs. She raised her free arm, spreading her fingers and flicking them at Carl. Icicles with sharp, pointy tips pinged through the air like frosty knives, aimed right at him.

Toni's stomach clenched, knowing she'd never make it to him in time. In her frustration, she set her sights on instead attempting to melt the icicles with her flames, inhaling and letting out the biggest stream of fire she could summon.

"Carl, my lad! Duck!" Jon ordered as he charged from out of nowhere at Carl, managing to knock him out of the way just as the icicles hit the wall, embedding themselves in a brocade tapestry.

Dannan appeared at the balcony's railing, now crumbling and cracked, his helium-filled voice full of anguish when he shouted a warning to Jon. "Behind you, lad!" he belted out as the balcony shuddered and he crashed to the ground, cracking the marble floor.

Toni's eyes flew to Jon just as the crystal chandelier above them let go, dropping from the ceiling, swinging wildly to and fro and headed straight for the man she loved.

She ran toward him, tripping over chunks of wall and slipping on the water from the melting ice sculptures, sliding and cracking her head against a heavy toppled chair.

Just as she was about to push her way up from the floor, Jon roared a triumphant cry, as he ran and leapt for the chandelier, grabbing the weighty chains that once mounted it to the ceiling, directing them and riding them straight toward Angria.

Using his feet, he rammed the bottom of his boots up under her chin, knocking her backward momentarily, but that didn't slow her down for long.

As the queen recovered from the blow, she rose up bigger, higher, filling the ballroom with her presence until it seemed there was nothing but her in the room. Her howl of fury filling the space, forcing pictures to fly from walls and candelabras to crash to the ground.

And then it happened.

Okay, so it wasn't flying monkeys, but close enough.

Hundreds of black bats with almost human-like heads, their wings humming in a racquet of sound, swirled in circles, diving, plucking at the air until they began to dive-bomb like an ebony swarm of aerialists.

"Bibbidi-bobbidi-boo!" Angria screamed.

A batch of them zeroed in on Nina, snatching a bluebird from her hair and lobbing it almost across the room.

"You motherfuckerrrrrrs! I'll drain you bastards dry!" she screamed, racing after the bluebird, scooping it up and shoving it down the front of her dress.

But Toni noted with panic, through the haze of black-as-night wings flapping furiously, Nina was just a little slower than she had been even earlier today. Her gait was sluggish even though she jumped into the fray, balls to the wall, as the bats attacked.

They began scratching at her flesh with their claws, tearing, ripping small holes in her skin while she howled her anger.

Wanda screamed, too, as the bats soared around her, tearing at her wings. She opened her mouth wide and roared, her fangs flashing, her face distorting as tufts of hair sprung from her face and arms.

But she couldn't shift fully any more than Marty could; it was as though the longer they stayed in Shamalot, the weaker they grew.

"Wanda, get out of the way!" Toni screeched just before inhaling again and spraying the bats with a stream of molten fire.

"Her heart, milady!" Dannan bellowed over the noise of the squealing bats, using the king's dropped scepter to swat at them. "You must get Angria's heart to stop her!"

Toni stopped then, right in the middle of the madness, as the bats and the women screamed in unison, as the walls fell about her and the room turned from magical to a nightmare.

Her heart? How the hell was she going to get her heart?

Seriously?

But Toni's body said, *Hello in there, Sissy-Pants. You killed a GD dragon while riding on his back. And let's not forget, you whacked the head off a sea bitch. Surely you can figure out a way to get your hands on an organ.*

Now her mind? Well, it had other ideas. *Are you fucking nuts? Did you lose every last brain cell you ever had back in that damn forest? The queen's ten times the size of you and she's got a bag o' tricks that even David Copperfield would envy. She'll jack you up so hard you'll feel it in the afterlife. Like Wanda said. Stop, drop and roll right on outta here, kid!*

No. This time she would not run away. No matter what happened, she would not let someone else have control over her life.

Not. This. Time.

Angria rose again, like some demented Thanksgiving Day parade float, wavering back and forth, swiping her arms above her, directing the bats in a bizarre dance just before a bitter wind began to rip through the room and chunks of glacial ice crashed to what was left of the ballroom floor.

Racing toward a very weak Nina, Toni ducked the falling ice while Marty and Wanda made an attempt to stop Angria by hacking at the knees—literally, with swords they'd grabbed from the fallen guards who'd unsuccessfully attempted to stop her.

Toni skidded into Nina, who wobbled and gripped her arms. "Listen to me!" she yelled to the bedraggled vampire above the noise. "I have an idea. When I say go, help knock her down. Do you still have the energy?"

Nina's mouth twisted in pain, her eyes riddled with the agony of her lack of nourishment. "No, kiddo, don't try anything crazy!"

"Nina! Trust me, please. I trusted you, now you have to trust me! On the word go!" she bellowed as she yanked her arm from the vampire's and ran, waving her hands at Jon.

Jon swiped his sword at Angria, striking uselessly at her midsection.

"Jon! Go for her legs! Get Marty and Wanda and Dannan and knock her down!" she hollered to him, dropping to the floor where the king was sprawled.

She dragged him upward out of the line of fire, sweat pouring down her face, shivering violently from the merciless wind and snow pelting at every inch of her exposed flesh. "King Dick, stay out of the way. Stay right here," she ordered, spitting her hair from her face.

"Nay! I shall help!" he said, giving her a shove. "Go! I'll aim for her legs as instructed!"

Dannan came crashing toward her then, his suspenders hanging from his big body, his arms and chest covered in gashes, his sword swinging.

"Dannan! Pick me up!" She held her arms up to him and as he ran by, he scooped her up, tucking her to his chest.

"Milady, what do ye plan?"

"I need to knock her down to get to her chest!" she yelled, pressing a quick kiss to his cheek. "Don't fight me on this, just throw me right at her head and then take the bitch down! Be safe! On the word go, okay?"

As they neared Angria, her hands throwing out one torture after another at them, her eyes wild with hate, Toni sent up a little prayer.

Dear Realm,

I could really use a win. Whatever you want, take it—even if it means taking me.

Preparing her body for launch, she yelled to everyone, "Gooo!"

Dannan dropped his sword midstride and grabbed her at the waist, propelling her at Angria's head.

Toni landed on her shoulders with a thud, her heels sinking into the queen's flesh, her feet finding that familiar tingle. She grabbed her hair, knocking the queen's heavy crown to the floor in the process. As it crashed and broke into golden pieces, Nina, Marty, Wanda, Jon, King Dick, and

Dannan all began hacking at Angria's legs as though they were chopping trees.

Angria screamed her outrage, rearing her head back while Toni hung on to her slick black hair, bellowing a long, furious howl as the queen began falling to the ground.

Pulling the knife from between her breasts with one hand, slipping down along her shoulder, Toni clung to the front of the queen's gown and, when she landed with a thud, debris flying up all around them from the impact, she raised her arms high, gripping the long knife, preparing to sink the steel deep into her heart.

The queen's irate eyes rolled to the back of her head, her mouth opening wide as she wailed a protest just as Toni lifted the knife to embed it in her flesh.

In that crucial moment, the queen's arm rose, her fingers sprouting long, brittle nails, preparing to swipe Toni.

But Jon screamed a warning in sync with Dannan. She saw Jon run toward the queen's hand, waving his arms at her. "Toni, no!" he hollered in a raw cry of anguish, just before he struck the air with his sword, narrowly missing the queen's arm and falling in front of her sharp claws.

Everything happened in slow motion for Toni then.

Dannan toppled, skidding across the floor on his butt and crashing into a wall, his head snapping back and forward before lolling to the side.

But it was seeing Jon, thrown high into the air, deep gashes of crimson across his neck and chest, that made Toni scream her fury, cry out in utter despair.

She saw Nina hiss from the corner of her eye, heard her scream the word "No!" as she flashed her fangs just before sinking them deeply into the queen's neck. She fell backward to the floor, collapsing against the broken marble.

Angria reared her head back and screeched a mournful wail as Marty and Wanda used their swords to slice her head off.

With everything Toni had, she rammed the knife into Angria's chest, plunging deeply, using her legs to push the blade in as far into her as she could, until only the carved handle was left exposed.

The queen's body shrunk right before her eyes, shriveling and trembling until she returned to her former size.

A sneer crossed her lips as Toni used her last ounce of energy to widen the wound with the blade, driving her hand into the queen's chest, her anguished cry echoing throughout the decimated ballroom when she pushed her way through bone and vessels and blood and yanked the queen's heart out, throwing it to the ground with a sob.

Her shoulders slumped as sorrow sank in, deep and gnawing, making her body weak, her bones melt as she fell from the queen's bloated body to the floor and scrambled to reach for Jon's lifeless hand.

She gripped it tight, tears pouring from her eyes.

So close.

She'd been so close

Chapter 17

Toni blinked, her gaze taking in the disaster area the ballroom had become. Flowers, torn to shreds and wilted, covered the floor, ice melted in enormous puddles filled with chunks of marble and broken candlesticks.

The grandfather clock lay on its side, smashed, its springs spilling from the guts of its body. Dannan's big blue frame was crumpled in a corner, unmoving after the blow he'd taken when he'd tried to distract Angria for Jon.

The queen's body had disappeared into the ether, and Toni was glad for it, or she might have been tempted to fry her to a crisp.

And she still held Jon's hand—or the real Prince Iver's hand—and that was all she needed, she thought, as she lay unmoving amidst the rubble.

She gripped Jon's cold, unmoving fingers tight, refusing to let go as tears filled her eyes. He'd taken the hit for her, taken it like the stand-up guy he was, and she was never letting go.

She'd stay on this damn floor until she rotted and Angria's mutated bats picked the flesh from her bones, but she wasn't letting go. She'd failed him. She couldn't bear that she'd failed him.

"Dannan? Please say he's all right?" she asked on a croak to anyone who cared to answer.

"He's okay. Still breathing, just passed out. Now, kiddo...I need you to hear me," Nina said, kneeling on the floor next to her, her pale face haggard as she leaned over Toni's body to look down at her, her eyes full of anguish and weary with exhaustion. "Let go of him. *Please* let go."

But she shook her head. They likely all thought she was insane, but she didn't care. She would never let go. "No. No, I won't. I finally found somewhere to be, *someone* to be with, and I'm not leaving him. I left once. I won't do it again."

Marty muffled a sob, her hair topsy-turvy, her once-beautiful lavender dress all but hanging off her body. "Sweetie, give me your hand. You're not making sense right now. You'll come back with us. I swear to you, Toni, we'll take care of you. You'll come to Buffalo. You'll stay at the house with me and Keegan and Hollis. Eventually, you'll work at Pack—that's our cosmetic company. You'll be amazing. Harry, my brother-in-law who works in accounting, will train you. He'll love you, too. I know it hurts right now, honey. I know it hurts almost more than you think you can bear, but we'll help. You'll never be without us. Please, Toni. Please let go."

Wanda was there then, her perfect face covered in smudges of soot, her hair lopsided and mashed to her face, her dress sodden from the snow.

She brushed Toni's hair from her eyes with a trembling hand. "Honey, listen to me. Please, *please* listen. We have to go. It's going to be okay. Not now. Not a month from now, maybe not even a year from now, but someday...someday it *will* be okay. It will. I'll make sure it will. Arch will cook for you. He'll coddle you. He'll *love* you. Darnell will sit with you. He'll take walks with you. He'll rock you until you fall asleep on my porch swing. But you have to let go. I'm begging you, come back with us."

Carl sat down on his haunches, letting his front legs slide forward until he was resting against Toni's side, his chin on her arm. He whimpered, nudging her, and still she held Jon's hand.

Nina hooked her arms under Toni's and pulled with a grunt, her tug weak. "Come with us, Toni. I'll do whatever you need."

"Will you be my BFF?" she asked weakly, tears gushing from her eyes and streaming down her face.

"Forever and ever. Swear it on Marty's life."

"Will you braid my hair? Talk to me for hours on the phone while we watch *The Bachelor?*"

Nina nodded in earnest, giving up on trying to move Toni. "I'll do sleepovers and fucking hair salon appointments, and GD shopping until your legs fall off. We'll see rom-coms till your flippin' eyes bleed, but you have to come with me now. We need to see the king and go home."

"I...I can't," she managed to husk out without sobbing.

"You can. You fucking will. The hell I'm leaving you here," Nina insisted, sitting back from her kneeling position to flop on the floor tiredly.

199

She gripped Toni's free hand and pressed it to her stone-cold cheek before setting it in her lap. *"You can."*

Marty placed her hand over Nina's, and Wanda repeated the act. They held her hand that way for what seemed like forever, stroking her fingers, whispering to her, soothing her.

"Why do you sit upon the floor when the prince's life hangs in the balance?" someone asked with an outraged yelp.

"Lady, shut the fuck up. I don't know who the hell you are, but Jesus and fuck, we've been through some shit here, okay? Nothing's hanging in the balance. Now blow," Toni heard Nina say before she caught sight of an elderly woman.

"Are you mad?" the woman wailed, making a fist of her wrinkled hands and wringing them.

"Do you mean, like, mad as in I wanna rip your head off? Yeah. I'm mad. Or do you mean crazy like belong-in-a-straightjacket mad? Because then no. Though, after this crap, you'd think I'd be headed in that direction. Now go away and let the kid mourn her man!"

"No, no! You misunderstand! She is his one true love—she and only she can save him! I saw her face in my mirror. She is the one!"

Toni gasped at the woman's words just as King Dick appeared above her. The arm of his fancy jacket ripped completely off, his hair hanging in his regal face, dripping droplets of water mingled with the blood from the cut on his forehead down on her.

"Roz speaks the truth! You must save him, Antonia!"

She sat upright so fast it made her head spin. Looking up at the old woman, her wrinkled face so sincere, Toni asked frantically, *"How?* Tell me how!"

Whatever it took. If she had to eat frog's legs, turn tricks in the Garden of Wings, whatever.

Roz looked at her as if *she* were the one who was crazy. "True love's kiss, of course!"

Toni blinked, because this really was madness. A perfect, incredible insanity to be sure, but utter madness. So much so that she began to laugh at the irony, her head falling back on her aching shoulders, her eyes filling with tears. Marty, Nina and Wanda joined her in her laughter until they were all holding their stomachs.

Of course it was true love's kiss that would save him. Of course.

Toni rolled toward Jon—or Iver—or whoever, resting her torso upon his as she brushed his wet hair from his face. His handsome, flawless face, with eyelashes that swept over his ruddy-colored skin in ebony perfection and cheeks a Kardashian would kill for.

Toni smiled at him, her heart swelling in her chest, her fingers trembling as they traced his mouth.

"Ye must wake now, Stable Boy, for 'tis I, your one true love," she whispered, before she placed her lips on his, his mouth cold and unyielding, and kissed him.

With everything she had. For all she was worth, with all the growing love she'd thought was crazy to have felt after knowing him for so little time.

There was a moment of silence, a slight intake of air when Wanda and Marty held their breath. A moment where she did indeed think Roz might be out of her mind.

But then Jon's chest heaved and his eyes popped open. His beautiful sapphire eyes. "Milady?" he croaked, his deep voice cracking.

"If you ever do that to me again, I'll show you what wrath and swords are really all about, *Prince Iver Daring*," she murmured, tears falling from her eyes to land on his chest as she ran her hands over his face.

He used a thumb to swipe at the salty drops. "I did owe you one, did I not? I suppose we can call it even now, eh?" he asked on a chuckle.

Toni fought a sob. "You know what I think? I think we should just wipe the slate clean. Let's start all over. I'm Toni Vitali from the land of intor-nets, phones, cars that go vroom-vroom and dating—better known as Jersey. Pleased to meet you, *Iver*."

Iver smiled up at her, flashing his white teeth. "That's prince to you."

Toni poked him in the ribs while she laughed, making him groan as Marty and Wanda helped them from the floor, throwing their arms around them and hugging the couple hard.

Nina roused Dannan, gripping his big fingers and pulling him to a standing position.

He smiled and scooped Toni up in his big hand, holding her in front of his face. "Aye, lass, you are a fine friend and a mighty wench."

She gripped his fluted ears and kissed the end of his big blue nose before he set her down next to Iver.

Toni took a deep breath as she addressed everyone with a smile, knowing what had to happen next, even as she dreaded it. "Whaddya say we return some shoes and get you guys home?"

King Dick cleared his throat and pointed to the shoes. "About the shoes. I do not know how you came upon them, my lady Toni, but I owe you the deepest of gratitude for their return. They are dangerous when in the wrong hands, which is why, I assume, the good witch Brenda gave them to such a fierce warrior." He bowed in front of Toni then rose to smile at her.

Toni held up a finger and waved it. "Yeah. Can I get an explanation on these, please? Because trust me when I say, I was the last person on earth someone would nominate to slay dragons back in Jersey and now I'm suddenly fairytale villain slayer of the year."

King Dick barked a laugh, his eyes twinkling with amusement. "Those shoes once belonged to a very powerful queen. She gave them to me upon her death when she could no longer trust they would be guarded with caution. I have kept them a secret for many years now. Simply the knowledge of them could cause great upset in my peaceful land. They allow you to absorb your enemy's powers, but in the wrong hands, they can be quite dangerous. Which only goes to show, you are honorable and kind."

Toni ran a hand over her forehead to squeeze her temple. "Just for the sake of security, a drunken witch stole them from you. Maybe you might want to consider tightening your ship?"

King Dick grinned. "Indeed I shall." He knelt in front of her and asked," If I might?"

Toni nodded, almost hesitantly. She'd had these things on for almost three weeks. What would she do when her feet were no longer in arched Barbie position?

The king placed his hand at her heel and pulled first one then the other shoe off, leaving her feet finally free. Toni wiggled her toes in gratitude as the tingle she'd grown used to fizzled and dissipated entirely. "Thank you."

King Dick smiled as he rose. "And now, for your wish. I shall grant you each one. Will it be that you leave Shamalot, Toni, and return to your homeland of Jersey? I wish nothing but love for my son, but I have learned a very hard-won lesson today. I cannot force the heart to do what it does not wish, and I sense your heart is torn."

Her throat tightened, her stomach clenched. The dreaded eleventh hour was upon her and she had to make a choice. How would she ever choose between the love of her life and her beloved brother?

Damn you, realm!

But Iver stepped forward, his eyes full of determination, his jaw rigid. "I would have this known—if Toni chooses to return home, I shall go with her, Father. I will not leave my true love under any circumstances."

Marty and Wanda's wings began to flap wildly. "Fan me, Wanda," Marty ordered with a breathy demand. "Before I pass out from all this man."

But now Toni shook her head, bracketing his face in her hands. "No, Jon." She shook her head and corrected herself. "*Iver.* I can't let you do that. I won't ask you to leave your family, your kingdom, your everything for me."

"You *are everything*," he whispered, gripping her wrists. "None of it matters if you are not by my side to share it. And I will not be denied the chance to know you."

Roz stepped in then, letting the hood of her coat fall to her shoulders, her craggy, lined face smiling. "I must tell you what I have seen in my mirror, children. I did not understand last eve when the vision came, but now I do. Listen close. You are, indeed, the prince's one true love, milady. I did not tell falsehoods when I counseled the king of such. He was right to send Resplendant away. And your happiness Brenda spoke of indeed lies with Iver. Yet, the prince's one true love must stay here in Shamalot in order to remain safe from those who wish to harm her in her homeland." She turned to Marty, Wanda and Nina. "*You* three must return to your families, and help the maiden save her brother—for he is in great danger."

"*He's alive?*" Toni almost screamed as relief flooded her veins, forcing her to lean back against Iver, who held her steady and strong.

"Aye," she said, her gravelly voice thick. "But he is in dire need of help, and the maidens must assist where the moon is high over the forests, where the wind blows endlessly and the trees and water are in abundance."

"But what does that mean? Will I ever see him again? I can't see him if I'm not there, and I want to help find him."

Roz placed a hand on Toni's and stared deep into her eyes. "You must heed my warning. 'Tis urgent you do so. There are hunters who seek you, milady. Ugly hunters who will take your life if they locate you. I can assist with a means for you to see your brother and your newfound friends again, but for now, you must stay here and learn to rule the kingdom with the prince, and they must return."

"And you must give me your word you speak the truth, Roz. I will not have my lady's heart suffer," Iver said.

Roz instantly bowed in reverence. "My word, my prince. She will see her brother again. This I swear to you."

"Welp, I guess that's settled, huh, kiddo?" Nina asked with a nudge, her voice weak and trembling. She began to pull the bluebirds from her hair and the one from inside the bodice of her dress, setting them on the edge of a broken chair, where they continued to chirp. "Promise me you'll take care of these little buggers. I'm fucking attached."

Toni threw her arms around Nina's waist and hugged her hard. "I promise. Now, we need to get her home, Roz. How do we do it? She's sick and—"

Nina thwarted Toni's words by hugging her back with a weak squeeze. "You be good, kiddo. Whatever we need to do back in Jersey, consider it done. Okay? Go be happy, Sparkly Pants," she gruffed out before letting go and knocking Dannan in his thigh. "You look out for Red here."

Dannan rumbled his consent, his wide chest expanding as he sucked in a breath of air.

Tears fell from Marty and Wanda's eyes as they held out their arms to her and gathered her and Nina into their embrace. "What Nina said. We'll find Cormac, I promise. We'll do whatever it takes to help him. But you have to promise us something. Stay put. Try not to fret. Become part of this world you've fallen in love with—learn it—learn how to be a good princess. Most of all, find your joy again, honey. You've been so long without."

Toni inhaled a shuddering breath as Iver tucked her back by his side. "So this is it?" she asked Roz on a squeak.

They'd all been so tightly bound by the chore of getting her to the castle, she wasn't sure what she'd do when she didn't wake up to Nina complaining about her stupid hair, or when she could no longer tell Carl one of her mixed-up fairytales. "Everyone can go home now?"

Roz nodded her silvery head, tucking Toni's hand into hers. "For now, yes. But you will meet again and again. This I promise. All you have to do is ask."

Toni turned to face the women and Carl, leaning down she pressed a kiss to the top of his head as tears fell from her eyes and her heart swelled in her chest.

"You be good, and the next time you read a story, think of me, huh, buddy?"

Carl stomped his hoof and nudged her with his muzzle as she stroked his soft jaw.

How did she say goodbye to these women? How did she let them go after everything they'd done for her? How did she tell them how much they meant?

But she would. Because it was important to say it as often as she could, whenever she could. "And you three? How do I even begin to say thank you? I…" She choked on her words, almost unable to get them out. "I never would have made it here without your support. I haven't had anyone on my side for a long time, but I'm damn glad it was you three and Carl who showed up when I needed someone the most. So…thank you. *Thank you.* All of you. I'll never forget what you did for me—*ever.*"

"Nor I, fair maidens," Iver said, his voice cracking ever so slightly. "You are brave and noble, and I shall never forget what you have done for Shamalot by helping to save the good people and Toni from Angria's destruction. You are always welcome, honored guests in our kingdom." He bowed before the women then stroked Carl's head.

Nina balled her fist and gave Iver a gentle slug to his arm. "You be nice to Red here, Prince Flawless. Or I come back. Then I kill you. Got it?"

Iver barked a laugh and pulled Nina into a hug. "I shall wait in fear of your reprisal, Discontent One."

Marty and Wanda, both smiling through tears, hugged him, too. Dannan gathered them all up and squeezed. "Come back soon, lasses, and I shall show ye the town as my guests. We'll chase elves and drink thistleberry wine."

Everyone laughed, wiping their eyes.

"If you are ready," Roz prompted, pulling a hand mirror from the pocket of her lush coat.

Toni hugged them all hard, one right after the other, pressing kisses to their cheeks. "Be safe. When you find Cormac, tell him I love him, and that I'm happy. So happy."

Toni stepped back then and whispered, "Merry Christmas," smiling at Carl and the trio, their hair falling in wet clumps around their faces, their gorgeous gowns torn and soot-covered, tears glistening in their eyes. She waved, blowing them a kiss as Roz held up her hand mirror against one of the walls still standing in the ballroom.

"Mirror, mirror in my hand—send them home to their land!"

There was a second's worth of a pause as Toni watched a spiral of green smoke twist upward and then a door appeared. A door that looked just like the door to the dressing room in the outlet store.

They each stepped over the threshold, with Nina last in line. Clinging to Marty's hand, she turned back and gave Toni the thumbs-up sign and grinned before the door disappeared into the smoky mist and they were gone.

Iver pulled her close to his side as she let her cheek rest against his broad chest, tears spilling from her eyes. While she was thrilled to begin this adventure with her prince, she felt like a piece of her had just left.

"Don't be sad, milady. For they will return and we shall throw them a ball the likes of which they've never seen. I shall see to it myself."

Toni barked a laugh, drying her eyes with a torn piece of his shirt. "Hah! Bet Nina can't wait to put on another ball gown."

Tipping her chin up with his fingers, he whispered down at her, "You are one fierce opponent, milady. You saved Shamalot today. I burst with pride."

She smiled up at him, loving the way she fit against his hard frame. "You saved *me*. You *sacrificed* yourself for me."

"And I'd do it again and again. You and your safety, your happiness, will always be my first priority." He pressed a gentle kiss to her lips, making her warm all over.

When she pulled away, leaning back in his arms, she said, "So I guess we have some talking to do, huh, *Prince Iver*? Owner of a castle the size of Hoboken, wielder of the sword of wrath and, I'm assuming, richer than God?"

He grinned, lifting one eyebrow. "Was my heartfelt apology not enough?"

"I think you skipped some serious details, Reindeer Whisperer," she teased.

"Maybe one or two," he hedged on a chuckle.

"So here's what I was thinking. Why don't we get to know each other a little better while we clean up this mess?"

Iver looked around at the debris-filled ballroom and winced as frightened servants began to poke their heads into what was left of the entryway.

"I do not know if we possess a broom large enough in all of Shamalot, milady."

Toni giggled, grasping his hand and pulling him over an enormous chunk of cracked marble. "Why don't you show me your broom closet and we'll see?"

But he stopped her and pulled her tight to him. "Is this a saucy euphemism from your land of Jersey for something other than cleaning the castle?" he asked, wiggling his eyebrows.

"You wanna find out?" she teased, running her tongue over his lower lip, loving that he stiffened against her.

"Oh, indeed, milady. Indeed, I do," he said, before stealing her breath and her heart by kissing her soundly.

And as Iver held her close, Antonia Vitali from the land of intor-nets and cars that went vroom-vroom, knew without a shadow of a doubt, she'd found her one true love.

**

And this storyteller is thrilled beyond words to tell you, the prince and the soon-to-be princess rode off into the broom closet to discover the joys of euphemisms from the land of Jersey.

Ahem.

And they lived happily-ever-after.

They really, really did!

Epilogue

Some time later in Shamalot time—and eleven and counting implausible paranormal accidents gone by—a not-so-vampire anymore vampire; a beautiful halfsie; a gorgeous blonde werewolf; a cuddly demon who'd discovered he had a kindred spirit in a blue ogre; a manservant who'd raised hell in the royal kitchens when he'd found out they knew nothing about garlic infusion; a sweet zombie who suddenly had the gift of a limited but thoughtful vocabulary; a blue ogre who was in the process of teaching his beloved princess the art of the sword; a king named Dick and his queen Jane; a former faux prince turned successful reindeer farming entrepreneur and his beautiful, expectant wife Resplendant; one very happily getting-to-know-her-prince, soon-to-be princess Antonia of the Fiery Hair; and one even happier, flawlessly gorgeous Prince Iver, all gathered at the under-construction Castle Beckett for a belated Christmas/Princess Party gathering...

As Toni looked down the long table, set with beautiful china and silver, red and white flowers spilling from small vases on a lush tablecloth, at her friends and *their* friends, her prince at her right, the king and queen at each end, she beamed with gratitude.

As promised, to wipe out the horrible memory of the last celebration gone awry, Iver had indeed hosted a ball for them, a belated Christmas ball fit for princesses Hollis, Charlie, Naomi, Noa, Penny and the twin princes, Alistair and Daniel; a ball set right in the middle of Castle Beckett's recreation room—which was closer to the kitchen and, according to Arch, easier on his aging knees.

They'd found out the world of Shamalot really was in a different time, and back in Jersey it was the week after Christmas, even though at the castle, it was now well into a bitterly cold January.

The girls of OOPS hadn't missed any of the Christmas festivities, according to Nina. They'd gotten back in plenty of time to uphold all of their traditions, and now they were here, with Toni and Iver, laughing, chatting, getting to know one another as they feasted and celebrated the miracle of friendship between two very different worlds.

But who needed a reason to celebrate Christmas twice in one year anyway?

Toni reached to her left and patted Nina's hand as she dug into a full plate of chicken wings, smothered in buffalo sauce and ranch dressing.

Toni lifted her red napkin and swiped at the vampire's lips, wiping a smear of buffalo sauce. "So how's human treating you, Nina?"

Nina smacked her lips and grinned. "Fuck, it's the bomb. Do you have an idea how long it's been since I've had a chicken wing I didn't upchuck? For-fucking-ever."

Toni observed Marty and Wanda, who looked to each other, their eyes worried, but they covered it up quickly and smiled at Toni.

"It's so funny how Nina suddenly doesn't have plans when we want to shop these days, don't you think, Wanda?" Marty asked, her eyebrow lifting.

Wanda folded her hands in her lap. "Funnier still? The fact that we're always shopping right near the *Wing Stop*. Crazy, right?"

Nina threw another chicken bone down on her plate, where the carcasses of at least a dozen wings lay, and licked each and every one of her ten fingers with delight.

"Shut the eff up, you two. I'm your damn dream come true. Isn't this the shit you've always wanted? Me sharing in all your bullshit girl-bonding? Only now, I don't have to sit and watch you two scarf down half a side of beef while I doze off from all that boring talk about lip gloss and cold cream. Now pass the damn mashed potatoes and shut it."

Toni barked a laugh and patted Nina's thigh. "Girl-bonding achievement unlocked. I'm glad you're enjoying food again, but don't you miss being a vampire?"

Nina plopped some mashed potatoes on her plate and shook her dark head. "Like I'd damn well miss the clap."

"So no...?"

"Not even a GD little."

But that wasn't ringing entirely true for Toni, so she waved Marty and Wanda over to the table where Arch had placed his equally infamous weenies in a blanket, an eye-rolling delicacy almost on par with the bedsport, if you listened to Iver.

"How is she *really*? I mean, she's all 'yay wings and hamburgers', but is that just a front?" Toni asked.

Marty sighed, her shoulders lifting. "I don't know. I can't tell. I worry once she gets past the honeymoon stage of this, when she realizes what's really happened, she'll flip a nut. It's like she didn't even skip a beat."

Wanda nodded, tucking her hand to the side of her face. "Exactly. 'Oh I'm a human again. Whatever' has been her attitude since this happened."

Toni sighed long and bit the inside of her cheek. "How's Greg taking it?" she wondered as she looked at the handsome man who sat beside Nina, chatting with Iver and Heath and Keegan.

Wanda's eyes became sympathetic. "He's worried, too. He told Keegan the other day that she's behaving like nothing's any different. Except she calls Arch a hundred times a day to get recipes from him. It's like she's on a mission to scarf as much food as possible because she missed out on eating for eight years."

"Do we still think it was because she drank some of Angria's blood that this happened?" Toni asked as she watched Nina cut into a slab of rare prime rib.

Marty nodded, smoothing her hands over her red knit dress. "We do. It's the only explanation."

After they'd returned to their homes in New York, everything had come to a head for Nina. One ugly, failed attempt to fly, where she'd landed in a thorny bush, got scratched up from head to toe and didn't heal, the inability to use her fangs, and an almost broken wrist from trying to move a car illegally parked in front of her castle later, and she'd found out she was human again.

"Can't Greg just bite her and make everything vampire again?"

Wanda shook her head. "Absolutely not. It goes against everything they believe in. And even if he was willing, she's not. Or so she says."

"Hey!" Nina interrupted them, a napkin tucked into the neck of her hoodie, a bottled beer in her hand. "Quit talkin' about me like just because my hearing isn't supersonic, I don't know you're damn well doing it. I'm fine. Now let's go celebrate this shit and quit whining. Isn't that what we're here for, framily?"

Toni threw her arms around Nina's neck. "That *is* what we're here for, and if you're happy, vamp, er...human, I'm happy. I love you no matter what."

She planted a wet kiss on Nina's cheek, making Marty and Wanda laugh when she batted Toni away and stomped off with a grin to the table to attack more chicken wings.

"Nina's right. We're here to celebrate being together again, and that's all that matters right now. Have I mentioned how happy I am for you two lovebirds? Because I'm thrilled," Marty said with a wide grin before heading over to help her daughter Hollis catch a fairy as they buzzed throughout the room.

"Lady Wanda," Iver said, wrapping his arm around Toni's waist. "Any word on Cormac?"

Toni sighed a happy sigh as she leaned into him. Iver had been very supportive in their efforts to locate Cormac. In fact, he was supportive about everything she did. He didn't care when she ate something too spicy and hiccupped fire, burning his hair—or when she made his nose grow when she asked him if he'd been the one to leave his towel on the floor in the bathing chamber.

He didn't even mind when she jumped into the ocean and swam with Muriel. She'd retained the powers of the shoes once they were removed, and she'd set about helping King Dick secure them so no one ever got their hands on them again.

Iver also encouraged her to learn how to use a sword, giving her tips when he wasn't learning the business of running Shamalot from his father, who he'd become quite close to since he'd returned home.

Iver had made his peace with King Dick for making the deal with Jon with the help of Queen Jane, who smoothed the way. And Toni and Queen Jane had rather hit it off, spending their afternoons together while she taught Toni the fine art of being a princess and someday queen.

Jane was funny and bright and far more than a woman who wore fancy dresses and had lavish teas. She was warm and loving and most of all, she loved Iver as much as Toni realized she did.

Wanda reached out and squeezed his arm. "I think we have a location, if Roz's vision is right. We're on it as soon as we leave here."

Toni's stomach jumped into high gear. "You will let me know if I can help, won't you?"

"Nope. I will not. You heard what Roz said, right? You're in danger. You stay here at Castle Beckett for as long as necessary and we do the heavy lifting. Now, let's focus on this awesome celebration. Did I tell you two kids how happy I am for you both?" Wanda asked, her smile beaming.

"Did I tell you how happy I am that Archibald brought coffee grounds to last me a lifetime?"

Wanda chuckled, giving her a hug. "You look beautiful and happy and healthy, and that's all I can ask for. Now, if you'll excuse me, I heard the words roast and beef. They call my name." She blew them a kiss followed by a wink and wandered off to the far end of the table, where her husband smiled at her as she took her place beside him.

Iver wrapped his arms around her waist from behind, nuzzling her ear and making her shiver. "I declare this particular ball a success. Well done, Lady Toni."

As Toni watched the people who'd become so dear to her eat, laugh and pass food, as she watched all the new faces she'd met today interact with each other while the children played, the girls in their princess costumes and tiaras, the boys with their plastic swords, fencing.

As fairies buzzed about and Ellesandra read to the children, and Resplendant and Jon Doe smooched in a dark corner, and Dannan and Darnell told old war stories, she burrowed in closer to his chest.

"It's been an amazing day. Thank you for this. You're a good prince. Have I told you that today?"

He turned her in his arms. "Nay. I think the last I heard such praise was this past eve, during the bedsport."

Ah. The bedsport. It went against all royal Shamalotian rules, but it wasn't as though they hadn't broken a half dozen of those already. What was one more?

And it was amazing. Fulfilling. Everything she'd always dreamed it could be, and as Iver became more skilled, as he tempted her with what he joked were his smooth new moves, she fell deeper in love with each passing second.

Their royal wedding was set for the spring when, according to Iver, the hills beyond the castle would eventually roll with green, the honeysuckle and sugared pears would scent the air, and the breeze would warm their souls. He promised her a wedding the likes of which no one in Shamalot had ever seen.

Until then, they talked long into the night and the better part of the days, they laughed, Jon taught her all the shortcuts in the enormous castle, and they conspired to find a way to bring phones, Netflix, and the Internet to Shamalot.

But mostly, they loved. They grew as a couple. They made plans for a future filled with children and their version of a happily-ever-after.

Looking up at his beautiful face, tracing the outline of his jaw, her heart fuller than she could ever remember, Toni said, "How could I be so remiss? You, my one true love, are the best prince a girl could ask for—bar none."

But Iver frowned. "Have you asked for others?"

She pushed her arms up under his and laughed. "It's an expression, silly. It means, there's no one else like you in the world and I wouldn't trade you—not even for a lifetime of Starbucks and a flushing toilet."

"Not even for your beloved, most revered Starbucks? Milady, it must be true love," he murmured against her lips, making her sigh.

"Ya think?" she asked on a giggle.

"Nay, princess in training, *I know*," Iver whispered back as he swept her up in a kiss.

Oh, and it *was* love.

Everlasting—true—the kind fairytales are made of.

The End

I so hope you'll come back to find out what's going to happen to Nina now that she's a chicken-wing-eating, beer-guzzling, bona-fied human again as the girls of OOPS search for Toni's brother, Cormac, in *Bearly Accidental*! Coming winter of 2016!

Note from Dakota

I do hope you enjoyed this book, I'd so appreciate it if you'd help others enjoy it too.

Recommend it. Please help other readers find this book by recommending it.

Review it. Please tell other readers why you liked this book by reviewing it at online retailers or your blog. Reader reviews help my books continue to be valued by distributors/resellers. I adore each and every reader who takes the time to write one!

If you love the book or leave a review, please email dakota@dakotacassidy.com so I can thank you with a personal email. Your support means more than you'll ever know! Thank you!

About Dakota

Dakota Cassidy is a *USA Today* bestselling author with over thirty books. She writes laugh-out-loud cozy mysteries, romantic comedy, grab-some-ice erotic romance, hot and sexy alpha males, paranormal shifters, contemporary kick-ass women, and more.

Dakota was invited by Bravo TV to be the Bravoholic for a week, wherein she snarked the hell out of all the Bravo shows. She received a starred review from Publishers Weekly for *Talk Dirty to Me*, won a Romantic Times Reviewers' Choice Award for *Kiss and Hell*, along with many review site recommended reads and reviewer top pick awards.

Dakota lives in the gorgeous state of Oregon with her real life hero and her dogs, and she loves hearing from readers!

Connect with Dakota online:

Twitter: https://twitter.com/DakotaCassidy

Facebook: https://www.facebook.com/DakotaCassidyFanPage

Join Dakota Cassidy's Newsletter, The Tiara Diaries:
http://mad.ly/signups/100255/join

eBooks by Dakota Cassidy

Visit Dakota's website at http://www.dakotacassidy.com for more information.

Accidentally Paranormal, a Paranormal Romantic Comedy series

Interview With an Accidental—a free introductory guide to the girls of the Accidentals!

1. The Accidental Werewolf

2. Accidentally Dead

3. The Accidental Human

4. Accidentally Demonic

5. Accidentally Catty

6. Accidentally Dead, Again

7. The Accidental Genie

8. The Accidental Werewolf 2: Something About Harry

9. The Accidental Dragon

10. Accidentally Aphrodite

11. Accidentally Ever After

12. Bearly Accidental

13. How Nina Got Her Fang Back

14. The Accidental Familiar

A Lemon Layne Mystery, a Contemporary Cozy Mystery Series

1. Prawn of the Dead

2. Play That Funky Music White Koi

3. Total Eclipse of the Carp

Witchless In Seattle Mysteries, a Paranormal Cozy Mystery series

1. Witch Slapped

2. Quit Your Witchin'

3. Dewitched

4. The Old Witcheroo

Wolf Mates, a Paranormal Romantic Comedy series
1. An American Werewolf In Hoboken
2. What's New, Pussycat?
3. Gotta Have Faith
4. Moves Like Jagger

A Paris, Texas Romance, a Paranormal Romantic Comedy series
1. Witched At Birth
2. What Not to Were
3. Witch Is the New Black
4. White Witchmas

Non-Series
1. Whose Bride Is She Anyway?
2. Polanski Brothers: Home of Eternal Rest

The Hell, a Paranormal Romantic Comedy series
1. Kiss and Hell
2. My Way to Hell

The Plum Orchard, a Contemporary Romantic Comedy series
1. Talk This Way
2. Talk Dirty to Me
3. Something to Talk About
4. Talking After Midnight

The Ex-Trophy Wives, a Contemporary Romantic Comedy series
1. You Dropped a Blonde On Me
2. Burning Down the Spouse
3. Waltz This Way

49084576R00123

Made in the USA
San Bernardino, CA
12 May 2017